THE BABA YAGA

Also by Una McCormack

NOVELS

Star Trek
Deep Space Nine: The Missing
The Fall: The Crimson Shadow
Typhon Pact: Brinkmanship
Deep Space Nine: The Never-Ending Sacrifice

Doctor Who
The Way Through the Woods
The King's Dragon

AUDIO

Doctor Who: An Eye for Murder
Blake's 7: The Ministry of Peace
Blake's 7: Risk Management

Eric Brown &
Una McCormack

WEIRD SPACE

THE BABA YAGA

**ABADDON
BOOKS**

WWW.ABADDONBOOKS.COM

An Abaddon Books™ Publication
www.abaddonbooks.com
abaddon@rebellion.co.uk

First published in 2015 by Abaddon Books™,
Rebellion Intellectual Property Limited,
Riverside House, Osney Mead, Oxford, OX2 0ES, UK.

10 9 8 7 6 5 4 3 2 1

Editors: Jonathan Oliver & David Moore
Cover Art: Adam Tredowski
Design: Simon Parr & Sam Gretton
Marketing and PR: Lydia Gittins
Creative Director and CEO: Jason Kingsley
Chief Technical Officer: Chris Kingsley
Weird Space™ created by Eric Brown

ISBN: 978-1-78108-364-2

Printed in the US

To my beautiful daughter

Una McCormack

PART ONE

RUNAWAYS

CHAPTER ONE

Braun's World

"*MARIA! MARIA! WAKE up!*"

Someone was shaking her awake. She didn't want to be awake. Too early. She didn't fall asleep till late. She couldn't get comfortable. She always needed a full nine hours—

"*Maria! You've got to wake up!*"

Kit. Home early. Still dark out there. Kit shaking her. Waking her up. Waking her up *early*.

Maria shoved her head beneath the pillow. "Trying to *sleep!*"

But Kit only shook her harder. "You can sleep on the road. Come on, Maria, I need you now."

He pulled the pillow away, gently, but inexorably. He clearly wasn't going to give up. Besides, Maria was awake now and past the point of slipping back to sleep. With ill grace, she reached for her dressing gown.

"Leave that!" Kit snapped, pulling it away from her and throwing it onto the bed. "Come *on*, Maria! We don't have much time!"

Maria grabbed the dressing gown back. "Kit Emerson," she said. "It's..." She checked the time. "Four in the morning." *Four in the morning? What the hell is going on?* "My alarm doesn't go off for another *three* hours. You're not due back for another four."

She peered at his face, pale and starkly shadowed in the glow of the streetlights.

"Kit?" she whispered. "What's going on? Why are you back early? You're meant to be on duty till seven—?"

He took her hands between his. She could see he was trying to be calm, but his hands were trembling, and freezing cold. "I need you to do what I say," he said. "Don't ask questions—just get up, get dressed, pack a few essentials. Then wake the little one and get her out into the skimmer. We're leaving, and we need to leave as quickly and as quietly as possible."

"Kit, are you going AWOL?"

Still holding her hands, he gently pulled her up from the bed. "Love. No questions." He was pleading with her. "We need to go—"

"If you think that you can wake me up in the middle of the night, drag me out of bed, and make me wake up Jenny for no good reason at all—"

"They're here, love," he said softly. "There's not much time. We've got to get away. We've got to get away *now*."

After that, she barely stopped for breath. She was dressed in seconds—good, practical clothes, clothes that would last a journey—and the bags were out and packed in short order. Kit went into the kitchen, to sort out supplies. They had always been good like this, she thought through her daze and the growing, gnawing fear. They had always been a team: one of them stepping forward when the other reached their limits. She remembered going under the knife when Jenny came: he had held her hands between his then, too, and his confidence and calm had enfolded her as her whole world narrowed and numbed. She hadn't been afraid, because she knew that he was there and that he would look after them. It meant that she knew he wouldn't wake her or the child for a bad reason. And she knew for certain that he would not go AWOL without an *excellent* reason.

They're here... Maria shuddered. She had known the risks when he had taken this posting, but she had never believed, not really, that they might come.

The worst threat humanity had ever known. Worse than plague, or the second great measles epidemic; worse than any atrocity humans had inflicted upon themselves, and worse even than the Vetch, those enigmatic aliens and their bitter, bloody war against humankind.

The Weird...

"Have you packed everything you want, Maria?"

Maria looked around their little flat. They had only been here six months, and it still had a temporary, institutional feel. They were still living out of suitcases. Everything they owned that she really liked was in storage. She'd regretted not making the space more like a home, for Jenny's sake, but now it seemed to be a blessing. It would not be as much of a wrench to leave. "I think so."

"Get Jenny. And make sure she understands that we need to be quiet."

As soon as he was missed, they would be sending military police after him, and there would be a court-martial, and then...

Maria sobbed. Kit, already heading towards the doorway with bags in each hand, stopped and looked back at her. "I'm so sorry," he said, awkwardly, his voice rough and dry. "I should never have brought us here. I just wanted a good life for us."

Maria shook her head. "We agreed," she said. "Together. We made the decision together." She rubbed her tired eyes, and smiled at him. "That's the last squeak you'll get from me. If we have to go, we have to go. I trust you, Kit. I always have, and I always will. Get those bags in the skimmer, and I'll get Jenny, and we'll go wherever it is that you've got planned." She raised her eyebrows. "I assume there is a plan?"

"There's a plan," he said. "Not sure if it's a good one."

"We'll work on it," she said, and turned towards their little girl's room.

This at least, she thought, felt like a home. Jenny, like any four-year-old, was good at taking a space and bending it to her will. Maria was from a big family—fifth of six—and so the mess was nothing compared to what she'd been used to as a child. She had thought that Kit—orderly and careful in everything—would find the child tornado stressful, but he was a patient man, and while he did not indulge excesses, he understood how Jenny needed space to roam free and explore.

"Come on, sweetheart," she crooned, softly, like she did when Jenny was tiny, and she lifted her from the bed. "Time to get up. Time to get up."

The small warm body curled around her, little head nestling into her shoulder. "We can be cosy in a minute, sweetheart," she said. "We need to get dressed first."

Jenny began grumbling, but Kit was there in the doorway, holding clothes: little grey t-shirt, blue jeans, socks and shoes and stripy jersey. "Come on, pet. Time to get dressed."

The complaints stopped at once, and Jenny started to pull off her pyjamas. Jenny would do anything for Daddy.

The chattering began, and Maria said, "We need to be quiet, Jenny. Can you do that?"

Jenny eyed her. "What's for breakfast?"

"Banana."

"Is that all?"

"You can have something else once we're on our way."

"Okay," said Jenny. She lifted her arms to her father. "Up."

"Please," said Kit.

"Up, please, Daddy."

He lifted her, and she put her head against him. He nodded at Maria. "Time to go."

She nodded back. "I'll leave on the lights," she said. "It'll look like we're here."

"Okay."

And that was it. They were gone, slipping out of the flat and down the stairs, away from the routines that had served their whole married life, and into a dangerous, unknown future.

They got into the little car. From the back, Jenny—wide awake now, bright-eyed and bushy-tailed—looked at them with sharp inquisitive eyes.

"Where are we going, Daddy?"

Maria looked over at Kit. He gave her a strained half-smile.

"Somewhere new, pet," he said, to Jenny. "Somewhere we've never been before."

Somewhere safe, thought Maria, and then her blood went cold. *If we're not already carrying the danger with us...*

Hennessy's World
Later that day

A LITTLE SOUTH of the equator on Hennessy's World, the most populous world in the Expansion, lay a vast archipelago. Spread across these hundred thousand islands were the offices, playgrounds, and palaces of the Expansion's richest and most powerful.

The waterways had been a challenge to the founders of the great city, but one which they met with confidence and panache. Taking lessons from the past, they sunk the foundations of their city deep, and they built with new, lightweight metals, which reflected back the water and the sunlight in triple harmony. The towers shot upwards—but they built downward too: great cavernous buildings of strong plastics developed for this purpose, some opaque, some transparent, so that the deep ocean could provide a backdrop for the days and nights of the people who lived there. No city as big or as ambitious had existed before in the history of humanity: but then, no empire of this scale had existed before to match the great reach of the Expansion, stretched out over hundreds of worlds. The city's founders wanted a capital fit for humanity's greatest empire, and they got it, naming their creation Venta, after another great city of old.

But the lightness of the city was deceptive. A great darkness was approaching Venta, and a gloom hung over the Expansion's most senior servants. One of these is now making a journey by flyer from the outlying island where she has spent the night to her place of work.

The flyer is on autopilot. It takes a smooth path, mostly uninterrupted: air traffic around the capital is tightly regulated, and at this height, permits are restricted to senior officials and military personnel. Few people really see Venta from above; either they hug the ground, snarled up in everyday traffic, or they're packed into near-orbit craft, so expensive and uncomfortable that few can be bothered to travel in them. But the passenger in the flyer is a person of great importance. Her name is Delia Walker and she is a senior analyst with the Expansion's intelligence agency, the Bureau. On another day, she might enjoy the view her privilege gives her. But today she has a great deal on her mind.

The flyer continues to its destination: a large square building on Santa Maria, the capital's largest island. It comes to a halt over the top of the building, hovering there as a great hatch irises open beneath it. Then the flyer falls, in a swift but controlled descent, into the heart of the building. It is a long time since Walker found this part of her journey exhilarating. These days, arriving at work fills her with dread.

The flyer decelerates, and then gently lands. The hatch has sealed above her and the bright sunlight is gone, replaced by the gloomy artificial light of the carpark. Walker leaves the flyer quickly, grabbing handheld and briefcase, and heads to the dropchute. The chute takes her down—further down—deep into the bowels of the great square building, and Walker doesn't step out until it reaches the bottom floor. She walks along a bright white corridor interrupted only by colourful but unimpressive paintings, and, reaching the big double doors at the end, presents her datapin to gain entrance to the big meeting room beyond.

It is one of those great caverns that the builders of the city liked so much. On one wall, many viewscreens are stacked in rows, pumping out information from across the whole Expansion; the other three walls are transparent, at least to the people inside, and beyond them deep sea creatures swim about, staring around them with huge unblinking eyes.

KINSELLA, WALKER SAW, was already there. Sometimes they varied it, so that she arrived first, but today he had left half-an-hour earlier than usual. Walker passed behind him on her way to the coffee and tapped his shoulder in greeting. He twisted his head slightly in acknowledgement, nothing more. *What a farce*, she thought. *Why do we keep up this pretence?* Surely everyone in this room knew exactly what they were up to in their spare time. She certainly knew everything about them. It was their business, after all. Walker herself could compile dossiers on the private lives of pretty much everyone in this room; it made for an interesting if sly office culture.

Three colleagues—for want of a better word— were gathered by the coffee dispensers, deep in conversation. They fell silent when Walker came near. No surprises there; they would be her chief rivals in this morning's debate. She ran through what she knew about them. All ex-Fleet, part of the inrush of personnel from military intelligence who had come in during the war with the Vetch, and after. They were a bureau within the Bureau: a different culture that sat uncomfortably with the careful civil servants, brilliant analysts, and enabled boffins who historically had filled the ranks of the department. Chief amongst the ex-Fleet people was Commander Adelaide Grant, who stood now in the middle of the three, stirring her coffee slowly and studying Walker in turn. There were, Walker thought, more Fleet officers here than a few years ago. The Weird threat had breathed new life into Grant and her ilk, providing a focus for their hawkish outlook.

Walker turned away. What Grant wanted was not what she wanted—either for the Bureau, or for the Expansion. The war with the Vetch had ended in an uneasy truce, which, with the Weird providing a common enemy, was turning into an equally uneasy alliance. And even if it had taken the Weird to bring the old enemies together, the fact remained that peace—or détente—*had* happened, when, twenty years ago, nobody would have believed it. And this was why Walker believed that the same had to happen with the Weird. There had to be another way, even with something as alien and destructive as the Weird. *Because God knows we won't destroy them with brute force...*

We have to be smarter than that.

But Grant and her people wanted the end of the Weird, by any means necessary, and for this they wanted money and resources to go towards their current cause—developing the 'superweapon' that Vetch scientists had devised, and which had hitherto proved unsuccessful.

Walker's stomach turned, suddenly. She took her hand off the coffee pot and instead poured herself a glass of water. She sipped, swilling the water round her mouth, washing away the sour taste, and watching her enemies—her colleagues—watch her in turn. *We know about you*, they seemed to be saying, *and we will not hesitate to use what we know*. She knew what they were thinking, because she was thinking the same. She looked around the room, taking stock: the doves, on this side; the hawks, gathering across from her; and, here and there, the undecided—a combination of the waverers, not quite able to make up their minds, and those who simply enjoyed making their colleagues in both camps sweat. The Bureau employed a lot of people like that, and a substantial proportion made it to this level. Walker had done the same, when it served her ends.

She sat down in her usual place next to Andrei. Andrei Gusev, one of oldest of the old-school at the Bureau, sly and clever, and thoroughly ill-disposed towards the military types starting to fill the upper echelons of the Bureau these days. Goose-steppers and heel-clickers, he called them. No nuance. No subtlety. Only one set of weapons for every kind of problem—and no sense of the long game. No sense that while persuasion might take longer, it could be a considerably less costly way of doing business. Walker had been one of Andrei's deputies for several years during her thirties. He had taught her what low cunning could do that brute force couldn't, and—slowly, surreptitiously, and entirely according to his principles—had sold her this vision of what the Bureau was for and how it should operate. A tool more complex than any weapon. *Find the common ground*, he would often say. *Enemies beget enemies. So turn your enemies into your allies.*

"Good weekend?" Andrei said. It was beneath him to gesture even slightly towards Kinsella.

"The usual."

"I dread to think," he murmured. Andrei did not approve of the affair, Walker knew, clearly thinking it a lapse of both judgement and taste. "I hope you weren't too—how shall I put it—otherwise involved to be able to put some thought to our forthcoming imbroglio?"

"Don't be pert, Andrei."

"I ask only for the benefit of our cause."

And for your own voyeuristic amusement, you nosy old bugger, Walker thought fondly. "Well, of course," she said. "Rest easy. I'm not going to lose this one."

Andrei sighed. Under the guise of reaching for her glass, Walker took a good long look at him. He seemed tired, as he often had in recent months, as if the thought of the fight ahead wearied him. *Not long,* she thought, coolly, but not entirely without compassion. *Not long before he quits all this and goes back to his island to potter around on that little boat.* She had seen it many times: officers for whom the fight lost its allure; who became wearied at the thought of yet another round of chilly, committee-room combat. They sickened, sometimes suddenly, and then they were gone, a lifetime of effort all brought to nothing. But the battle went on, and Walker, at least, hadn't tired of it yet. Not with people like Grant on the warpath.

The heavy double doors swung open, and the room went quiet as Latimer entered. Everyone— hawk and dove alike—studied the man carefully as he made his way round to the head of the table. The newly appointed head of the Bureau was an outside man, parachuted in by Council to unite what had always been a hotbed of personal rivalries in the face of the Weird crisis. It had not yet done the job. The competition remained, although now just two groups were competing for Latimer's attention and approval. At some point he would have to show his cards and back somebody. Walker was damned if it was going to be Grant's lot.

Latimer settled in his seat, taking his time. He was tall man, austere, like a Benedictine monk. He didn't laugh much—in fact, he didn't laugh at all—and he didn't talk much either. He watched. As he laid out his handhelds and screens, the rest of the room shuffled impatiently. Walker saw Grant roll her eyes. If the people in this room had one thing in common, it was resentment at how Latimer was playing them: biding his time; keeping them guessing. This was not how it was supposed to be. Council was supposed to jump when the Bureau ordered, not the other way round. What was the point otherwise of having all that dirt on the political class?

Latimer looked round the room and gave a thin smile. The assembled elite of the Expansion's spy corps smiled back, wanly. Walker's stomach lurched again. *It has to be today,* she thought. *What Latimer decides today will affect the Expansion for decades to come...* Beside her, Andrei sighed again, as if letting a little more of his will leave him. "Let the revels begin," he murmured.

THE BATTLE LINES were clear from the outset and, throughout the morning, the hawks seemed to have the upper hand. Certainly they were making the most of available evidence, in the form of graphic and gruesome images from worlds where the Weird had attacked. Hardly anyone in the room could watch them in full. The Weird—in their ambulatory forms as Sleer—were repulsive to look at, like mobile, human-sized afterbirth, and their destruction was without conscience, although clearly with purpose. In the images Grant was now showing, the hideous creatures—human-shaped but palpably other—ravaged a city on the world of Rocastle, tearing the human population apart, limb from limb. The hideous Flyers, vast monstrosities of bulky grey flesh, flanked with tiny eyes and suckers, had come in waves, landing and disgorging a relentless tide of pitiless, hideous Sleer. It was carnage, and of the bloodiest kind.

Walker forced herself to watch the devastation for as long as she could, but eventually she had to look away. Instead, she started to watch Latimer. He gazed steadily at the screen, hardly seeming even to blink. Walker glanced across the table at Kinsella, who was looking at her with a question in his eyes. *When*, he seemed to be saying, *are you going to step in, Walker? When are you going to respond?*

Walker shook her head, almost imperceptibly. Not now. Not in the face of this. But her moment would come.

The footage came to an end. Grant, turning to her rattled audience, said, "This is the enemy we face. This is what we are up against. And what we must all understand is that the Weird might be amongst us now—here, in this room. They can infect human minds—any of us in this room, right now, could be an agent of the Weird. For this purpose, I am proposing that we introduce mandatory screening of all government employees: a test that will enable us to discover who has been infected and prevent them from accessing positions of power—"

Now Walker spoke. "A test? You mean a telepathic scan, don't you?"

Grant turned to look at her. "It can take the form of a telepathic scan, yes."

"Do we have another way of testing for mind-parasites?"

Grant studied her carefully. "Not as yet, no."

"So you're proposing a mandatory telepathic scan for all government employees. Have you ever undergone a telepathic scan, Commander Grant?"

"I have not—"

"No, I imagine not. You wouldn't be proposing them so lightly." Walker addressed the room. "We need to take a step back. Compulsory telepathic tests are a huge invasion of privacy. What's next? Mandatory scans for all citizens?"

There was a pause, during which it became patently clear that, given the chance, Grant would certainly introduce such a policy. Eventually, Grant said, "There are always costs during war."

"But we're not *at* war," said Walker. A few voices started to object, but Latimer raised his hand, and they subsided. "We are not at war," she said again.

"In fact, we have never communicated with the Weird, and we have no idea *what* they want."

Now the disagreement would be heard. "Surely we know they want to destroy us?" one of Grant's associates said. "Even if they don't, their very existence is manifestly incompatible with ours—"

"We know nothing of the sort," said Walker clearly. "We have barely any experience of the Weird. I don't deny that our experiences thus far have been appalling, but surely we don't want to rush headlong into another war—"

"The Weird have brought war to us!"

"In fact," said Walker, "there's evidence to suggest this might not be true—"

Latimer held up his hand again. "I won't have this turn into a slanging match."

"I agree," said Walker. "But Grant and her team have had their say. She offers a superweapon, which may well not work, and compulsory medical procedures. I have another suggestion. May I present my case?"

Latimer nodded, and the room fell silent.

"Thank you," said Walker. She stood up and took her place at the head of the table. "We are fresh from a costly war with the Vetch," she said. "We cannot afford another one. Our experiences with the Weird have been brief, bloody, and brutal, but in truth we know very little about them. Yes, our instinct is to fight back. But what if the Weird *cannot* be defeated by superior force? What if we direct all our energies and resources, and place all our hopes, on a weapon that cannot save us? We have to take a longer view, and we have smarter weapons in our arsenal."

Looking down the table, she saw Andrei nodding.

"What do you suggest, Walker?" Latimer said.

Walker smiled. "We communicate."

There was a silence, and then the room collapsed into chaos. "*Communicate?*" said Grant. "You can't communicate with the Weird! They are a force for destruction! You've seen the images from Rocastle, from everywhere the Weird have been! They murder—nothing more! That's all they do! You can't communicate with that!"

Another of Grant's associates called out, "You might as well try to reason with a crimopath!"

"What harm could it do?" Walker shot back. "Why reject this idea out of hand?"

"Because it's a fantasy!" said Grant.

"I disagree," said Walker. "And in fact, one of my assets has recently returned from Satan's Reach with some fascinating information." Satan's Reach—a region of space beyond the control of either the Expansion or the Vetch Empire, where lawlessness, theft, and rumour were rife. "This asset reports that there are stories of a Weird portal somewhere in the Reach where a human colony lives alongside it without being absorbed or enslaved—"

"'Reports'? 'Stories'?" Grant snorted. "You're condemning yourself, Walker. This isn't *evidence.*"

"But it is another option." Walker turned to address Latimer directly. "We have no evidence either that the weapon that Grant proposes can do what she claims. Are we going to back only one horse in this race?"

Latimer was tapping his finger against the side of his nose. "What do you need?"

"Ships," said Walker, quickly, sensing her moment. "We need to send out ships in search of this world to find it, and to determine whether peaceful co-existence with the Weird is possible."

"Ships?" Grant laughed out loud. "You'd be moving them from the defence of the core worlds. This is insanity!"

"What can a fleet of ships do if a portal opens here on Hennessy's World?" Walker shot back. "If the Flyers emerge and the Sleer hatch? What could ships do? Blow the portal from the sky and take us all with it? If we knew how to communicate with the Weird, we might have a way to bargain with them."

Grant had turned white. "You're talking about surrender," she said.

"You're stretching the definition of surrender beyond reasonable limits," Walker said. "I want to prevent mutual mass destruction and, more importantly, our own extinction. A superweapon— by definition—cannot do this."

Latimer held up his hand. Everyone went quiet. Slowly he began to gather his papers up in front of him. "I'm interested," he said, at last. "We can at least explore what can be done. Commander Grant—see what ships can be spared."

Grant shook her head. "I'll look into it. But this is a mistake. If the Weird arrive and we have depleted our defences—"

"If the Weird arrive, we're all dead," Walker said. "Guns and ammo won't help us. Communication— that might."

Latimer brought the meeting to a close. Walker, coming back round the table, sat down again next to Andrei. He was nodding, and Walker heard him murmur, "Good, good."

* * *

LATER, SHE WENT to Kinsella's apartment.

He opened a bottle of wine and Walker took the offered glass automatically, cradling it in her hands. He bent to kiss her forehead, and sat down beside her, the picture of satisfaction. "A good battle," he said. "Well fought and well won."

"Hmm." Walker put down her wine, untouched.

"You don't sound as pleased as I thought you would be."

"That's because I don't think Grant and her gang are likely to give up very easily. If we want to send out those ships, they're going to have to be from Fleet, aren't they? Where else can we get them?"

He rubbed the palm of her hand with his thumb. It felt good; relaxing. "You think there'll be a price?" he said.

"There's always a price."

He sat and thought for a while. "You think the price will be mandatory scans?"

"That's right."

"Then let that be the price. I call that a good bargain."

"I won't do it, Mark."

He put his own glass down in frustration. "What's the problem? In the great scheme of things, it's nothing."

"It's too far. What about dignity? What about privacy?"

"*Privacy*? Sweetheart, you're in the wrong business if you're worried about privacy! Or has it really never struck you before that what we do, on a daily basis— on an *hourly* basis—is invade the privacy of others?"

"Within limits. And with no automatic assumption that we have the right."

He frowned. "You sound like Andrei."

"That's not a bad thing," Walker said. Kinsella was silent a moment, and she narrowed her eyes. "What?" she said. "What are you thinking?"

"I'm thinking... that sounding like Andrei Gusev isn't necessarily always going to be a route to success."

She turned to look at him. "You know," she said, "under other circumstances, that might sound like a threat."

"I didn't mean it that way."

"No?"

"Look, I know how much Andrei means to you—he's meant a great deal to a lot of people over the years—"

"Jesus, Mark, you sound like you're delivering his eulogy!"

Kinsella held up his hands. "I don't understand why you're getting so angry."

"I don't like hearing Andrei written off like that!"

"I'm not writing him off! God knows, I wouldn't dare! All I'm doing is making sure we've planned for the inevitable!"

"You want to plan his funeral while we're at it? He adores Beethoven's late string quartets, but given the occasion would probably prefer Rachmaninov."

"Christ, Delia, what's come over you?"

He was cut off by the chime on his comm. "Who is it?" he snapped, impatiently.

Like a supernatural force invoked by his name, Andrei Gusev's face appeared on the viewscreen. "*Delia,*" Andrei said, looking past her lover and straight at her. "*Get in, now.*"

"Andrei?" she said, caught off-guard. "How did you know I was here?"

"*Don't be ridiculous*," he said, sharply, and she was embarrassed to have asked. "*Get yourself dressed and get yourself in. Something bad has happened.*"

"What's going on?"

"*We'll talk about it when you're here. And for the love of God, the pair of you, get here as quickly as possible, and don't bother with those pointless separate routes.*"

He cut the line. Walker and Kinsella sat for a moment or two in silence, still reeling from their argument. "Well," she said at last, "so much for privacy." She stood up. "We'd better do as we're told."

Typical, she thought, as they sat together in the back of her flyer, *the only time we share a car to work, and we're not talking to each other.*

CHAPTER TWO

THEY WENT THROUGH the double doors together, their argument still unresolved. Andrei was standing in front of the banks of viewscreens and their array of visual data. He nodded to Walker and Kinsella when they arrived, and directed their attention towards the screens.

"What's happening?" said Kinsella.

Grant, standing near Andrei, replied. "A Weird portal has opened on Braun's World." She gave a bitter smile. "Nobody had even heard of the place, before tonight. Quite dull, all told. A few military installations left over from the war."

This, Walker knew, was not true. Braun's World had come to her attention several months ago, when her team had noticed the movement of a number of men and supplies into one of the desert bases. A team of telepaths had been sent there too. She'd struggled to find out what was going on, and still didn't have answers. What was Grant not telling them?

"How far is this place from the inner worlds?" asked Andrei.

"Considerably closer than we would like." Grant gestured at the coordinates onscreen.

Kinsella whistled as Walker said, "Well within Expansion space."

"You see our problem." Grant pointed at another display. "I want you to look at this," she said. "You in particular, Walker." With a flick of her wrist, Grant switched content on the viewer in front of her. "This is Dentrassa, the largest urban centre on Braun's World, less than an hour ago."

The onslaught of images that followed nearly made Walker throw up her supper; footage of the Weird was enough to unsettle even Fleet veterans. But to think that this was happening *now*... And then there was the sound. The sound of people being consumed, in fear and terror. Walker turned away.

"Is that shame?" said Grant. "You should be ashamed. This is *your* fault."

"Adelaide," said Andrei, with a warning tone to his voice, "I advise you to be very careful about throwing that kind of language."

"You know what I mean."

There was a short silence. "How are we getting these images?" said Kinsella, before the argument started again.

From behind them, a quiet voice spoke. "Police and Army on the spot. On the frontline, by the looks of it." It was Latimer. Pale and shaken: shocking to see from someone usually so controlled. He tapped his brow. "Their helmets are fitted with visual recording devices." He turned back to the screen. "And sound, it seems. Someone turn that off."

Grant signalled to someone to cut the audio feed, and the room went mercifully quiet. Everyone waited for Latimer to give some guidance. Walker and Kinsella exchanged glances. A crisis often made or broke people at Latimer's level—and this was no ordinary crisis. Was he up to it?

"Advice," Latimer said at last. "I want to hear advice." Walker and Andrei both opened their mouths to speak, but Latimer held up his hand. "Grant—talk to me," he said.

No, thought Walker, *I'm not going to let her seize the momentum...* But Andrei's hand was upon her arm, holding her back for the moment: *Let her say her piece. She might have something worthwhile to offer.*

"Make sure the news blackout is in place," said Grant. "Seal off Braun's World—we can't risk anyone getting off-planet and spreading the infection."

"Those seem like reasonable actions to me." Latimer looked around the room. "Any objections?"

Andrei shook his head. "All wise. Shall we get on with it?"

Grant held up her hand. "I haven't finished yet," she said, and turned to Latimer. "Braun's World is finished. You have to understand. And you have to understand the consequences of it. We can't risk infection. Nothing must escape that planet."

"We're sealing the ports now," Latimer said. "I can have the best part of the Eighth Fleet there in a matter of hours. Nobody is going to get past them—"

"But somebody might," said Grant.

"Nobody will!"

"But somebody *might*," Grant said again.

Quietly, Andrei said, "I fear you're going to have to be more explicit, Adelaide. People here don't seem to be quite understanding what you mean. And I for one want to hear you say it out loud."

Grant looked coldly back at him, and suddenly Walker understood what she meant. "You've got to be joking—"

"What?" said Kinsella. "What does she mean?"

"Go on," said Andrei, contemptuously. "Say it out loud."

Grant turned away from him and addressed Latimer directly. "Braun's World should be bombarded from space. We can't afford to let anything that may have been touched by the Weird survive—"

"We can't do that!" said Kinsella. "There are millions of people there!"

"Let's be clear," said Walker. "You're proposing mass murder?"

"And if somebody infected by the Weird escapes Braun's World and makes their way towards the inner worlds? What then? How many dead then? It's no distance from there to the inner worlds. And only a short jump to here. To Hennessy's World... to Venta. Do you want to see the Weird here, Walker?" Grant gave a short laugh. "Perhaps you do."

"I am not casual about the lives of others," said Walker softly. "I would not, for example, recommend the unnecessary slaughter of millions upon millions of people—"

Grant turned away from her, back to Latimer. "We have no time for this. The longer we debate, the more likely it is that somebody, right now, is escaping that planet." She jerked her thumb towards the visual display. "Do you want to see that happen here?" She leaned in. "You've listened to these people, and they can offer you nothing. This is a threat beyond our comprehension. The Weird *will* destroy us, unless we destroy it first."

Andrei was becoming more and more angry. Coldly, he said, "I have seen many things in my time at the Bureau. I've perpetrated a few outrages in my time, too. But nothing—*nothing*—compares to the sight of you trying to make capital from this tragedy in order to secure your power—"

Grant turned on him. "How *dare* you!"

"Be quiet, all of you!" Latimer raised his voice over them all. "This is not the time. Now listen." He seemed back in command of himself now. "First of all—mandatory scans for everyone within the Bureau. Taking immediate effect. Kinsella—see to that. No, Walker," he said, raising his hand as she tried to speak, "I've heard your case already, and the situation has changed. As for you, Andrei..." He looked at the older man coldly. "Anyone would think that *you* were the using this opportunity to discredit your colleagues from military intelligence. They are making hard choices in an impossible situation—"

"I'll warn you now, Latimer," said Andrei, "that if you go ahead with Grant's obscene suggestion, I will resign with immediate effect."

Latimer turned to leave. "Then I'll thank you for your long service, Andrei, and I hope you have many hours' happy fishing. Commander Grant, I'll expect to see a detailed plan of action on my desk within the hour."

*　　*　　*

"...AND I TELL you something else, Mark—Latimer can take his bloody scan and shove it where the sun doesn't shine—"

"The *scan*? Why are you still talking about that damn scan?"

They were back in Kinsella's apartment, mere hours after they had left together. Their whole world had remade itself around them in the meantime, and now Kinsella was staring at her as if she had gone mad.

Walker took a deep breath. "I'm still talking about the scan because it matters," she said. "It's a symbol of everything we have to take a stand against."

Kinsella fell back into his big leather chair. "Sweetheart, have you lost track of what's happening? There's a Weird portal open right by the core worlds, it is now apparently acceptable policy within the Bureau to recommend the wholesale slaughter of *millions*, and Andrei Gusev has been forced to resign. And you're baulking at taking a simple scan?"

"It's not a simple scan! And, besides, it's the *principle*—"

"Damn the principle! If there's any chance that someone has got away from Braun's World carrying that infection, then I say go ahead! Scan everyone on all the core worlds, and start doing it now!"

"You should know better than that!"

"Delia, let them scan you and have done with it! We've got more important things to worry about."

"I *can't*."

"Why *not*?"

"Why do you *think*?" she said, with some irritation. All these spies, she thought, all watching each other, and not a single one of them had managed to guess what was happening to her. "I'm pregnant."

He gaped back at her, like one of the fish that swam beyond the walls of their headquarters. So ridiculous. She pressed a hand against her mouth to suppress her laugh. If she started laughing now, she wouldn't stop until she started to cry. "Fourteen weeks, in case you're interested. So that's why not. Because it would mean that people would find out."

But Kinsella wasn't at the 'fourteen weeks' part yet. "How?" he said. "What... I mean, how?"

"I suspect you had the same sex ed classes that I did."

"You know I don't mean that—"

"This," said Walker, reflectively, "is the exact opposite of how I wanted this conversation to go."

There was a long silence. She looked at him as he stared at the carpet. After a while, she looked at the carpet too, and she realised how much she disliked the colours. Too pale. Showed the dirt. Not that Kinsella regularly cleaned up after himself.

"I'm sorry," he said at last. "I'm behaving abominably."

"No shit."

He rubbed his forefinger across his top lip, a habit when he was thinking that she had hitherto found quite endearing. Then—gently, almost cautiously— he took her hand. Her fingers curled instinctively around his. "Really," he said. "I'm sorry. You have my unconditional support. Um, what do you want? I'll do whatever you want. Do you want me to call Kay?"

Kay Larsen was a colleague of theirs at the Bureau and, more significantly, a qualified doctor.

"She'll know what we need to do next, surely," Kinsella said. "Where we can go to... to sort this all out." He held her hand even more tightly. "I'll come with you. You won't be alone."

"I haven't decided what's best yet."

A flicker of doubt twitched across Kinsella's face. "You're not thinking of going through with this?"

"It's a possibility."

"It'll finish you. They'll fire you."

"Not necessarily."

"Delia—don't delude yourself. If Latimer doesn't fire you on the spot, you'll be out within weeks. They have ways and means of doing these things. Altering organisational priorities. Moving your staff away. Internal reshuffling. Particularly right now. This attack—it's appalling, it's grim, and it means Grant and her gang will be able to push through whatever they want—up to and including your head on a platter. Don't give them any more ammunition. Sweetheart, please, listen—"

"Don't 'sweetheart' me! Don't you *dare* 'sweetheart' me, you bastard!"

They didn't speak again for a while. They sat in silence, side by side, looking out at the lights of the city shimmering on the dark water. The night seemed oddly, incongruously peaceful. The news from Braun's World wouldn't break for days yet. In one thing, at least, the whole Bureau was in agreement: bad news needed good management.

"I don't want children," he said, eventually. "I'm sorry, but that's the way it is. I never have. There's too much I want to do. I thought we felt the same way..."

In fairness, that was what she had always thought too. She was not a romantic: she knew the hard work involved in bringing up a child; the trade-off between time at her desk and time with the child; that one or both of these might suffer, even if she wasn't fired on the spot. She was not sentimental either, not about a collection of cells, and suspected that a few years ago she would have ended this pregnancy immediately, without even telling Kinsella, and moved on. But something was holding her back. Was it her age? The sense that this might be a last chance? Something tightened in her stomach (*not her, not yet, surely*). After a moment she realised it was anger.

I want what I want, she thought. *And that's not what Mark wants, or what the Bureau wants, or even what I myself thought I wanted, or ought to want. I have changed my mind. And that is permissible.*

Or should be. But there it was: some people's bodies had never really been their own to dispose of as they wanted. They had always been something to be policed and controlled. Not even she, amongst the most privileged of the most advanced technological society, really had that power over herself. She remained powerful as long as she obeyed the rules. But now she no longer wanted to obey the rules...

Kinsella, she realised, was still holding her hand; awkwardly, and yet oddly lovingly, as if was trying to reel her back from making a disastrous mistake and plunging into water too deep even for her. Calmly, Walker took her hand away. "It's all right," she said. "You don't owe me anything."

"Delia," he said reproachfully. "That isn't fair."

"I didn't mean it that way. I meant it honestly. I'm trying to be honest with you. This is my decision and I'll live with it. I won't force you to do anything you don't want to do." *And I hope you'll pay me the same courtesy.*

He hesitated, then: "If you'll let me give you some advice..."

This should be good, she thought. "By all means."

"Please don't throw away everything you've worked for. You're brilliant, Dee, among the smartest in the room. Andrei's besotted with you—he always has been. He's gone now. And you—you were always the heir apparent. You're meant to replace him. You have"—he stretched out his hands—"you have a *responsibility* to him. Especially now."

Now that their rivals were in the ascendant. A responsibility to a greater good? When he put it that way, there was only reasonable course of action, wasn't there? Anything else would be self-indulgence. Anything else would be irrational.

"I'll think about what you said," she said. It sounded to her ears as if she was speaking to a colleague rather than to a man she had loved. Kinsella seemed satisfied, however. At least she wasn't telling him a lie.

"Will you stay?" he said.

She looked out at the dark city, and then back to him. Could she, for old times' sake? For a moment, she wanted, more intensely than she had wanted anything in her life, to be able to stay here with him, safe in this cocoon. But the world had changed around them, and there was no escaping that fact.

She stood up. "I think I should go home."

BY THE MIDDLE of the second day, Maria knew they were in far greater trouble than she had bargained for. As yet, she wasn't sure exactly what that trouble *was,* but she had no doubt that the spaceports weren't sealed off just for Kit. Something else was happening on Braun's World and runaway junior officers weren't the only ones being prevented from leaving. *Nobody* was getting away.

Kit had taken one look at the barriers going up across the road to Dentrassa's second spaceport and turned the car round again. By dusk of the second day, they were out in the wilds. What greenery there was on Braun's World tended to be near urban centres and, as the suburbs disappeared, the landscape quickly became scrubland: rough grass and sturdy brown shrubs. The scrub in turn gave way to desert: great red empty plains where the sun beat down and there was little to no cover. Jenny groused from the back of the car; too tired to be awake, too tired to sleep. The aircon buzzed and hummed, and kept the temperature not quite on the right side of comfortable. As night settled and it cooled outside, they threw open the windows and let air gush in as they sped along the empty track. Maria had long since stopped asking where they were heading.

When they were sure that Jenny was asleep, Kit pulled over and got out of the car. Maria got out too, to stretch her legs, but Kit said, "Wait here. Don't follow me."

Maria looked around. There was nothing for miles—miles upon miles—apart from the dim light from their car. Overhead the stars were incandescent. "Where on earth are you going?"

"Not far. I'll be back soon."

He walked a little way—not far; she could still see the light from his torch quite plainly. He wasn't quite out of earshot. She heard snatches of his end of a hushed but heated conversation, enough to get the gist of the quarrel: he wanted to get them off Braun's World; he believed he was owed help. The exchange lasted only a few minutes and, by the end of it, it seemed that Kit's contact had agreed to offer them some assistance.

"All good?" she said, when he came back.

He eyed her cautiously. "Did you hear all that?"

"No," she said, which was technically the truth. She hadn't heard it *all*.

"All's good," he said. "Get back in, love. We've a way to go yet."

"Which way?" she said. "East?"

That meant back to civilisation, or at least to Dentrassa. So she wasn't particularly surprised when he shook his head. "West."

KAY LARSEN HAD originally been Kinsella's friend (Walker didn't know whether that was with or without benefits), but over the years the two women had drifted together. If you have to go up two flights of stairs to find the toilets with the skirted figure on the door, you quickly discover who else gets this extra compulsory exercise. In an institution like the Bureau, where women were thin on the ground, you either made friends with each other or else segregated yourself entirely. Even someone as private by nature (and profession) as Walker didn't care for total exclusion from female company. Larsen provided companionship, and was someone who understood, without having to explain. And here they were again, in the ladies', where they had shared many a quiet confidence in the past.

Larsen was struggling, Walker could see, watching her friend closely as she packed away her kit.

"Well," said Larsen. "Now I know why you weren't keen on being scanned for infection. I don't think it would have done any harm, for the record, but there's no way for knowing for sure. You're fit and healthy, and there's no point in doing anything to change that."

"And the…" Walker's tongue tripped over the word. "The baby?"

"We'd have to do some tests to be sure of that." Larsen looked at Walker sharply. "Is that something I need to arrange?"

"I don't know yet."

"Hmm." Larsen fiddled with the clasp on her bag. "Have you talked to Mark?"

"Yes, I've talked to Mark."

"And?"

"And he's clear this is my decision and my responsibility."

Larsen was staring down again into her bag, apparently fascinated by what it contained. "I can arrange whatever you need," she said in a neutral voice. "Very private. Carry on as you were. Nobody will find out."

"Somebody will find out."

"Perhaps, but it will be just a little mark in someone's little book. There alongside the alcoholics and the pill-poppers. No real harm done. I can tell you that for sure." She shot Walker a quick look, under her eyelids. A confidence for a confidence, Walker thought, and a sign that Larsen could be trusted. "Discretion is all that's required—that and a speedy return to work. Particularly now."

"And if I choose another option?"

Larsen looked up from the bag. "Then I'd advise you to start considering how your skills might be transferable to the private sector."

"Nothing else? You don't you want to tell me it would be a terrible, dreadful, life-destroying mistake?"

Larsen fiddled with the clasp on her bag. Open and shut. Open and shut. "Do you want me to tell you that?"

"I want you to tell me what you think."

"Do you need to hear that? You're not a fool, Delia. You surely know already what the consequences will be. They won't let you stay. Even under ordinary circumstances, this would probably mean the end of your career. As for now..."

She didn't need to go further. Carnage on Braun's World. Andrei gone. Adelaide Grant on the warpath and controlling the narrative. "I know," Walker said. "I know."

"May I ask where this sudden desire for motherhood has sprung from?"

"I don't know. Circumstance. Age. I'm as surprised as you are. But there it is."

"Hmm." Larsen closed her bag, decisively. "Mark may be a bloody idiot, but he's right about one thing. Ultimately, it's your decision." She held up her hands, as if each one was a weight upon a scale. "Two alternatives. Utterly incompatible. I know my choice—but I'm not you." She lowered her left hand. "As I say, though—it might be a good idea to start looking for other sources of income." She nodded at Walker's belly. "Because soon everybody will be finding out."

WHICH HAPPENED SOONER than Walker had anticipated. Late morning, she slipped out for some air, taking a long walk along the central waterway where other officials—junior and with less to trouble them—were gathering to enjoy the sunshine and lunch. It was a scene she had observed many times, and had, in the past, enjoyed watching, reminding her, as it did, that she was at the heart of things, and that all was well. Not all was well now, but being amongst the impromptu picnickers did ease her mind for a while. This great civilization—this great Expansion—that she had served so assiduously. Surely nothing could destroy it?

Comforted a little, she returned to the Bureau, but found that the doors did not respond to her retina scan. She stood back, rubbed her eye, and tried again. Still no luck, and by now the entrance to the building was blocked by two security guards whose patience, sense of humour, and state-of-the-art weaponry Walker wasn't inclined to test. "There wasn't a problem this morning," she said, pulling at her lower lid and feeling rather foolish.

But there was clearly a problem now. One of the guards, after a quiet conversation with someone via the headset in his helmet, said, "Your clearance has been revoked."

From the corner of her eye, Walker saw his colleague tighten his grip on his firearm. Only a little, but enough. She took a deep breath and stepped back. "All right," she said. "Not your problem."

One of them nodded his agreement. She walked down the block, conscious of them both watching her, and stood on the corner looking around. Some mistake, she assumed; some piece of paperwork she had neglected to complete, some password she had forgotten to change. She reached for her handheld to send Kinsella a message—and then she saw Latimer sitting at a table outside the café across the road and knew there had been no mistake.

He gestured to her to join him, and she slipped through the queuing traffic. He watched her impassively as she sat down. "Sorry for the scene," he said. "The problem is... Well, I simply don't know who can be trusted these days."

"Is this about that bloody scan?" Walker said. "For God's sake—"

"It's not about the scan."

"Then what's the problem?"

"It's not about *that* scan, I should say."

Walker felt her shoulders slump. "Ah."

"Do you see my dilemma?"

"Actually," Walker said, "I don't."

"And there lies my problem." He picked up his coffee cup and drained it. "Divided loyalties. New priorities."

"You're saying that having a child would stop me from doing my job?"

"I'm saying that I'm not going to take the risk. Not as things are now." He stood up. A black flyer, sleek and unobtrusive, had pulled up. "I've got you a ride. Go home. Think about your future. I'll have your personal effects sent on."

Personal effects, she thought, as the car rose and then sped towards to her flat. It made her sound like she was dead.

Back home, she sat for a while with her head in

her hands, until her anger got the better of her. Then she put a call through to Kinsella.

"You son of a bitch," she said, when his face came up on the screen. "You couldn't wait, could you? What did you think? That I'd cause a scene and embarrass you in front of everyone?"

"*I've no idea what you're talking about,*" Kinsella said. He glanced sideways. There must be someone in there with him. "*I've never had you down as the kind of person to cause a scene. Not until now—*"

"I've been fired, Mark!"

She realised immediately that she had made a mistake. You couldn't feign that kind of shocked expression. He hadn't known, and he hadn't said a word.

There was a pause. Walker heard voices in the background; she couldn't distinguish who was there, but she could hear the questions being asked, the sound of the rumour mill starting to grind... "I'm sorry," she said.

"*Christ, Delia, are you okay? Do you need me to come over?*"

Walker ended the call. There was only one other person it could be and, to be fair, she had even warned her. *Soon everybody will be finding out...*

"*I'm sorry, I really am,*" said Larsen. "*But what's happened on Braun's World—it's changed everything.*"

"I trusted you, Kay! Not only as my doctor. As my friend!"

"*Delia, you know the score. None of us can afford to be showing divided loyalties right now. You shouldn't have put me in that position—*"

Walker cut the line. So much for professional

ethics. So much for the fucking sisterhood. She stared around the room. A call came in, from Andrei, but she directed it to messages and, when his gentle civilized voice came through asking her to pick up and speak to him, she silenced it and deleted his message unheard.

So this is what it feels like to be outside, she thought, dazed. Twenty-five years of effort, of hard work and dedicated service, and for what? All over, in the time it took to pop out for lunch.

She lay back against the cushions and, half-consciously, half-instinctively, rested her hand against her stomach. *What do we do now?* But the little collection of cells multiplying within her didn't have an answer either. Only demands. *Think about your future*, Latimer said. But outside of the Bureau, she didn't know what that could be.

THE LITTLE SPACECRAFT had been waiting for them in the middle of the desert. Maria hadn't asked how Kit knew it would be there. What mattered was that it was there, ramshackle and ancient, looking like it hadn't flown in decades, and didn't plan to ever again. But Kit was working it on it anyway, and Kit knew what he was doing when it came to getting battered old pieces of junk airborne.

But would it matter? Maria thought to herself. *Would we simply carry the danger off with us?* She looked at the little ship, its tiny hull and smaller cockpit, and thought of the three of them huddled in there, with nowhere to go, no way of putting space between them and any infection they might have brought with them... *What would it be like?*

What would happen? Would we know what was happening? Or would we all suddenly be gone?

She reached out to the little girl, fast asleep on a rug on the bare red earth, and stroked her hair. Jenny stirred slightly, and muttered, but didn't wake up. Maria twitched the shade so that the girl was safely out of the sun, and then stood up. Picking up the water bottle, she walked over to her husband and offered it to him. He stopped and drank gratefully, then turned back at once to his work.

"Kit," she said, softly.

"Love, I have to get on with this. We don't have much time."

"Kit, please. You have to tell me what's going on." Seeing his face, she amended that.

"You have to tell me *something* of what's going on." He hesitated, so she pressed on. "I know we're in trouble," she said. "I'm thinking more kinds of trouble than I can even guess."

"Yes," he said, sliding through the hatch back into the cockpit. She followed him down. Inside, it was hellishly hot and there was nowhere to go.

"I think you're AWOL," she said. "I think you're running now from the military police. And I think we don't have long before we won't be able to get away."

He stared down at the control panels in front of him, not answering.

"Am I right? Kit, am I right?"

"You're right—as far as it goes."

"Somebody's been helping us, haven't they?"

He shook his head. "Love, don't ask. I can't talk about that."

"All right." She sighed in frustration.

"Yes," he said, unexpectedly. "Somebody has been

helping us. They told me where to find this ship."
He held up a finger to stop her questions. "That's all
I can say. It's not safe otherwise."

That frightened her. "Will they continue to help?
Kit! Will they keep on helping us? If we get off
Braun's World?"

"I don't know."

She watched as, wearily, he rubbed his eyes. She
touched the back of his hand. "I guess we'll have to
cross that bridge when we reach it," she said. "What
will we do when we get away? Where are we going?"

He smiled. "You've got a lot of faith that I can get
this bag of bolts flying."

"If you can't, nobody can. And it seems a lot of
risk on the part of our mysterious helper to send
you to a ship that won't fly. That, or some sort of
baroque plan that I can't understand."

He grunted.

"So where do we go? We can't go core-wards.
Where are we going?"

"Satan's Reach," he said, without looking at her.

"Satan's *Reach?* Kit, we can't go there! It's
dangerous! It's no place for a child!"

"It's not as bad you think. Some of the worlds are
supposed to be fairly safe..."

But Expansion propaganda had its hold on both of
them, and there was only one thing that Expansion
citizens knew about Satan's Reach, that part of
inhabited space that remained stubbornly beyond its
jurisdiction. "It's lawless," Maria said.

"I know!" he said, desperation in his voice. "Do
you think I'd drag you both there if there was
anywhere else? Maria, we'll be lucky to get away
from this damned world with our lives!"

Suddenly, the control panel fired into life. Maria took Kit's hand. "Said you could do it."

"Not quite sure *what* I did..."

"Don't ask too many questions," she said dryly. "Come on, all aboard. I'll get Jenny."

They were up and flying over Braun's World within the hour. Maria watched and listened carefully: no air traffic control; no friendly messages directing ships around the planet. The occasional curt order from the military. It was if a thick black cloud was descending over the world. A shroud.

And Kit—whenever he was asked—offered codes that somehow, miracle upon miracle, let them pass whenever they were challenged... *Don't ask*, he'd said. *I can't talk about that...* She studied her husband's weary, grey face. *Who is helping us, love? And why?*

They saw the bombardment of Braun's World from a great distance: pinpricks of light at first, hitting the ground, and then great flares of white, pluming upwards. For a few seconds, Maria didn't understand, and then she turned to Kit and said, "*Everyone?*"

"Everyone," he said. "There'll be nothing—and nobody—left alive."

He turned to the controls, and lay in a flight path for Satan's Reach. And, unnoticed, a little ship peeled away from the fleet sent to wipe out whatever infection was loose on that damned world, and began to follow their trail.

CHAPTER THREE

THE SKY WAS blue and the water on the lagoon calm and green. The dark shapes of strange fish could be seen below the surface, shadowy and mysterious, darting about on weird purposes impenetrable to the human mind. At Andrei's bidding, Walker stopped the engine on the little boat, and then watched patiently as he arranged himself for an afternoon's quiet fishing. He unpacked his kit, assembled his rod and wire, unfolded a rickety canvas deckchair, and settled down comfortably. With a flick of his wrist, the music stored on the main datacore in the cabin was activated, and Andrei selected some Mozart, which floated out across the water. The fish disappeared.

"Well," Andrei said. "This is pleasant."

Walker poured them both cold drinks and took her seat next to him in the other deckchair, looking out across the water. They were about half a mile out from Andrei's private island, where he was apparently enjoying his retirement immensely or, at least, putting on a good show. She herself would have found the quiet unbearable: the absence of city noises, even muted behind sound-proofed windows, the sense of being cut off from everything that had ever mattered to them. Their current position gave them a striking view back to downtown Venta. Gleaming white towers dominated the skyline. The tiny black shapes of flyers could be seen swarming between them, like insects. High above even the towers glided a handful of government flyers, moving at a statelier pace. Walker could not hear the city, but she could feel its low steady *thrum*, like blood in the veins, or a quiet heartbeat, or the soft plashing of a fish.

Andrei gestured with his fishing rod. "The most stirring sight in the Expansion," Andrei said. "Or so the tour guides would tell you. Are you stirred, Delia?"

Walker contemplated the city whose schemes and concerns had consumed her entire adult life. There had indeed been a time when the view made her catch her breath, but looking at it now, she realised that she felt little of the old awe, the excitement rising from the knowledge that she was at the heart of the greatest civilisation humanity had ever built, and she was one of the people shaping it. What she chiefly felt now was vague regret, at the time and energy spent on it. Somewhere along the line, it seemed, she had started a process of detachment, of separation. She was slipping off the hook.

"I, at least, must confess to an unaccustomed tremor of emotion," said Andrei. He raised his hand to shade his eyes from the glare of the white sun off the water. "This was not where I thought we would be, only a few days ago. Indeed, it's hard to think how events might have turned out better for our colleagues." He made a low hum at the back of his throat. Walker looked at him in interest. That was the sound of Andrei thinking, and one was wise to pay attention.

"Something on your mind?" she said.

Andrei remained absent for a while, his clever brain plainly ticking over, and then he turned his brilliant smile on her. "Only you, dear lady. One thing for an old man like me to find himself in early retirement. Something else for someone like you. What do you intend to do now?"

Now Walker herself became absent, as she considered whether or not to tell him her plans. Would it be better for him to know, or should she let it go? He should be untroubled now, surely, left in peace after a lifetime's struggles, as calm as the waters supporting this little ship... "I'm going to Satan's Reach," she said.

She rarely got the opportunity to surprise Andrei, so it was always enjoyable when it happened. His bright blue eyes widened. "Well," he said. "That was not the answer I was expecting."

"No?" She smiled. "I thought you knew me."

"You've surprised me in many ways in recent days, Delia."

Walker stretched back in the clumsy little chair, letting the sun warm her arms and legs. "Your first lesson. We don't serve the institution. We serve the principles that the institution embodies. The corollary of that being that if the institution no longer embodies those principles—"

"One must continue to serve them from the outside."

She smiled at him. "You had it easy, you know, your generation. Superiors who shared your values—"

"Ah, yes, very easy. Merely the outbreak of war with the Vetch to contend with."

"A war with a clearly defined enemy and a clearly defined goal. But now..." She gazed into the water, trying to catch a glimpse of a fish. "Is it inevitable, do you think, that without an enemy to unite us we must fight each other?"

"You don't consider the Weird an enemy? There are many who would disagree with you. I'm not sure that *I* agree with you."

"The point is that I don't know! We don't know enough about them! We don't yet comprehend them, in any way. Yes, they consume; yes, there has been terrible devastation..." The thought of Braun's World made her stomach churn, but she steadied herself. "But what do we know about the Weird, really?"

"We know they kill in great numbers, and in ways horrible to contemplate. We know that they enslave and can control minds—infect minds, so that people are no longer able to make their own decisions but must act according to the will of the Weird."

"Yes, they kill in great numbers—but so do we. So do the Vetch. You talk about controlling minds—so do we, with our relentless propaganda, our mind-numbing culture, our news blackouts. Every single person in that city"—she pointed towards Venta—"has their freedoms curtailed in some way. They cannot send their flyers above a certain height. They cannot leave this world without passing through all the hoops we can throw at them. They can choose between one indistinguishable council-member or another—"

"The Weird are in a different category, Delia."

"And yet most of the people on Braun's World didn't die at the hands of Sleer, did they? They died when Fleet bombarded their cities."

"You've seen the footage, just as I have," Andrei said softly. "Would you have wanted to live that way? Mind-numbed by drugs, surrendering oneself to be consumed by a monstrous creature? Some people on Braun's World might consider it a mercy that they have not had to live that way."

"Even so," she said, "just because the Weird that we have encountered kill does not mean that all our encounters with the Weird must end in devastation. If I only ever see white swans, it doesn't disprove the existence of black swans."

Andrei laughed then. "The Weird are rather less lovely than swans!"

"You get my point." Softly, urgently, she said, "I believe this colony exists, Andrei. That there is a place where humans are able to live harmoniously with the Weird—not enslaved, not farmed, but in genuine cooperation. It wasn't something I simply made up to see off Grant and her cronies. Somewhere out in the Reach, they exist. I'm going to find them."

"Indeed," he said dryly, "you have a moral imperative."

"Well, yes," she said, and laughed. "That always helps."

He pondered the absent fish for a while. "You may find that people will try to stop you in your quest."

"I'm not beholden to anyone now."

He looked at her sharply, but with compassion. "No, Delia?"

That caught her unawares. "I'm beholden to the future. I always was. More so than ever. And that's why I want peace. Not news blackouts and compulsory scans, and bigger, faster, wilder superweapons. Something else."

"You may be asking a great deal of Satan's Reach," Andrei said. "I can't stop you. I can only give you my blessing—and warn you again. There are people who are going to try to stop you. Play your cards carefully. Keep your own counsel." He smiled at her. "Like I taught you."

She smiled back. He turned back to his fish and they sat together in companionable silence. Tentatively, uncertain about the gesture and what it might mean, she laid her hand softly upon her stomach. *Little minnow,* she thought. *I hadn't forgotten you.*

A TRIP TO Satan's Reach meant a ship, and someone to fly the ship—and that meant funds. Cold, hard cash; or, at least, cold, hard credit in the bank.

Her apartment was her main asset, and very desirable: on one of the most secluded inner islands, with a handful of pleasant, discreet neighbours, excellent facilities, and fantastic views over the waterway. Walker made a few enquiries, and by mid-morning had a great deal of interest from agents and private buyers alike. She set a bidding war going, and turned her attention to trying to charter a ship. Something at the back of her mind said: *What will you do without this place when you come home? Where will you live?* Another, harder part of her mind replied: *If you go to Satan's Reach, you're not coming back.*

By mid-morning, she was not sure the journey was ever going to happen. If you offered enough money, someone would be willing to take you almost anywhere, but whatever enquiries Walker made ended in refusal. They would sound interested, take a few details, and then, if they did get back to her, it was to make an apology and say that the ship she was interested in had already been chartered, or there must have been a mistake, or there were no pilots available at such short notice, or the risks were too great, or the insurance too expensive... She tried a few of her old assets, but none of them returned her calls. No doubt word had got loose that she was burned. They wouldn't dare speak to her for fear of reprisals.

She slipped into her flyer and went for lunch at a nearby café. Her appetite was off, she noticed, with cool, almost scientific, detachment, so she pushed food around for a while, and then sat sipping water and watching the foot traffic. After a while, a familiar figure emerged from the crush. Kinsella.

"What exactly are you playing at?" he said, sitting down opposite her.

Walker felt the anger that had been simmering within her all morning start to flare. "Hi, Mark," she said. "How are you? I'm okay. No sickness, thank goodness. Some fatigue."

"I know you're okay. Do you think I'm not keeping track of you? Of course I know you're okay."

"I guess Kay must have told you. She told everyone else."

"You put her in a very awkward position."

"Poor Kay," Walker deadpanned. "Things must be difficult for her right now."

Kinsella flushed. "I'm not here to talk about Kay," he said, in a softer voice. Walker was coming to hate this voice. People trying to speak calmly and reasonably to the mad woman whose hormones were turning her brain. Only Andrei had managed to be concerned without slipping into patronising.

"Not here to talk about Kay, not here to talk about me—I guess you must be here to talk about yourself."

Kinsella sat back, looking genuinely hurt. "I don't know what's got into you," he said. "You were never like this—"

"I've had a short fast course in who my friends are."

"All right then, Delia, we'll play it your way. But if you'll listen to someone who once considered himself your friend—whatever you may think of him—then you'll take the apartment off the market and abandon any plans you might have to leave." He must have seen her swallow: he leaned in and spoke softly. "What did you think was going to happen? Did you think that Latimer would let you walk away?"

That would explain the difficulties she was having chartering a ship. "Are you here at Latimer's bidding?"

"I'm here because I care about you."

"So he did send you. You can go back to him this afternoon and tell him he can get lost. He didn't exactly go out of his way to keep me."

"You can't just walk away, you know. You were on the inside—as deep as it's possible to go."

"And I've signed legally binding documents that prevent me from revealing any of it to anyone without serious repercussions."

"Legally binding documents which are not enforceable in Satan's Reach."

So he knew that—or was making an educated guess. She composed herself and gave away nothing.

"Where are you heading?" he urged. "What's the plan?"

She stood up. "Whatever my plan is, it's my business. I'm a private citizen now—"

"You know as well as I do that you're not. You can't be. Never." He rubbed his hand across his mouth. "Besides," he said. "The Reach? What about... What about the *child?*"

"The *child?*" She turned to him in anger. "How dare you, Mark? You have no *right!*"

"I know," he said. "I know..."

They stood facing each other, not touching. His hands were pressed against his forehead; hers were balled into fists by her side.

"They won't let you go, Delia," he said, at last. "They can't."

A cold desperate feeling welled up within her. But she was damned if she would let him see that, and she went on her way. "We'll see," she called back over her shoulder.

But could well be right.

So what would she do next?

In the event, she didn't need to come up with another plan. As she strode along the sidewalk back to where her flyer was parked, a slight figure, rushing up past her on the outside, slipped and fell against her, then dashed off. "Sorry!" they called back, over their shoulder—and then they were gone, before she gather much sense of what they looked like.

Walker could tell when a fall was deliberate. Instinctively she checked her wrist for her ID and datapin. All still safely there. Puzzled, she checked the pockets of her jacket.

Where she found a small piece of paper, covered in a familiar scrawl.

Andrei's.

Heartbroken. But since I can't stop you, I may as well help you.

She flipped over the piece of paper. More scrawl. Directions. Down to the docks. A name: *Yershov.* And something else, which she didn't understand: *Baba Yaga.* She puzzled over that. Some kind of code? It would become clear, no doubt; Andrei did not waste your time. Walker smiled. Some friends you could always count on. And if Andrei, by helping her travel to the Reach, happened to put a spanner into the works of Commander Adelaide Grant—then all to the good.

THE WOMAN WAS nondescript, nothing special. The only point of interest, as far as Yershov was concerned, was that was that she plainly had money. Not vast amounts, no; not one of the idle super-rich, who swanned around the core worlds and sometimes even ventured to the edge of the Reach. But her clothes were good, her teeth were white and even, and her manner suggested she could be a right royal pain in the bloody neck. Yershov didn't like the rich—Yershov didn't like anyone, really, including himself—but he did like money, and he hadn't seen enough of it in recent years. Money didn't, in general, come to this part of St Martin's Docks, and when it did, it was usually keeping close company with trouble. Yershov chewed his bottom lip. He could do without trouble. But he was short of money.

The woman drew closer. No, he thought, nothing special. Too old, for one thing—he sniffed, as if her age was a personal affront—and dressed too mannishly for his taste. Women should look like women. Still, at least she was smart. She'd be something professional, he guessed—a teacher or a lawyer or a doctor or... Yershov frowned; his knowledge of the professions ran out round about here. Probably a doctor. Next question was: What would bring someone like this down to this part of the world? Husband worries? Boyfriend worries?

She came straight up to him. Nice necklace. No rings. Two small bags that he thought might be designer. Tired looking. Could make more of herself. She spoke quietly, her Anglais clipped and precise. Posh. "I gather you have a ship to hire."

Yershov tugged his earlobe. "Mebbe."

The woman leaned back on her heels and gave him a good long appraising look. Then she looked behind him at the snub-nosed pile of junk she was trying to hire. "It's not state-of-the art, is it?"

"S'all right," he said. Loyal to his knackered old ship, he added, "Does the job." More or less.

"That's all I want." She sighed and looked past him once again. "It *will* fly?"

"It'll fly."

"If it'll fly, then you're hired." She offered him her handheld. "That's what I'm paying."

He looked at the amount on the screen, sniffed

a couple of times and pretended to consider it. "There's some last minute repairs," he said.

She added a few hundred units extra. "That's as far as I'm going."

He sniffed again, but he knew he wasn't fooling her. Of course he was going to take the offer—it was the first he'd had in over eighteen months, and he'd barely been making ends meet from repair work. "I mean it about the repairs," he said.

"I mean it about the money. I'm not going any higher."

"No, you're not getting it, lady." He jerked his head back at the ship. "She's dry-docked. Uncertified. What I mean," he said, because she was posh and probably hadn't ever had to worry about this kind of thing, "is that the phase technology is out of date. It's not technically legal for this ship to fly."

The woman closed her eyes, very briefly, then seemed to regroup. "That's all right," she says. "I don't particularly want anyone to know that I'm leaving."

He rasped out a sour laugh. "Like that, is it?"

She gave him a very cool look. "Whatever you're thinking, Mr Yershov, probably doesn't even begin to cover it."

For a moment, Yershov was almost frightened by her. *Bitch*, he thought. Then he remembered that he was the one with the ship, and while she was the one with the money, she was also the one with the trouble.

She too seemed to be weary of the exchange. "Is any of this a problem for you?"

"No problem," he said. "I know a few tricks." He fair bounced towards his ship, scuttling up the metal ladder and opening the hatch, glad to be leaving Hennessy's World. Spots even on the crummier docks were not cheap. "So where are we going, lady?"

She followed him neatly up the ladder. Her bags didn't slow her down. "Satan's Reach," she said. "If you're man enough."

YERSHOV BOUNCED AHEAD of her like a proud father showing off his baby. A particularly foul-smelling, greasy, and unpleasant baby. Sliding down the ladder inside the ship, Walker almost gagged. The space was confined; the air stale and sweaty. As soon as she was sure Yershov couldn't see her, she put her hand over her mouth and willed herself not to be sick.

This ship that she had hired for half of what she had made from the sale of her apartment was not big. Yershov pointed one way down the single corridor in which she now stood and mumbled, "Engines," then he went off in the other direction. Walker followed him; the narrowness of the corridor prevented her from walking alongside him. There were two doors on either side of the corridor— leading to crew cabins, she guessed—and a couple more hatches underfoot which led, presumably, down to the hold. She wondered which cabin was Yershov's. She'd take the one furthest from that.

She looked round with a sinking heart at the ship's general state of disrepair. *What the hell have I let myself in for?* She hadn't been expecting much, but she'd been expecting more than this. She wasn't entirely convinced that it could in fact take flight. "When did you last get any work done?" she said.

Yershov looked back over his shoulder. "I do what's needed. Other people are expensive."

But had the benefit of competence. Yershov pushed aside a nasty-looking curtain, and Walker followed him onto the little flight deck. If she had been harbouring any hopes that here, at least, where the pilot must spend most of his time, would be comfortable, she was quickly disappointed. It wasn't so much the disrepair that she found depressing, she realised, as she walked slowly round the small space, it was the dirt and the grime, the grubbiness of every surface, the general air that nobody cared. Yershov lived here—this place wasn't only his livelihood, it was his home—and yet he couldn't care enough to clear up around him.

The sight of the half-empty bottles lined up behind the flight controls did nothing to make Walker feel better. Yershov mistook her attention for interest, and reached for two glasses. They weren't quite empty, so he tipped the contents into a third.

"We should toast our new partnership," he said, pouring out some brown liquid from the nearest bottle into the two glasses.

"I don't drink," she said, shortly.

He frowned, as if this wasn't something he quite understood, then shrugged and drank—first from one glass, then from the other. While his attention was diverted, Walker grabbed her handheld from her pocket and sent a fast and furious message to Andrei: *Who the hell is this guy?*

She put her hands in her pockets. That way she didn't have to touch anything. "You said the phase technology was out-of-date. What does that mean? Can this ship fly?"

"Sure it can fly," he said. "I've got all the gear." He turned his head sideways and lifted up a lock of lank hair to show the inputs where the flight jacks went in. "But then those bastards at space traffic control decided that the whole set-up—the software, the hardware, the interface with the wetware—was... now what did they call it? Obol... Obles..."

"Obsolete."

"That was it."

"And is it?"

"Is it what?"

Walker was starting to lose patience. "Does the fucking ship fly, Yershov?"

He glared at her. "Don't get shirty with me, lady. Of course it flies. But it's not legal to fly it within the Expansion." He gave her a crooked smile. "I won't tell if you don't."

Walker's handheld buzzed softly. She dug it out, conscious of Yershov checking out the device, putting a price on it, and read the message from Andrei: *Trust him.* A second message came almost straight away: *Correction: don't trust him at all, obviously. But believe me when I say he can get you where you're going.*

Walker shoved the handheld back in her pocket. Andrei's word was going to have to do. Because, really, Walker thought, as she looked round the battered shell of the ancient ship in which she was proposing to visit one of the most dangerous parts of known space on a wild goose chase for a colony that may not even exist, how many other options did she have? She couldn't charter anything on the books. So it would all have to be firmly off the books, which meant trusting herself to something that looked like it could barely heave itself up from the ground.

"All right," she said. "You're hired. When can we leave?"

"When do you want to leave?"

"How about now?"

He nodded at her two bags. "That's all you're bringing?"

"That's all I need."

"Didn't think people like you could pack light."

With a conscious effort of will, Walker relaxed. She folded her arms in front of her, and smiled at Yershov. After a moment or two, he began to get uncomfortable. "If we're going to travel together for a while," she said, "you'd better get one thing straight. You've never met anyone like me."

He looked at her like she'd sprouted an extra head. "Huh?"

"Get in your sling, Yershov. I want us off Hennessy's World within the hour." She followed a hunch, and reached into her pocket for her handheld. "Don't make me tell Gusev how disappointed I am."

Andrei's name, as ever, did the trick. Yershov hastened over to his pilot's sling, strapping himself in and busying himself with the flight controls. Walker, with deliberate casualness, took the other sling. But her heart was pounding. Andrei's name would hold him for a while—but as the distance between them and the core worlds grew greater, the threat of the Bureau would diminish. She would need to find another way to control this man.

"Yershov," she said, suddenly.

He glanced up from the controls. "What?"

"What's it called?"

"Huh?"

"The ship. What's its name?"

Yershov ran his hand lovingly over the panel in front of him. For a moment, Walker almost liked him. "This old girl? She's the *Baba Yaga*."

He went back to plotting their escape from Hennessy's World. The *Baba Yaga*. It meant nothing to her. But it would.

JENNY WAS CRYING again, but silently, her head tucked into her mother's shoulder, her small body shivering with sobs. Maria did not think it was possible to have experienced anything worse than what she'd been through over the past two days—fleeing their home in the dead of night; the long hot day in the desert while Kit had tried to fix the ship; the red-hot flare, strangely beautiful, of a whole world coming under fire... But the universe held even worse horrors. Jenny was now afraid of her father.

It was inevitable, really. Too long without sleep. Too much on his mind. And then they had realised that their escape from Braun's World had not gone unnoticed, and that a ship was in pursuit... The wrong moment for Jenny to discover that one of her favourite toys had not been packed, and that the only option open to her now was to start screaming... But Kit could shout louder, and the sight of her father angry and out-of-control had hushed the little girl at once. And here she sat, her hot little head pressed against her mother, sobbing away to herself.

Maria stroked the child's hair and watched her husband. Kit's mouth was set in a thin straight line; his eyes were fixed on the displays; his knuckles were white where they gripped the controls. "That's it!" he whispered, suddenly exultant.

"You've shaken them off?"

He turned to her and gave her a tired smile. "Yes. Well, for the moment. Long enough to give us a head start." His eyes fell on the child in her arms. "Jenny," he said. "Sweetheart."

But the little girl shook her head and burrowed deeper into her mother's arms.

"Leave it for the moment," Maria said softly, and he nodded. She stood up, Jenny still in her arms, to carry the child to bed. From the doorway, she mouthed, "I love you."

It took a little while for Jenny to settle, but eventually exhaustion did the work, and the little girl fell asleep on the cot she was sharing with her mother. When she was sure her daughter was in a deep sleep, Maria went back to join Kit.

He was still sitting in the same place, staring at the display, but he was holding a toy in his lap: a grubby little teddy. He held it up as Maria came towards him. "I found this in the bag," he said. "I know it's not Monkey..."

She bent to kiss the top of his head. "She'll be fine. She'll be pleased with Bear."

"I'm sorry," he said. "I didn't mean—"

"I understand. These things happen. This is not... it's not the easiest of situations."

"I'm only trying to keep us alive."

"I know." They sat in silence for a while, and Maria listened to the gentle humming of the ship's engines. Regular. Steady. "Where are we going?" she said.

"Shuloma Station."

"Where's that?"

He looked away. "On the edge of the Reach."

Her blood went cold. "But not *in* the Reach?"

"Not quite."

"Kit, I don't want to take Jenny there—"

"Love, please! We don't have many options—"

"So how have we settled on this one?" When he didn't reply, she pressed on, "It's this contact of yours, isn't it? Whoever he is. Are you going to tell me who it is?"

Kit looked at her steadily and then, very slowly, shook his head.

"You can trust me, Kit."

He leaned forward in his seat, and reached out to put his hands around hers. "It's not about trust, love. It's about your safety."

"Oh, Kit, darling. What are we mixed up in?"

Again, he didn't answer.

"I wonder if there's anything I can ask you that you'll answer."

He gave a watery smile. "Try me and see."

But she turned away, afraid to ask the questions that were most pressing on her mind, because then she might have to admit more truths about their situation than she would like.

"Please, Maria—perhaps I'll be able to answer."

"They're there, aren't they? On Braun's World?"

He gave a puzzled frown. "Who?"

"Not who. What." Her voice dropped. "The Weird…"

She felt his hands tighten. "What makes you say that?" he said, his voice light and false.

"I'm not an idiot! Fleet bombarded the planet! I watched them murder *millions!* What else could it be? Some kind of portal…"

His fingertips were tapping against her wrist. "Would it make any difference if that were true?"

"A difference? Of course it would make a difference!" Her voice had crept up, so she lowered it again. "They're parasites too, aren't they? The Weird. They get into your head. You don't know you have them but they're inside you, making you do things you don't want to do until you're not yourself any longer. You're..." She shuddered. "You're one of them."

He was looking at her in frank horror. "How do you *know* all this? It's meant to be classified!"

"Oh, Kit. Some secrets are too big to keep, you know." She swallowed. "But if there's a chance we're infected, the slightest chance, then we shouldn't have left—"

He let go of her hands. "We're not infected."

"What? How do you know? How can you be sure? You dashed away from the base as if..." As if he had been trying to outrun a plague.

"There's a test. A scan. I took it."

"But I didn't. Jenny didn't—"

"I can tell you for certain, Maria—you and Jenny are not infected."

She supposed she would have to trust him. "So," she said. "Shuloma Station. What will we find when we get there?"

"I don't know," he said honestly. "But I trust my friend, and I know that we'll be safe. If we're careful."

"Then by all means let us be careful."

He gave her a beautiful smile, and her heart warmed within her. They would be safe, she thought. Yes, she trusted him, absolutely, and so she would trust whoever he trusted. She reached out and took his hand, and they sat together, peacefully, almost as if they were at home, and it was evening, and they were enjoying the time that they were spending together before it passed.

And, not far behind them, but beyond the range of their scanners, a little ship corrected course, and began to follow them again.

CHAPTER FOUR

IF WALKER HAD harboured any illusions that the Expansion enjoyed total control over its citizens, a few hours in the company of Yershov on the *Baba Yaga* put that notion to rest. Administering a large empire was a difficult task, and it was much easier, on the whole, if citizens stayed put. Travel between worlds was expensive, the permits and passes needed were cumbersome, so that on the whole people tended not to bother, and enjoyed what their home worlds and immediate systems had to offer them. It made life easier all round.

But some people always manage to find a way to slip past the authorities, and Yershov, it seemed, was one of those people who had the knack. But then people did get away sometimes, Walker reflected: renegade telepaths exhausted from the strain of being used for governmental purposes; the odd libertarian who wanted to live out the fantasy of the open road... And it was easier to let these people go than try to prevent them all from leaving. They were better out of the Expansion than spreading their dissatisfaction within, infecting others with their resentment. Whether this courtesy extended to senior officials from the Bureau who, until only a few short days ago, had been privy to some of the Expansion's most sensitive secrets was yet to be determined. But Andrei, at least, seemed to think that Yershov was up to the job.

And so it proved, incredibly. The *Baba Yaga* rose clumsily from her berth in St Martin's Docks, lumbered halfway around Hennessy's World at high altitude and then, when she was as far as she could be from Venta and her troublesome air traffic control, heaved herself up into orbit.

"Why is nobody stopping you?" asked Walker.

"She's old," said Yershov. "Nobody quite believes the ion traces she's leaving. So they write it off as noise." He gave a toothy smile. "Sometimes being old means you're invisible." So slowly, steadily, and—apparently—invisibly, the *Baba Yaga* made her way to the edge of the system. "Helps we're going out," Yershov said. "Early warning defence systems point outwards. Not as concerned about people escaping as they are enemies invading. Trying to get back to Hennessy's World would be a whole different ball game. But leaving? There's a few blind spots here and there. We'll get to one of those, then phase."

"How do you know Andrei Gusev?" Walker said, suddenly.

Yershov gave her a sly look. "I was wondering when you'd ask that."

"And your answer?"

"We met during the war with the Vetch. Gusev needed the odd cargo taking from point A to point B, no questions asked. I obliged."

Gunrunning, Walker assumed; arming the human populations of worlds overrun by Vetch invaders. A dirty job, making money from the suffering of others.

"You got a problem with that?"

"What you do in your off-hours is your own business." Walker shifted slightly forwards in her sling to show him her handheld. "Here's where we're going."

He nodded at the coordinates. "Shard's World." He grunted, and she watched as his gnarled hands scampered over the flight controls, and then he leaned back in his sling and fixed the flight jacks into place. "Get yourself comfortable, lady," he said. "This might be bumpy."

The beautiful starscape of her home system gave way to the empty grey swirl of the void. Walker closed her eyes. "Remember, Yershov," she said, "I'm no lady."

ABOUT AN HOUR later, Yershov lay snoring in his pilot's sling, exhausted from the rigours that the phase had demanded of his shrunken old body. The three or four shots he'd drunk right after must have helped too, Walker thought. Still, it was better than having him awake and his small dark eyes following her and inching across her body, judging and appraising. In the half-light and the quiet, the *Baba Yaga* was almost peaceful. Walker felt alone for the first time in an age:

without a communicator buzzing, or a colleague needing urgent answers, or Kinsella, sending her love notes... her mind inevitably turned to the inescapable fact that she was not alone. She was...

She stood up abruptly, banishing the thought and its implications. She stretched each limb carefully, then worked the muscles of her neck, trying to get sensation back into the top of her spine. Her work in recent years had kept her on Hennessy's World, and she had forgotten how space travel constrained one's body. It would be several days before they got to their destination in the Reach: the mining planet Shard's World. A former asset was there, pretty much the only person Walker knew within the Reach, although it had been some years since they had met face-to-face. Still, she doubted that he would have forgotten her. You didn't forget a brush with the Bureau, and his brush had been particularly unpleasant. A petty thief, he had fallen in with some fairly nasty gangsters whose rackets the Bureau had wanted closed down. Walker had been the one to question him, to run his undercover operation, and then to provide him with the cover identity that sent him out of the Expansion and away, they all hoped, from the reach of his former paymasters. She had heard nothing from him since she had put him on a shuttle for Shuloma Station, one of the crossing points between the Expansion and the Reach. All she knew was that he was now going by the name of Fredricks, and that he was on Shard's World.

She punched his codes into the comm. An automated service tried to prevent her from getting through to him, until she said her name, very clearly. Then his face appeared on screen. He looked older than when she had last seen him (but then, who didn't?), but his time away from the Expansion had clearly been good to him. He looked slick, and prosperous.

"Hello, Fredricks," she said.

The man now known as Fredricks blanched. "*Hell's bells, Walker. Is it really you?*"

"It's me."

"*I didn't think you were going to darken my days again. Where have you sprung from?*"

"Your dreams."

"*My nightmares, more like.*" He looked at her anxiously. "*You're not here, are you?*"

"On Shard's World? No."

"*Thank Christ for that.*"

"Not yet."

He took a deep breath and ran his hand across his eyes. "*I see.*"

"I'm passing through in a few days. I won't stay long."

He studied her thoughtfully. "*What do you want from me, Walker?*"

"Let's save that for when we meet."

"*I paid my debt to you, you know. I put myself in danger for you. Cost me everything I had back in the Expansion—*"

"You seem to be doing pretty well out in the Reach."

"*I've worked hard. I started with nothing, and I've earned everything I've got—*"

"I'm not coming to take any of that away from you," she said. "I won't take up much of your time. But I am coming. It would be a shame if a number of our old acquaintances found out your new address."

"*An hour?*" he said. "*I think I can manage that.*"

"I'm glad to hear that. I'll reach Shard's World by the end of the week, your time. Where can I find you?"

He sent over contact details, and her expensive little handheld, still diligently working this far from Hennessy's World, started assembling a little dossier on him.

"All right, I'll see you soon."

"*I'll put the kettle on,*" he said, and cut the comm.

She let her handheld go about its business for a while, and then began to read what it had found. *Merriman Fredricks. Specialist Import Services.* She found company accounts, saw exactly how successful he had been, but she couldn't find any specific details as to the nature of his business. Importing what, exactly? What did one import to a mining world? Flowers? She was digging for more information when she heard a rattling cough behind her.

Yershov was wide awake in his sling and staring at her glassily. She wondered how long he had been awake, and how much of that conversation he had heard. She would have preferred none at all—although it would do no harm, she thought, for Yershov to see that grown men were frightened of her.

"Shard's World," he said.

"That's where we're going. You set the course, remember?"

"I know Shard's World."

"You've been there?" She looked at him, irritated. "You didn't mention it."

"Long time ago. Good money, mining. Then the law changed and the union-busters came. Brought a load of slaveys with them. That was the end of that."

He'd been lucky not to get indentured himself, Walker thought.

"I said I'd never go back to Shard's World, not for any money."

"We do a lot of things we said we'd never do."

"I know," he said, and fell asleep again.

And although she was glad of the peace, she supposed she was glad too that he'd woken up and spoken. Because now she thought she had an idea what business Fredricks was in, and how she needed to take care when visiting the world where a one-time petty thief could make a home and a fortune.

DOCKING AT SHULOMA Station posed no problems: it was the kind of place where the fewer questions were asked, the happier everyone was. Still, Kit had told Maria that they needed to pack everything, and not assume that they were coming back to the ship.

"It's better," he said, haltingly, "if we try to... Well, we should be discreet."

They should cover their tracks, he meant, Maria thought, but she did not press him. He had promised her they weren't infected—and she couldn't believe he would take any risks with Jenny's welfare—so why would they be chased? Who would come after them? Surely his superiors had more to worry about, given the situation on Braun's World, than one junior officer who had gone on the run? Or perhaps the fear of infection was so great now that they would pursue people beyond reason... That was a frightening thought, as was the sight of Kit constantly looking over his shoulder.

But someone, at least, was looking after them, and

Maria was glad of it, in this godforsaken place. All her preconceptions of the worlds beyond Expansion control were true: dirty, frightening, unkempt places, with an underlying sense of lawlessness. Maria was used to the brisk order of military bases: small but well-kept homes and gardens; friendly, generous people, who would help you if you were in distress. People who wouldn't see you as an opportunity for self-advancement. She had known nothing like Shuloma Station.

The station lay on the very edge of the Reach, at the point where the rule of law imposed by the Expansion gave out, and the overlapping and contradictory jurisdictions of the many independent worlds of the Reach began. It had been a scientific research station, once upon a time, cutting-edge; where scientists who couldn't quite get permission for their research within the Expansion had come, finding it a place where nobody really bothered to ask questions, as long as the results were good. And since even research scientists need food and entertainment, and sometimes even want to enjoy the finer things in life, and since there seemed to be a good deal of money sloshing around, the traders moved in to offer whatever was wanted. Soon the place acquired its own momentum, and the great market of Shuloma Station was born. The place now had the feel of a bazaar; it had been running for more than thirty years, and had no intention of packing up soon. There was little original scientific work conducted on Shuloma these days, but business was still booming.

Maria, clutching Jenny's hand, stood at the intersection between two busy walkways and stared around at the booths, and the traders, and the people... and the *aliens*... Maria had never left the Expansion before. She'd seen a few pictures of non-humans—the Vetch, of course, were the staple villain of popular war vids—but nothing had prepared her for the great diversity of the universe beyond her former little world, in all its messy, stinking, oozing glory, with its tentacles and multiple eyes and excess legs and hands and fingers. She stared round until suddenly a little head came to rest exhaustedly against her. Turning to Kit, she murmured, "Jenny's getting tired."

"I know." Kit frowned into his handheld, and then looked down at his daughter. "Can you manage a little longer, sweetheart?"

The little girl clung to her mother's leg and stared at the ground. Kit sighed, and lowered himself down to her height. "Hey, Jenny," he said. "Think you can manage a while longer? For me?"

The little girl, bless her, smiled gamely and held out her small arms. "Carry, Daddy?"

Kit glanced down at the handheld.

"I can take that," said Maria, softly.

He hesitated.

"Pick her up, love."

Kit handed over the device and lifted his daughter into his arms, kissing her soft hair. "I'm following the directions I was given," he told Maria.

"You don't know where we're heading?" Maria said. "We don't have an address?"

He shook his head. Maria wondered, for a moment, whether it had crossed his mind that whoever was helping may well have decided that they were a liability, and was sending all three of them to an unpleasant fate. Then she decided that if it had occurred to someone as inexperienced as her, it had probably occurred to Kit too, and that it was a mark of their desperate situation that he was prepared to take the risk.

"Then I guess we'd better do what this thing tells us. Everything will be fine," she said firmly. She nodded towards a passageway on the right, where a huge birdcage hung on the wall, with a great scarlet bird inside. Its eyes, bright and sharp, glittered like gold, or fire. "Down there, I think."

A HEAVY GLOOM lay over Shard's World: a thick industrial smog that settled on the lungs and made every breath laborious. Walker had only been planetside for a matter of hours, and was already eager to leave. She could not imagine living out her life in this murk.

They had landed mid-morning, local time, at the spaceport outside Roby, the main city on Shard's World. They had had no trouble passing through customs and boarding a city-bound shuttle. Nobody checked documents; nobody asked for permits. The worlds that made up Satan's Reach did not trouble themselves with the baroque bureaucracy and tight controls that typified the Expansion; indeed, they prided themselves on their freedoms. Walker rubbed her hand against the window of the shuttle and looked out across a grim, depleted landscape: grey sky, oily river, heavy machinery, cheap housing. The freedoms enjoyed by the inhabitants of the Reach included, it seemed, the freedom to smother themselves in thick smog and choke themselves to death. This would not have been allowed within the

Expansion. For all the petty corruption of its senior officials, or the tendency of its police to shoot first and ask questions later, the Expansion did maintain a certain quality of life for its citizens. She looked at her hand where it had touched the window. It had come away black and damp.

"Fucking shithole," said Yershov, and Walker was inclined to agree.

After a couple of changes, the shuttle dumped them in the centre of Roby, a small square built around a fountain (dry). Here an effort had been made, once upon a time, at civic pride: there were numerous red-brick building with ornate fronts and the proud names of their one-time benefactors emblazoned across grand doorways. Some were quite fanciful— turreted, even, or with ornate tilework. But the bricks and the tiles were all soiled and blackened, and the locals scurried around the place with eyes down and shoulders hunched.

Fredricks had given Walker an address here in the main square. Walker got her bearings, and then led Yershov over to one of the larger buildings, which, it seemed, had once been a public library. Walker doubted such a thing operated on Shard's World now. They passed through high main doors (hinges rusty and the paint cracked) into a huge vestibule, whose size and ornate decoration gave it a faded glamour. Two big men waited there, smartly dressed and armed with lasers. One stepped forwards to meet them.

"Are you Walker?"

"Who's asking?"

He rested his hand upon his weapon. "Don't push it, lady."

"I'm Walker," she said. "Where's Fredricks?"

The other man gestured behind him to a grand stairway. "He's waiting upstairs."

Walker made to follow, but found her way blocked. "I can't go upstairs with you in the way, gentlemen."

"We were only expecting one of you."

Walker looked back over her shoulder at Yershov. "Don't worry about him. He's no trouble."

"Not a chance, lady."

Walker shrugged. It wasn't like she was relying on Yershov. He'd surely be gone at the first whiff of trouble. "Yershov," she said. "Wait here. I'll buy you something nice on the way back to the ship."

One of the men gestured Yershov towards a big sofa at the far end of the lobby, and stood guard by him, arms folded. The other man led Walker upstairs. Here any remains of the building's former glory were not to be seen. The paint was cracked, the carpets worn and scarred. They stopped outside a closed door, and the man tapped gently against it. "Mr Fredricks, sir. Your guest has arrived."

A voice called from beyond the door. "Bring her in! Bring her in!"

Walker's guide pushed the door open, and she stepped inside the most hideous room she had ever seen. Fredricks had hardly been the classiest person of Walker's acquaintance, but this place outdid even his standards of conspicuous consumption. The gilt candelabra was a low point, Walker thought, although the purple and silver brocade curtains were also particularly unpleasant. Behind a huge wooden desk, the man now known as Fredricks was sitting like a supervillain in his lair. Walker looked round the room, trying to think of something to say. She settled for, "Nice eagle," nodding at the bird, stuffed and housed within a glass dome. It had a gold collar round its neck.

Fredricks beamed at the thing. "Cost a fortune to ship in."

"I can imagine."

"I'm after a panther."

"When it comes down to it," said Walker, "who isn't?" She took a seat across from Fredricks. He was portlier than she remembered too (more conspicuous consumption, no doubt), but then the last time she had seen him, he had been sitting in a holding cell quivering in terror that his ex-employers might know where he was. He had, it seemed, thrived in exile.

"Have to say, Ms Walker"—he spread out the title: *Mzzzzz*—"you're the last person I would have expected to see out here in the Reach. You were always so..."

"Sensible?"

"Respectable."

Cheeky bastard. "Nobody in my business," said Walker, softly, "is entirely respectable."

Fredricks subsided. His brush with the Bureau had brought him briefly into contact with some of Walker's less salubrious colleagues, the kind whose offices didn't have windows but where the chairs had straps. Walker had always kept a... well, a *respectable* distance from the unpleasant but necessary parts of the Bureau's work. But it never did any harm to remind people like Fredricks about them, and that they were at Walker's disposal, should she need them. Or they had been, until recently. Not that there was any need to tell Fredricks that. Let him continue to think she was as well-connected as she had ever been.

Particularly given Fredricks' current business. Walker had continued digging, and her hunch had proved correct. Fredricks brought in people to work in the mines. But the poor sods who arrived here thinking that they were going to get honest paying work found on arrival that the costs had somehow racked up while they were in transit: phase technology was expensive, after all, and accommodation was at a premium on Shard's World these days, and of course Fredricks himself had to make a modest profit (those panthers didn't buy themselves)... And then there was the interest and the administrative costs and the authorities (such as they were) on Shard's World *would* charge so much for resettlement fees... Before you knew it, you were looking at a debt that would never be paid off, no matter how long you laboured underground. Fredricks called his business 'providing unrivalled solutions for personnel problems.' Walker called it people trafficking. No wonder there were bodyguards downstairs.

"I have to wonder," said Fredricks, "what brings you out this far when there's a crisis back home."

So the news blackout about Braun's World was over. It would be hell in the Bureau right now. "You know I can't say anything about that."

"No? So why are you here?"

"The Weird," Walker said, after a moment. "I'm interested in the Weird."

"We're all interested in the Weird. Those who aren't terrified want to work out how to make some money from them."

"I doubt they're interested in money."

"No? I didn't think we knew that much about them." Fredricks eyed her thoughtfully. "You've come a long way, Walker, so I'm sorry to say that I don't know anything," he said. "Yes, I've heard about the Weird, and I've heard stories about what they can do. I never want to come any closer to them than I am now." He frowned. "You're not looking for a close encounter, are you?"

"I've heard," said Walker, "that somewhere in the Reach there's a world where humans are living in harmony with the Weird."

"Living in slavery, more like, if the stories are true."

"Yes, I know about that. Not that. Genuine co-operation."

Fredricks thought about that. "Now that would be interesting... There might be opportunities in that." He shook his head. "I doubt such a world can exist. Humans and the Weird..." He shuddered. "It couldn't work. No way of living together. Either they'd devour us, or we'd destroy them before we are devoured."

"That's precisely what I'm hoping to prevent."

"Is that idealism I hear?" He laughed. "I guess that would make sense. Other people did the finger-snapping and the kneecap-smashing, didn't they? You were more fastidious."

She was getting tired of this. "Have you heard anything that sounds like the place I'm looking for?"

"I'm sorry. I can't help you." He looked at her with something approaching pity. "You know, this isn't a good place to be. Not for a person like you."

"I suspect you have little conception of what kind of person I really am."

"You know what I mean." He smiled. "You're not cut out for the Reach. Not cut out for how business is done here. You should go back where you belong. Back to Hennessy's World."

She looked around the horrible room, and out of the window at the bleak sky. "Well, nothing about this place appeals. Thank Christ I'm not stuck here."

Fredricks leaned back comfortably in his chair. "You might be."

Walker stopped in the act of standing up. "Is that a threat?"

"An observation."

"Based on what?"

"Your pilot."

"What about my pilot?"

Fredricks' eyebrows shot up. "You don't know? Good God, Walker, you really have changed. I can't picture the woman I knew flying blind."

"Tell me what the problem is with my pilot."

"Drinks a lot, doesn't he?"

"So does most of the Bureau. I didn't see that alleviating any of your anxieties at the time—"

"The thing is," said Fredricks, "I did a few background checks while you were travelling here. I'm surprised that ship is up in the air."

"It's remarkably sound for its age."

"I'm sure it is. They built those things to last. The pilot, however..."

"What about him?" Walker said.

"It's not just the drink. His head, you see..." Fredricks tapped his brow. "Full of junk. The pain must be constant. Take a little look around the ship. You'll find the pills soon enough. He must be doped to the eyeballs."

Walker ran her hand across her eyes. She should have guessed this. Should have thought of it...

"But I'm sure you know your own business," Fredricks finished. "Good luck, Ms Walker. I'm sure you'll be successful in your quest."

AT LAST THEY reached what Maria supposed she should be thinking of as their 'safe house.' They gladly sealed the door behind them, and looked around the little room. A big bed. A battered old viewscreen on the wall. A cupboard that, when opened, revealed a place to cook. A tiny bathroom. "Well," said Maria brightly, "let's get washed and have something to eat."

Jenny, when her hands and face were scrubbed, found a game to play on her father's handheld: colourful fish with huge eyes swimming through bright blue waters filled with various perils, collecting treasure from the ocean floor. Whenever Jenny hooked a treasure, a cheerful little *whoosh!* filled the small room.

Kit was lying awake on the bed, his arm across his face.

"Hey," Maria said, softly, to her husband and daughter. "Hungry?"

Jenny, with hardly a complaint, put down the game and scooted to sit on the edge of the bed. She dug into her supper with gusto. After a moment or two, Kit heaved himself up and took the bowl Maria offered with murmured, automatic thanks.

"When are we going home?" said Jenny suddenly.

Maria, seeing Kit's stricken face, said brightly, "Not yet, darling."

"I'm worried about Monkey. He's all alone."

"Monkey's clever. He'll do fine."

"But he's by himself. He'll be lonely."

"Not Mr Monkey. He makes friends wherever he is."

"It was mean of us not to go back for him."

"Maybe he'd like to hear about our adventure," Maria tried. "We could write it down or send him a message..." She glanced over at Kit, who was shaking his head. "Or else save it all up for when we see him again."

Jenny brightened visibly. "So we'll definitely see Monkey again?"

Maria ate a few mouthfuls of soup before replying. She made it a rule not to tell even the whitest of lies to Jenny, but how could she tell a four-year-old girl that the world where they had been living last week no longer existed in any meaningful sense?

"Mummy, will we see Monkey again? Mummy?"

"That's up to Monkey, really, isn't it?" she said. "He knows where to find us."

"How does he know where to find us? We didn't tell him where we were going?"

"Monkeys know these things," Maria said. "They know how to find their little girls. It might take him a while. And I think he might have some adventures on the way. Hey, I bet he'll have some great stories to tell us when he finds us!"

Jenny seemed satisfied by that: the idea of her monkey adventuring through space clearly appealed. Maria glanced over at Kit, who had been silent throughout the whole exchange.

There were tears running down his face. He looked, Maria thought, like a man who had reached the end. Maria was going to have to be the strong one now. Because Kit wasn't going to be around much longer.

She finished her soup, and then retrieved the bowls from her family, and put them on the side. Settling Jenny on the bed between her and Kit, she lay down beside the girl, who nestled into her. "Come on, Kit," she said. "Lie down. I have a story to tell, about a clever monkey who one day got left behind, so went looking for his little girl, and had some wonderful adventures..."

Kit lay down on the other side of Jenny. And Maria told her story, and savoured every moment, because she didn't think there would be many more of these to come.

THE *BABA YAGA* hung disconsolately in orbit around Shard's World. Walker, staring at the planet on the viewscreen, saw a world smothered in a grey haze. Ostensibly, she was contemplating their next move, but in fact she was wondering if this was the endgame. Her power bases had been centred on the inner worlds, Hennessy's World in particular; her strength had been in the leverage she could put on the civil servants and Council members and other glitterati of the central worlds. Fredricks had been her only contact within the Reach, and he had nothing for her other than the advice to turn round, go home, and get on with being retired.

Get on with being a mother...

Retirement, however, was not an attractive option, despite Andrei's apparent easy transition, chiefly because there would surely be consequences arising from her departure. Walker was not clear to what extent she was *persona non grata* back at the Bureau. In the current atmosphere, she might be facing worse than a slap on the wrist for a few traffic offences and failure to notify the travel office of her journey. To the more paranoid of her ex-colleagues, her sudden—and illegal—disappearance was sure to appear suspicious. Treasonous, even. No, a return to Hennessy's World, however appealing right now, was not on the cards.

Which meant staying on the *Baba Yaga*, or else looking for another ship and a pilot more to her taste. She risked a quick glance at Yershov, spread out in his sling. There was a little cup of something next to his left hand, as ever, and he was staring glassily at the display in front of him. *Doped to the eyeballs*, Fredricks had said. *Brain full of junk.* How had she missed that? It was almost as if she was preoccupied in some way... And what did it mean for her mission? Skipping past space traffic control was one thing. Putting her life in the hands of a washed-up, drug-addicted pilot with a headful of melting technology to fly her through some of the most dangerous territory known to man was another.

And hers was not only the only life she was putting at risk...

"Yershov," she said abruptly.

He jerked up in his chair. "What?"

"We need to talk."

"What about?"

Your head, you headcase, she thought; but his attention was already away from her. "Yershov! I'm talking to you!"

"Well, then, shut up!" he said. "Can't you see I'm concentrating?"

"Concentrating? On what?"

He didn't reply. Impatiently, she got out of her sling and edged through the narrow space to come to stand behind him. He was staring intently at the viewscreen in front of him. "What's the matter?"

"Look," he said, and jabbed his finger at the screen. "Look at that."

What, she wondered, was she supposed to looking at? There was a little red dot on the screen—was that it? "Tell me what the problem is," she said, in her best talking-to-junior-staff-members voice.

He looked round at her scornfully. "Can't you see?"

She repressed the urge to throttle him. She didn't want to be stuck in orbit around Shard's World for the rest of her life, and Yershov's melting brain was her only way out. "I see a little red dot," she said, very calmly. "Which could mean all manner of different things. So tell me what it means in this instance."

"Life signs," he said, darkly. "On board this ship."

"Well, I'm alive," she said, "and you're... here. So what's the problem?"

"*That's* us." He gestured towards two green dots to the far side of the screen, then jabbed at the red dot again. "*That's* someone else. There's someone on this ship."

Her first thought was the baby, but Yershov carried on. "Down in the hold. Hmm. Got to admit there's corners down there I've not looked at in years."

"Maybe it's spiders."

"Big buggers if so." He gave her a sharkish grin. "Want to take a look?"

Stalking around a decrepit space hopper with a junkie ranked pretty low on a list of what Walker wanted to be doing, but that was exactly what she found herself doing next. They left the flight deck and Yershov opened the nearest hatch to gain access to the hold. He handed her a torch and sent her off round to the left, before setting off to the right himself.

After about five minutes of shuffling round in near darkness and barking her shins on crates that seemed to come out of nowhere, Walker had had enough. She reached out to the nearest wall, feeling for a light and, when she found one, she switched it on, and looked round her. Nothing, only more crates on which she could do herself minor damage. "Yershov," she said, in a clear carrying voice.

"*Ssssh!*" Yershov hissed from somewhere across the hold and slightly ahead of her. He was still under the cover of darkness.

"For God's sake, there's nobody here! It was probably a false reading. Who would be desperate enough to stow away on a ship like this—"

Someone shoved past her.

"Oof!" Walker regained her balance, and twisted round. She saw a figure darting behind a stack of crates ahead. "Yershov! Over here!"

There were quick footsteps, and then Yershov appeared out of the darkness. "What?"

"Someone's here—"

"Told you."

"Yes, all right. Behind those crates."

They both moved forwards slowly. "Come out," said Yershov. "Come out, you bastard! Bloody cheek, stealing a ride off a man! Stealing his livelihood!"

Walker rolled her eyes. "Give over," she muttered. To their stowaway, she called out, "You're wasting your time. Do you realise how small this ship is? There's nowhere to hide. You may as well come out now."

There was a brief silence, and then, suddenly, the crates came crashing down towards them. Walker, who had been expecting it, jumped back and darted out to block any escape. She grabbed the figure's arm, pulling it back, stopping their flight. Her prisoner let out a high-pitched squeal. "Shut up," said Walker, and twisted her prisoner round to get a good look. She saw an ugly little creature with bulging eyes and blood-red tentacles hanging down from the middle of its face. It was clawing at her arm with a six-fingered, hairy paw.

Their stowaway was Vetch.

It was also very small.

It was a child.

CHAPTER FIVE

VETCH. HUMANITY'S ONE-TIME enemies, with whom the Expansion had been locked in a deadly war for years, and with whom an uneasy partnership now existed in light of the threat of the Weird. Walker, a product of the inner worlds, whose career at the Bureau had started after the end of the war, had not met many Vetch face-to-face. Of course, there were many images available, and the occasional diplomat passed through Hennessy's World: huge, ugly, and imposing. But this one—while definitely ugly—was tiny and trying to screw itself up even smaller. Walker had not thought of the Vetch having children before.

"Fucking Vetch!" Yershov snarled. "Fucking Vetch on my fucking ship! Well, we'll sort that out. We'll sort that out right now." He grabbed the child by its other arm and pulled. The child emitted that extraordinary high-pitched noise again, and Yershov belted it across the face. "Shut up, you little bastard!"

The squeal stopped abruptly. Walker, instinctively, wrapped an arm around the child's hunched shoulders and pulled it towards her. "What the hell do you think you're doing?"

Yershov tugged at the child, who whimpered. "Getting rid of this piece of junk."

"What?"

"I don't want it on my ship!"

"You're planning to *space* it?"

Another loud squeak, and then the child spoke, in a strange, rasping voice. "Don't let him do it, missus! I'm sorry I hid away! Don't let him push me out in the dark so I choke!"

"Nobody's going to push anyone anywhere," said Walker, and Yershov, taking this as a challenge, began the tug-of-war again. "Yershov, stop this right now—"

"It's dangerous!"

"It's a child!"

"It's *Vetch!*"

"I swear to God, Yershov, if you don't take your hands of this child, I'll find every damn painkiller on this ship and throw them out after it. We'll see how long you last then." She saw him flinch, and she pushed home her advantage. "Head *throbs*, doesn't it? All those rotting wires and rusting metal. Think how it would feel, if there was nothing you could take to ease the pain. Think how much that would *hurt*, Yershov, throb after throb after throb, getting worse and worse, and you're stuck in the void and can't get out—"

"Fuck you." Yershov shoved the child towards her. Walker released a slow steady breath, and then looked down at the child quivering within her arms.

"All right," she said. "It's all right. Nobody's going to hurt you. Not me, and certainly not him. My name is Delia. Who are you?"

"Me? Failt."

"Failt. All right. So we know each other's names now. That's a start."

Failt sniffed, sending the tentacles jiggling. "Don't know that one's name."

"He's Yershov. You don't need to worry about him."

"He wants to throw me out! Into space! Where I can't breathe!"

"You bet your fucking life I do," Yershov muttered. Walker lifted a hand to silence him, and he obeyed.

"You can't come on board people's ships without asking, you know," Walker said. "They're liable to take offence."

The child went sulky. "Didn't mean no harm by it. Wanted away from Shard."

"Well, I can't say I blame you, I thought it was pretty grim. But what about your parents? Won't they be worried about you?"

"There aren't any."

"You mean you don't have any? You don't have any parents?"

"That's what I said, Missus Delia. There aren't any."

"Then who looks after you? Who takes care of you? Won't they be missing you?"

Failt gave her an odd, calculating look. "You never been on Shard before, right?"

"This was my first visit, yes."

"Nobody takes care of me. I report to boss, he reports to next boss, and so on up."

Yershov was now angry again to speak. "Don't you get it, you stupid woman? This is *property*! Somebody *owns* this creepy little bastard—"

"I told you to shut up," said Walker, in a very soft voice, and, once Yershov had subsided, she turned back to Failt. "Let me see if I have understood this correctly," she said. "You're..." She hesitated over the world 'slave.' "You belong to someone, and you work for them. Is that right? And you hid away on our ship because you didn't want to belong to them and work for them any longer?"

"That's it," Failt said.

Yershov was fairly shaking now. Not with anger, Walker realized; he was afraid. "I've had enough of this! We've got to get rid of this... *thing*! Airlock, or else go back. This is someone's property. They'll want to recoup their investment. They'll come after us. Come after the *Baba Yaga*. These people aren't your nice types—they'll kill us, or drag us down with this one—" He lunged again towards the child. Walker caught his thin arm and twisted it down. Now it was Yershov's turn to squeal.

"Ow! That *hurts*! Let go, you fucking bitch! That *hurts!*"

"Listen to me," she said, in a clear voice. "Nobody is spacing anyone. Nobody is sending anyone back to slavery. For the love of God, this is a child!"

"It's Vetch!"

"It is a he, and he is a *child!*"

"Do I look like someone who's sentimental about children?"

"Do I look like someone who won't follow up on a threat?" She tapped a finger against his forehead, hard. Yershov winced, but he quietened down again.

"All right," said Walker. "I'm not murdering a child, and I'm not sending it back into slavery. Is that clear?"

"As crystal," Yershov said. "But if someone comes after us..."

"We'll deal with that if and when it happens." Walker put herself between Failt and Yershov, and pushed the child gently in the direction of the ladder back up to the main deck. "All right," she said. "Everyone's calm now. That's how we like it."

Yershov was muttering beside her. "I'd like to know how the little bugger got on board."

Failt stuck his head round. "Wasn't hard. This ship—anyone could get on board. Heap of junk."

"All right, Failt," Walker said firmly. "But why this ship in particular?"

"First ship came by since I came up from underground," Failt said.

"What do you mean?" said Walker.

"Worked down below," said Failt. "Pushing and pulling."

Walker understood. Children were docile, and easily cowed. Perfect labour. She doubted, though, that anyone would be coming after Failt to collect him. Children's bodies were cheap and plentiful. Fredricks probably had hundreds that he could slot straight into his place. "So what meant you couldn't do that any longer?" she said.

"Got too big." Failt waved his long arms. "So got sent up to the spaceport to push and pull there. Better than being down in the dark."

"Pity you're not still down there," Yershov muttered. "Pity the bloody roof didn't fall on you."

"Shut up," said Walker.

Failt grasped Walker's hand with his own furry paw. "Tell you what, Missus Delia, you're his boss, aren't you? You showed him what was what. He should be glad you're his boss. You're the kind anyone would want to slave for." He twisted his neck and looked up at her. His big bulging eyes were sad and loving. "I'll do anything for you, if you ask. I mean it. Anything. I'm yours, Missus Delia. Just you ask."

BEHIND THE BATHROOM door, Kit was once again on the comm with their benefactor. Maria stood close to the door and listened without shame. Kit was struggling alone, and had been since they'd left Braun's World. Maria should never have let him shoulder all the burden of their escape himself. She hadn't grasped the gravity of their situation, not at first, and she had always left the big decisions to him while she had taken care of their domestic life. She had become comfortable; lazy. But marriage was partnership, and when Kit had no more to give, it was her turn to step forwards, because she loved him and their daughter and she would do everything in her power to protect their frail little family. So she listened at the door, to take care of Kit, because he could no longer take care of himself, and because she did not think she would have many more chances.

The half of the conversation that she could hear did not make for happy listening. Their patron, apparently, seemed to think everything that could be done for the Emerson family had been done.

"You're not listening," said Kit. "I don't think we're safe here—"

There was a pause as the person at the other end

of the line presumably replied.

"From Braun's World. I think we must have been tracked leaving... What? No, no, of course I didn't! I wouldn't do something that stupid! How? Because they're bloody serious about nobody getting away!"

Maria sighed softly and wrapped her arms around herself. So it was exactly as she had feared and suspected: someone was following them, and had been following them long before they reached Shuloma Station, and they were getting close. They had been followed, and they had been found.

"Listen," said Kit. His voice had gone low and Maria had to strain to hear. "You've got to help. You can't abandon us! Not after everything I... No, *you* listen! My wife, my little girl—for God's sake, she's only four! No, I know that you said I shouldn't... For God's sake, what kind of a man do you think I am...? Yes, yes, it probably was because I went back. But I wasn't going to leave them, was I? They'd have been murdered—"

Maria clutched herself more tightly. So he'd had the chance to get away without them, and he hadn't. But that delay was the reason they were in trouble now. It'd given whoever was chasing them the chance to pick up their trail...

"You've got to help us!" Kit's voice was getting hysterical. "No, I don't want to put you in danger. But you're *already* in danger. What you know *puts* you in danger... No, you listen to me! I'm not playing around now. If they catch up with me, I'll tell them! I'll tell them it was you!"

"Mummy?" Maria looked down. Jenny was tugging at her arm. "Why is Daddy upset? Is he sick?"

"No, sweetheart, but he's very tired. Like you are."

And me too, she thought, *tired and very afraid.* She forced a smile onto her face, then reached into her pocket and drew out her little gold handheld. A gift from Kit for her last birthday: fashionable, and more extravagant than they could really afford. He could be silly like that, sometimes. "Hey, sweetheart," she said brightly, passing the device over, "why don't you draw me a picture of Monkey? Show me what you think he's doing now. I bet he's got into some kind of trouble!"

Jenny, thrilled, seized the thing and jumped onto the bed, hunkering down happily. Maria pressed herself back against the door.

"You can't threaten me with anything worse than the trouble we're in now, you understand that, don't you...? You've got to find them somewhere safe. *Really* safe... No. No. I know. But that's the way it is... Okay. Okay, I'm listening. Go ahead."

There was a pause—while the other person spoke, presumably—and then Maria heard Kit sigh and move. The call must have ended. Quick and light as a feather, she hopped onto the bed beside Jenny and began to admire the child's picture.

The bathroom door opened, but Kit didn't speak straight away. Maria looked up and saw him standing in the doorway, one hand pressed against the door frame, the other tugging at his upper lip. She smiled at him. "Everything all right, love?"

"Yes," he said. "I think things are going to be all right now." He gestured to her. "Quick word?" he said. "In private?"

She joined him in the bathroom and he closed the door behind them. She thought: *What would he say if I told him I'd been listening? Would he be angry?*

Relieved? But she wouldn't tell him. His pride... She would leave him his pride.

"This place," he said. "It's not safe. But I've found somewhere else."

"That's good," she said. "Not back to the Expansion, I guess."

"No," he said. "No chance of that. Still here, on the station." He took a deep breath. "Maria, there's something else..."

She put her fingers gently against his lips. "I know," she said. "You don't have to say it. I know what you're going to say." She took hold of his hand. "I love you, Kit Emerson. I loved you the first time I set eyes on you, when I thought all you could see was Katie Levinson in that stupid tarty skirt."

He laughed—couldn't help himself. "Sweetheart, I didn't even *see* that skirt!"

"So you say!" They were both laughing now, and crying, all at once. She loved him so much, and this was goodbye.

He was pressing a datapin into her hand. "Here's the address," he said. "It's not far, but—"

"We'll need to take the long way round."

He leaned back to look at her. "Ah," he said. "I see." He gave her a rueful smile. "I shouldn't forget how smart you are."

"When it comes to you and that little girl, I know everything."

He tapped the datapin she was holding. "There's more than an address on there, Maria. There's an explanation. That datapin. It explains everything. I can't tell you... And please, don't look, don't look..." He shook his head. "Someone will contact you, I'm sure about that. They'll want what's on the datapin. When they get close, it'll give you a signal. You'll know they're close, and you'll be able to trust them." He folded her hand around it. "Keep it safe, sweetheart. It's cost me…"

…everything. "I promise," Maria said. "I'll keep it safe."

"You're not going to ask any questions?"

She kissed him, full on the mouth. "I trust you, love. With my life."

In a halting voice, he said, "I know where the place is, if things go well here…"

She shushed him. "Don't make promises you can't keep. We'll stay as long as we dare, and then we'll move on."

"You can't go home, Maria." He had started to cry—noiselessly, tears slipping down his face. "You can't go back."

"We'll make do. We'll cope. Haven't I always made a home for us, wherever we've been sent?"

He pressed her hand. "On the datapin. There's a number you can contact. But only if things get really desperate. I've called in so many favours to get us this far…"

She kissed him gently on the cheek and then turned to Jenny. "Hey, sweetheart! Daddy needs to get some sleep. Let's go for a walk!"

It was a measure of how bored the little girl must be that she was off the bed in a trice, grabbing her mother's hand and pulling her towards the door. But it broke Maria's heart all over again. Kit started to say, "I'll come and find you—" but she stopped him before he could finish with a finger on her lips. She grabbed one of their still-packed bags, and was out of the door in no time. She looked up and down the long corridor, but there was nobody to be seen. She put the datapin into the handheld, and a series of directions began to unfold. She tugged at the strap of the bag until it was comfortable on her shoulder, then turned Jenny round to face the right way. "Come on, sweetheart. Let's see what we can find."

She led her daughter away into the unknown, and she kept a brave face on all the time while the little girl laughed to see all the new strange things in the strange new world crowing all around them. *Goodbye, Kit. I love you. I'll love you for as long as I live, and I'll never let Jenny forget you.*

WALKER ABANDONED HER reading on her handheld and stretched in her sling. Failt, who had been sitting on the floor next to her, as close as he could get, shifted to accommodate her. She looked down at him, curled up on the floor, staring at Yershov. Yershov was slumped in his sling, eyes closed, drumming his fingers against his chest and muttering profanities under his breath. After Failt had been brought up from the hold, there had been a short but very thorough and professional search of the flight deck and Yershov's cabin. The alcohol was now under lock and key, as were Yershov's painkillers, subject to Walker's control and administration. Yershov shifted slightly, and Failt gave a low growl. *Then there were three,* thought Walker. And a happy little band they were.

"Why are you here, Missus Delia?" said Failt, suddenly. "You don't belong."

She looked down at him. His gruesome little face was staring up at her. *Missus Delia.* She had no idea where he'd learned that form of address—perhaps it was something his overseers had insisted on—and she didn't have the heart to correct him. "What makes you say that?"

"You're not Reach-people. You're not slavey and you're not boss." He glared at Yershov. "Him now— he's slavey if ever I met one. But you? You're like boss—I bet when you say things people do them, and I bet that sometimes you'd have them hit if they didn't do what they were told. But you're not bad like the bosses."

That, thought Walker, was a pretty good assessment; apart, perhaps, from the final qualification. "Thank you," she said.

"So why are you here?" said Failt. "You should be home with famblee."

"With what?"

"Famblees," Failt said. "Isn't that what they're called? The human kids, sometimes, they talked about famblees. Two big ones and a handful of little ones altogether overground in one big room. Sounded nice."

Families. *Christ*, thought Walker, *out of the mouths of babes...* "Well, Failt, I'm looking for somewhere."

"All of us looking for somewhere. So what you looking for in particular?"

Walker sighed. Her searches through the datanet were proving fruitless, not least because her access to the more informative parts had been revoked. All her resources had disappeared—including her mode of working. Still, it was what she knew, and she couldn't stop now. The procedure at the Bureau when your analysis reached an impasse was to stop and present your thinking to a colleague, in case a fresh mind could see a way through. Walker was pretty short on colleagues at the moment. A runaway Vetch child would have to do.

"Have you heard of the Weird, Failt?" she said.

He swung round to face her, his little body suddenly all screwed up in tension. "Have I heard of them? Everyone's heard of the Weird, missus, even us underground! Everyone's scared they're coming!"

Well, at least she didn't have to explain that. "Back in the core—"

"What's that?"

"The core," she said, slowly. "That's where I come from. The main human worlds—"

"You're from there?" Failt goggled at her. "The big rich worlds? *Said* you weren't slavey! If I was from there, I would never have left. You should go back home, missus!"

"Perhaps I will, one day. In the meantime, do you want my story?"

Failt hunkered down. "Sorry, missus."

She rubbed the back of his paw. "I'm not cross. Just teasing. Anyway, back in the core, we heard rumours about a world where humans and Weird are living together."

Failt shuddered. "Bet that weren't good for the humans."

"That's the thing—it was good. It's co-operative."

His tentacles twitched. "What's that, missus?"

She sighed. "I mean, that on this world, the Weird aren't absorbing the humans. They simply... live alongside each other. Like humans and Vetch do now." More or less.

"Like you and me."

Walker smiled. "That's right, like you and me."

"I haven't heard of a place like that, missus.

Sounds make-believe to me."

Walker sighed. "I'm beginning to think that may be the case."

They were quiet for a while, and then Failt said, "There's a story on Shard. Everyone told it. About someone who used to smuggle people off Shard and take them away, take them away to be free, not make them work till they drop like the bosses do. They went to a safe place to 'live-in-peace-and-harmony.'" Failt chanted that in a singsong voice, as if the words were memorized rather than understood. "I thought that sounded nice, so I kept on asking. Some people said it was a trick, the way for bosses to find out who the troublemakers were. Show up those who were going to try and do a runner so that they could be put down below, as deep as deep can go, and could never ever get away ever. But some people said it wasn't a trick, it was true. And then others said be careful what you wish for. They said, 'live-in-peace-and-harmony' wasn't always as good as it sounded. Like the Weird-folk, those people who been done over in the head. They think they're happy, but they're not. They're slaveys like everyone else, only they don't complain any more. But I don't know what was true."

Walker stared down at her handheld. "Did you ever meet anyone who had been there?"

Failt shook his head. "Could all be make-believe, couldn't it? Everyone needs to think they got a hope, don't they? If you don't think you've got a hope, you give up, don't you?" He smirked at Yershov. "And some of us make our own hope and hide away on people's ships when they're not looking."

Yershov pushed himself forward in his chair. "You

filthy little bastard," he said. "I should've pushed you through that airlock the moment I laid eyes on you—"

"You'd have gone out straight after him, Yershov," Walker said calmly. "Sit down and shut up. Failt, is that all you know? Is there anything else?"

The child shrugged. "A name."

"Go on."

"Heyes. Everyone used to talk about Heyes."

Heyes... Walker jumped up from her sling and went over to the comm. It wasn't much to go on, but it was something. And if this was a story that went round the poor benighted workers of Shard's World, then perhaps Fredricks might be able to help. He was the kind of person that would have his ear to the ground...

Behind her, still sitting on the floor, Failt murmured to himself, "'Live-in-peace-and-harmony'..." Then he snorted. "Bet it's all make-believe, Missus Delia. Like famblees."

"*Hello, again, Walker,*" said Fredricks. "*Your pilot's head imploded yet?*"

"We're doing fine at this end, thank you," Walker said. "But I need some information."

"*Information, huh? Not a new ship?*"

"Not yet."

"*And what's in it for me?*"

He was, in Walker's opinion, starting to get cocky. "Gerhardt Lopez is due for parole shortly," Walker said; Lopez was Fredricks' erstwhile boss. "I'd be happy to put a word in for him. And then I'd be happy to pass on your new name and address so that you two could get together and remember old times."

Fredricks scowled. "*All right,*" he said. "*I was only having some fun. What do you want to know?*"

Remember who's boss, Fredricks, she thought. *Remember who's slavey.* "Do you have much of a problem with runaways at your end?"

"*Now why would anyone want to run away from here? The opportunities that Shard's World presents are unique within the Reach for anyone prepared to work hard—*"

"Parole board are waiting to hear from me," Walker said, shortly.

"*All right. No. Yes. Sometimes.*"

"Those opportunities not so great after all, hey?"

"*The work ethic isn't what it once was. But, yes— sometimes, people leave Shard's World without paying off their debts. Breaks my heart to say so— not to mention hurts my wallet—but there it is. Some people don't recognise an opportunity when they see one.*"

Or recognised when they'd been scammed into slavery. "This happen a lot, this sudden disillusionment?"

Fredricks looked at her cannily. "*What are you after, Walker?*"

"Have you heard the name Heyes?"

"*Heyes? You're looking for Heyes?*" Fredricks burst out laughing. "*Christ, Walker, if I didn't know better, I'd think the Bureau has lost the plot.*"

"I can assure you that we are as serious as ever we were. What's so funny?"

"*You'd laugh if you knew Heyes!*"

"Why?"

"*Well, you know, the whole business was before*

my time, but people round here still spit when you mention the name. Caused a lot of trouble. Cost a lot of people a lot of money."

"Oh, I see—when you say 'people' you mean the kind of bottom-feeding bastard who might traffic other people into slavery, yes?"

"Nobody," said Fredricks loftily, *"comes to Shard's World against their own will. That would be illegal, not to mention unethical."*

"I know, I know—and it's not your fault if they don't read the small print."

"Now you're talking like someone I can do business with, Walker."

"But Heyes had a different kind of business, yes? Ran some kind of underground railway?"

"That's what I said. Caused a lot of trouble helping people—"

"To escape?"

Fredricks glared. *"I was going to say 'abscond.'"*

Walker tapped her upper lip. So the part of Failt's story checked out. What about the rest? *'Live-in-peace-and-harmony'?* Was that all make-believe?

"You're talking about Heyes in the past tense. Dead?"

"I don't think so. But long gone."

Walker sighed in frustration. As soon as a lead presented itself, it was snatched away.

"Look," said Fredricks, *"I wouldn't do this for anyone, but because it's you, here's what I heard. Heyes got off Shard before people decided to put a stop to what was going on. Last I heard, he was heading for Shuloma Station. That's all I know."*

"Shuloma Station."

"I've got a friend there."

"A friend? Forgive me if I find that unlikely."

"*An associate, then, if that seems more plausible. DeSoto. I'll send over his details.*"

"Is he in the import business too?"

"*DeSoto? Of course not.*"

Fredricks cut the comm but, true to his word, contact details for DeSoto soon materialised on Walker's handheld. "Yershov!" she shouted, and the pilot jerked awake in his sling. "I want a course set for Shuloma Station."

Dutifully, Yershov obeyed.

Failt gave a low, throaty chuckle. "See what I mean? He's slavey."

THEY WALKED FOR about an hour, after which Jenny had to be carried. Maria had never felt so tired, not even in the early days of Jenny's life. Her every limb ached with a bone-deep weariness. They walked the length of one section of the station, and then a second, and most of a third. Then there were some steps to climb, and then a dropchute (mercifully) and then past a big interchange where some kind of festival seemed to be happening: great drums were beating, and reedy pipes cheeping, and a tall man in a flame-coloured robe held aloft a great golden artefact cast in the shape a fiery sun. People rushed past in excitement after the procession, and nobody, it seemed, had time or space for a lonely, frightened new widow and her exhausted little girl. They slipped away from the crowd down a wide, busy thoroughfare, and soon after found the neighbourhood they were heading for: a rather gloomy area, set back from the thoroughfare, with narrow hatch-like doors on either side of the corridor, and grimy orange light coming from strips in the ceiling above. Maria found the door by the string of letters and numbers marked on its surface. The door opened and, with great relief, she ushered the little girl inside.

The room was completely bare. Maria almost burst into tears, but she remembered Jenny, and got a grip on herself. "Well," she said cheerfully, "let's see what we can make of this!"

"There isn't a bed, Mummy."

"I know. Perhaps we're missing something." Maria held the door open with her foot to get some light from the corridor into the room, and, feeling around on the wall by the door, managed to find a light switch. A grubby yellow light made the room more visible, although it showed, too, the extent of its uncleanliness. Maria let the door close behind her, and saw that there were more switches on the wall. Turning one of these revealed that the room had a drop-down bed, and other switches opened up a water supply, a heat supply, and some meagre toilet facilities.

"Are we staying here long?" Jenny said, doubtfully. *I hope to God not*, thought Maria, but said, "Hop into bed now, Jenny. Time to get some sleep."

"I won't sleep till Daddy arrives," Jenny said, firmly, but the minute her little head touched the pillow she passed out, lying in a heap in the middle of the tiny bed.

Maria didn't sleep. She lay beside Jenny and listened to the distant beat of the drums from the festival. She heard people pass along the corridor outside, laughing and singing. One time she thought she heard someone scrabbling at the lock outside.

She sat up, wondering how she might protect herself and Jenny, and then she heard a mumbled curse, and whoever it was went on their way. She lay back. Her eyes were gritty and her head buzzed with exhaustion. Eventually, she realised that it wasn't simply her head buzzing. Someone was trying to get through on the communicator Kit had given her.

She moved to sat on the side of the bed and switched the communicator on.

"*Emerson?*" The voice coming through the little device was distorted and Maria could make out nothing about the person speaking: not age, not gender, not accent.

"Who is this?" she said, quietly.

There was a short pause, and then: "*Who are you? Where's Emerson?*"

"Kit," Maria said, passionately, angrily, and from a place of great, aching grief. "His name was Kit!" She looked back over her shoulder, afraid she had woken Jenny with her outburst, but the little girl was still deeply asleep. "I imagine he's dead by now. There were people following us, and he sent us away because they had found us."

There was silence from the other end, and Maria started to think that the communication had been cut. Then she heard a deep sigh. "*I see. I'm sorry. I wish it hadn't come to this—*"

"But it has," Maria said. "And it's because of you—"

"*Emerson chose to help me—*"

"And now he's dead. You'll forgive me if I don't have very warm feelings towards you."

"*You're the wife, aren't you? I told him not to go back for you. It's probably what cost him his life. He should have left you—*"

"So that I could die on Braun's World along with everyone else?"

Again, a short silence. "*What do you know about that?*"

"Only that the Weird came, so Fleet bombarded the planet, and now everyone there is dead."

Again, she thought she heard a soft sigh come through the communicator, but she couldn't decipher the meaning. Perhaps it was genuine feeling; perhaps she had been utterly mistaken and it had simply been a crackle of interference. "*If they've found Emerson, they'll be coming for you next, I'm afraid. You should try to get away.*"

"Away? To another safe house? Do you have one here? You sent us on here, I'm guessing—"

"*There isn't another safe house. I've done all I can. If you want, you can try to get away from the station. But I have to be honest with you—it won't make a difference, not in the long run. They're set on finding everyone. I'm sorry. Really, I am. This isn't your fault. But they can't leave anyone alive.*"

"For God's sake!" Maria said, frantically. "I have a little girl! You've got to help us!"

But the communicator had gone silent. Maria reached into her pocket and twisted the datapin around between her fingers. She had no way of accessing the secrets on it. But what was it that Kit had been willing to die for? What was it that people were willing to kill for? Kill even her, and her little girl? Beside her, Jenny sighed in her sleep. And Maria lay down next to her, and held her daughter close to her, curling around her as if she really could shield her from a terrible, hostile world.

PART TWO

BOLT HOLES

CHAPTER SIX

IT WAS BARELY a month since Andrei Gusev had been pushed, but his presence within the Bureau was all but eradicated. Four decades of service, and it was as if the man had never been there. A new dispensation reigned. Gusev's style, under successive Bureau heads, had been firm but almost collegiate: policy was decided in comfortable sessions in his office; minor infractions were treated with an arched eyebrow and a gentle word in private. (Major infractions, it was true, were more summarily treated. Even a man as genial as Gusev had his limits. He wouldn't have remained so influential without them.)

Now the air of bonhomie was gone. Latimer, ostensibly, was at the head—but nobody in the upper echelons of Bureau officialdom could forget how he had crumbled when the news from Braun's World had arrived. The tone of the Bureau, as ever, was set by the second-in-command. But Commander Adelaide

Grant, formerly of Fleet Intelligence, was a colder and more humourless person than Andrei Gusev. The Bureau was a colder, more humourless place.

Telepathic scans of all senior staff, to check for infection by Weird mind-parasites, had been carried out within days of Grant's ascendance. Kinsella still shuddered at the memory: sitting in a small, chilly white room while a hatchet-faced official telepath went through the contents of his mind and memory in orderly fashion. It was not that the experience had been brutal, but it had been brisk, bloodless, and horribly efficient. It had lacked everything that had made one loyal to Gusev: courtesy, subtlety, humanity. Afterwards, Kinsella had retreated to a cubicle in the toilets and wept silently for some time. It had been a few days before the fragments of memory dislodged and brought to the surface by the experience had been coaxed back to sleep.

There was another effect of Grant's sovereignty that Kinsella was now struggling with. The Bureau was now a place in which no meeting between colleagues, however casual, went unmissed. Finding a quiet corner in which speak to Larsen was proving a near-impossibility. Using any technological means to contact her was obviously out of the question: all communications were being openly monitored by Grant's new Information Transparency Task Force, and anything untoward suggested possible infection and invited yet another and deeper scan. As known associates of Walker—and protégés of Andrei Gusev—Kinsella did not doubt that Grant had her eye on both him and Larsen. There was no shortage of people lining up to curry favour with the power behind Latimer, and junior staff at the Bureau were learning quickly that offering to monitor the activities of a more senior colleague was an easy way up the ladder. Chance encounters walking along the waterways or buying coffee, even happening to find themselves in the same dropchute, were going to be noticed and recorded.

While Kinsella did not fool himself that even a doctor's surgery had the privilege of privacy, it was the best he could think of. A couple of faux migraines set the groundwork; after that an appointment to speak to one of the Bureau's approved doctors was not only reasonable, but in fact required by his contract. Sitting down in Larsen's office, he let her test his eyes and blood pressure, and then he lifted out the small black and silver device that had come in so handy so often during the course of his career, and placed it on the table between them.

"We have about two minutes," he said.

Larsen stared at him in horror. "Are you *insane?*" she hissed.

"This works with every bugging device I know— and trust me, I know more than a few."

"And what if they have ones you don't know about?"

"Then we're in trouble." He tapped his watch. "One-and-a-half minutes. Where's Delia, Kay?"

"I have no idea."

"Do you know how they found out about the baby?"

She hesitated. "I'd assumed it was you."

So she had known. That made three of them, and he hadn't told anyone, and Delia, he was sure, hadn't told anyone else... He let the imputation of guilt pass because he knew now what he needed to know: that Kay Larsen was probably not to be trusted. She meanwhile was looking down at his blocking device as if deciding whether or not to trust it, and therefore, him. "Have you heard from Andrei?" she said.

As if he would tell her anything. "Not a dicky bird," he said cheerfully.

"I assume he has something up his sleeve."

Fishing, he thought. She was fishing. Well, she wasn't going to hook a damn thing. "I doubt it. The last time I saw Andrei Gusev he was emptying his desk and he looked about fifteen years older."

For some reason, that seemed to terrify her. But why would she care, if she'd informed on Delia? He didn't believe that Larsen was one of Grant's people, but he did believe that she had seen which way the tide was turning, and that she had chosen to protect herself. Still, he was... *surprised*. He had liked Kay Larsen; had thought—briefly, a long time ago—that he might even have loved her. They had been very close. And then she had pulled away. He had put it down to experience, but he had always remained fond of her, and he wasn't used to thinking of himself as a bad judge of character.

"Andrei must have *something* in mind," she said. "He wouldn't give up..."

"Well, he has," Kinsella said, bitterly, and clearly startling Larsen with the venom of his response. "And if even the savviest, the smartest, and the most enduring of us aren't clever enough to beat this lot, where does that leave the rest of us, Kay? Have some of us been making some tough choices?"

She frowned at him. "What are you saying...?" she started, but he pointed to the device on her table, and lifted his finger to his lips.

"Time's up," he murmured, and slipped the little device into his pocket. "So what do you prescribe, Doctor?"

She studied him for a moment. Then she reached for pen and paper and wrote out a prescription. "We'll try you on these first. One at the onset of symptoms. Come back if they continue."

She shoved the slip of paper towards him. He turned it over to look on the back. She had written: *You need something for your head.*

SHULOMA STATION WAS pretty much what Walker had been expecting from the Reach: colourful, chaotic, and unresponsive to any official-looking card that she might have chosen to flash about. Perhaps it was to the good that her privileges had been revoked. It would have been frustrating to have her authority ignored. Here on Shuloma Station she had no more sway than anyone else—and no less.

They passed through a cursory customs check, and she found a booth where she was able to change some of her Expansion units into local scrip. She handed a bundle of these over to Yershov, and left the pilot safely ensconced in a bar on a thoroughfare along from the docking bays, almost happy with his lot. She didn't think he would leave: the cash in hand had mollified him, and the threat of finding himself stuck in space with no pain relief would hold him a while yet. If anything, it was tempting to find a new ship and pilot here on Shuloma—but Yershov clearly knew how to fly under the radar, and that might well come in useful on this quest.

"Better the devil you know," she muttered to herself.

Failt, skipping alongside her with his odd gait, looked up. "What's that?"

"Nothing. Thinking through my options."

"We ditching that slavey pilot here?"

Walker smiled. "Not yet."

"He wanted to space me, Missus Dee."

"Well, let's keep our eyes open in case we see something else we like, hey?"

Soon, however, they had left the docking zone, and were heading by dropchute and moving walkway into the heart of the bustling space station. When they had come out of phase into local space to make their approach to Shuloma, she had taken the opportunity to make an appointment with Fredricks' friend DeSoto. On a hunch, she had not mentioned the connection with Fredricks, merely presented herself as a trader looking to open offices here, where the Expansion met the Reach.

They navigated the station with ease, passing big open markets where anything, it seemed, could be bought or sold. Bright clothes for alien bodies; sweet and sour scents of food for alien mouths. Brash music that must signify beauty to someone here... Failt was in seventh heaven. He must never have seen anything like this in his whole short life, only the grim caverns and grimy hangars in which he had laboured. Did he even remember open skies, Walker wondered? Had he ever felt rain on his face, or sunshine? Perhaps that was something they should remedy, when this was all over...

When this was over. As if she had any idea how this was going to end. As if she had any clue what was going to happen. Apart, of course, from her body's agenda, progressing towards its inevitable endpoint, completely beyond her control...

They found the thoroughfare on which DeSoto's offices were located. Walker, sticking her hand into her pocket, gave Failt a little pile of notes and told him to explore the nearby market. "Don't go far," she said. "Keep within sight of this place."

He nodded, and then skipped off immediately to a little booth selling something bright and sticky. Walker smiled at the sight of him. Did children of all species always manage to find their way straight to the sweetshop? She left him to enjoy himself, and turned to the business in hand.

DeSoto was a small man, round, with curling moustaches of which he was plainly proud. "I have to confess, Mr DeSoto," she said, after the pleasantries were over and she was sitting opposite him in his office, "that I have come to you rather under false pretences."

He eyed her cautiously. "Oh, yes?"

"I'm not in any kind of trade. I'm from the Expansion, where I specialise in... information retrieval. A mutual friend of ours passed on your name."

"Mutual friend?"

"He goes by the name of Merriman Fredricks."

DeSoto stood up and gestured towards the door. "Could you go now?"

"Fredricks said you'd be able to help me."

"Anyone who is a friend of Fredricks is very far from being a friend of mine."

"Then let me reassure you on that score. As far as I'm concerned Fredricks is a necessary evil."

"Evil?" DeSoto snorted. "You're right there. But necessary? We can argue that."

"We could, but we'd be wasting our time. Let me speak plainly. I'm looking for information about someone called Heyes, who I believe came here some time ago from Shard's World. If you can help—that's good. If not"—Walker nodded to the door—"If not, I'll leave and trouble you no more. You're a busy man, I'm sure."

"I *am* a busy man," he said, petulantly. "And information isn't free, you know."

"Mr DeSoto, nobody knows that better than me. Did Fredricks not explain? I am in the information business."

She waited for the ramifications of that to sink in, and then watched with quiet satisfaction as DeSoto's features rearranged themselves into something considerably more respectful. He sat down again. The worlds of Satan's Reach—and the stations which served them—were all well outside the Bureau's jurisdiction, but the reputation of its operatives went before them. Walker was not going to mention that she had been more on the analytical side—and certainly not that she was no longer in the Bureau's employ.

"You're a long way from home, Ms Walker," DeSoto said, giving her a canny look.

"Our interests"—Walker put a slight stress on that lofty *our*—"stretch well beyond the core worlds."

"I bet they do. We hear things, you know. Troop movements. Problems on places like Rocastle. Cassandra. Braun's World."

She didn't blink.

"There's talk of infection—a plague on the loose. I've been seeing people wanting to get away from the Expansion—rich people, too; not your usual lot, trying to get away from debt. People much like you, in fact. Seems all isn't how it used to be back in the Expansion."

She remained cool.

"And now, here you are, asking for information. Well, Ms Walker—I have to ask myself, how much is it worth to you?"

The reputation of the Bureau went before it, and the tale grew in the telling. The truth was, nobody really had a clue what went on inside the walls of her old organisation, and everyone who worked there was invested in maintaining the shroud of secrecy. There were rumours, yes, and some of them were even true—disappearances, interrogations, dungeons in the deep. But a great deal of the power of the Bureau arose from its mystique, and the beliefs that people held about it.

"My employers, Mr DeSoto," Walker said quietly, "invest a great deal of time and money in their staff. They don't like to think of us being threatened, or blackmailed, or otherwise held over a barrel. And so they equip us properly. In my pocket," she said, tapping her jacket, "I carry a small but very useful device. The moment I walked into this room, it began tracking your vital signs. By now it has a very good picture of what makes you tick. Where the weak spots are. And if I reach into my pocket"— she rested her hand against her chest—"then a little pulse, inaudible to either of us, will start emitting. And within the space of a minute, your brain will be turned to pulp. A minute isn't that long, really, but I should imagine it feels like eternity."

It was bullshit, of course. If the techies at Bureau had managed to develop anything close to a technology like that, they certainly hadn't mentioned it to anyone. But the story was working its magic on DeSoto.

"There's a bar on blue level, section seven," he said, quickly. "The Crossed Keys. Heyes is usually in there. Otherwise, try the building next door. It's the church."

Walker frowned. "The *church?*"

DeSoto smiled at her. "What?" he said. "Didn't you know? Heyes is a priest."

A priest. Well, that might explain him running an underground railroad... "Thank you," Walker said. "You've been most helpful." She reached into her jacket pocket.

"Hey!" said DeSoto. "What the fuck are you doing? I've told you what you want to know!"

"And I'm rewarding you," said Walker. She drew out the bundle of notes. "Five hundred sufficient?"

DeSoto fell back into his chair, muttering something that might have been *bloody cold-hearted bitch*. She didn't mind. She *was* a bloody cold-hearted bitch. She counted out the slips of paper onto his desk with some ceremony, and then left his office and went back into the concourse. DeSoto escorted her out—presumably to make sure she really left—and slammed the door behind her. Failt, seeing her, hopped over. "Hey, Missus Dee!" he cried, shoving a stick of shocking pink gunge into her face. "You gotta try this!"

Cautiously, she touched her tongue against the bright abomination—and then spat out, to Failt's roaring amusement. The damn thing tasted of fish.

*   *   *

EVENTUALLY, THEY HAD to leave their tiny room to in search of food. Jenny was ravenous. But where, Maria wondered, wandering through the station in a daze, did you find food in a place like this? It was not like there were the clean but sumptuous palaces of conspicuous consumption that you found on the inner worlds, or even the brisk but well-stocked shops of the Fleet bases where Maria had spent her married life and done her shopping. Yes, there was so much on sale—but she had no idea what was *food*, much less what was safe.

Jenny, hungry and fractious, dragged her heels and complained. She wanted Monkey. She wanted Daddy. No, she didn't want Mummy. She was hungry. She was thirsty. She was tired and she wanted Mummy to carry her. She wanted Mummy to carry her *now*. That last came out particularly loud. A few passers-by glanced at them.

"Jenny, *please!*" Maria said, in desperation. She couldn't risk them attracting any attention. She had no idea whether the people who had come after Kit were anywhere near; had no idea what she was supposed to be watching for. She seized the child's hand and pulled her away, down a little thoroughfare where she hoped she would be able to calm the little girl enough to go back out in search of something to eat. But Jenny, struggling against her mother's increasingly forceful attempts to move her, began to sob.

"You need to shut that kid up," said a voice from further along the corridor. Maria looked up, but the lights ahead were dim and she could only make out shadows. "She's making too much noise."

Her daddy is dead! Maria screamed silently. "She's

tired," she said, and pulled at Jenny's hand to hurry her on. The child ground to a dead stop.

"If she's tired, put her to bed." Another voice, nearer. "Little brat."

"She's tired and she's hungry. We're looking for something to eat."

Someone ahead of her, still shadowed, gave a rasping laugh that turned into a hollow cough. "Everyone's hungry, sweetheart. Me and my friends here—we're hungry. But we're short on money. Fancy buying us dinner?"

"Jenny," said Maria, in a clear voice. "Come on."

"No."

"Jenny, I'm not playing any longer. Come *on!*"

"I *won't!*" yelled the child, and then the howls started in earnest. The laughter came again, from all sides. Maria heard footsteps moving closer. The lights behind her suddenly went out. *Oh, God,* she thought, *please let us get out of this alive...*

Two dark figures emerged from the shadows, heading towards them. Two men, leering and laughing. One had a little scar cutting his left eyebrow in half. The other was gloved.

"Mummy," whispered Jenny, "I'm scared. I want to go home."

Maria felt hot breath on the back of her neck. Someone's hand was on her shoulder. "Please," she said. "Please let us go. I swear we've got nothing."

"Nothing? Nothing at all? What? You were going to *steal* food?"

"Now that's terrible, that is. This place isn't what it was. New people arrive and they bring the place down."

"Fucking disgrace. Shouldn't be allowed."

"No!" cried Maria. "I wouldn't steal—!"

"No? Not stealing? Then you must have money— or something to sell. Let's have a look and see what it is."

Maria, in horror, realized that Jenny was being pulled from her arms.

"*Jenny!*" she shrieked, and tried to hold on—but her assailant was stronger. She could hear her little girl crying, "*Mummy! Mummy!*" but there was nothing she could do—

Suddenly, there was a bright burst of light and a flash of white heat. An energy weapon had been fired, overhead, and with great precision. It didn't hit anyone, but the force from the blast sent the three assailants flying. Maria, taking her chance, grabbed Jenny's hand and pulling her to safety.

"Wardle Springer," said a clear voice from behind them. "Are you preying off young women again? We've had words about this in the past."

One of Maria's assailants—presumably Springer— stood up again. Maria held Jenny close to her. She supposed she should run—but she wanted to discover the nature of her mystery benefactor.

"*You!*" hissed Springer.

"Always." And then the lights came on again and Maria could take a good look at her saviour.

She was a tall young woman of beauty and grace. She stood with one hand on her left hip; the other was pointing her energy weapon at the ceiling. "Time to disappear, Springer." She tilted the weapon slightly. "And take your stooges with you."

The other two men were still struggling to get to their feet, rubbing their eyes from the weapon's flare. Maria suppressed an urge to laugh: she doubted it would go down well and it struck her that it would come out sounding hysterical. One of them made a move towards the young woman, who smiled, shook her head, and levelled her weapon again. His friends pulled him back, and all of three of them disappeared off up the corridor into the darkness.

Maria turned to her guardian angel. "Oh, thank you! Thank you! I don't know what would have happened if you hadn't arrived when you did—"

"I doubt they'd have killed you," said the young woman, frankly. "But there would have been bruises and probably some broken bones." She glanced at the child. "At the very least. And unless you know the right kind of people, it's hard to find help around here." She stared at Maria with dark, intelligent eyes. "You're not from around here, are you?"

"No."

"From the Expansion?"

"Yes. Is it that obvious?"

"Well, nobody who knew Shuloma Station or was Reach-born would walk down here with a child and without a weapon. And your clothes." The woman gave a half-smile. "They're nice." With a fluid movement, she holstered the weapon. "I'm Amber, by the way. People round here often need looking after. So I look out for them. I take care of them." She smiled at Maria: a wide smile of great charm and loveliness. Maria thought she saw gold glint in the half-light. "You seem in trouble. Perhaps I can help take care of you?"

Maria smiled back. She felt dazed. *I seem to have been rescued by a superhero*, she thought. "Yes," she breathed. "Please. We're lost—we're hungry. Please—help us!"

Again came the golden smile. Amber held out her hand. "Then come with me. I'll take care of you."

W ALKER WAS NOT a religious person. The Bureau was not the kind of place where people troubled themselves too much about guilt, the afterlife, or the eternal verities, and the Expansion, on the whole, didn't encourage religion as it tended to turn people to radicalism and acts of conscience. Andrei Gusev, while not discouraging religion amongst his protégés, seemed to consider it rather a puzzling personality defect. If any of Walker's immediate contemporaries held religious beliefs, they had kept it quiet. Kinsella could have been a Buddhist, for all she knew. Probably could have done with some mindfulness training, she thought. He had a tendency to bottle things up. The upshot of all this, however, was that Walker had rarely been inside a place of worship (and, then, only to oversee arrests), so she had no idea whether this tiny cavern tucked behind the noisy bar was par for the course.

Following DeSoto's advice, they had tried the Crossed Keys first, but the old woman who owned the place—a wizened Gentinian with purplish skin and small tusks emerging from her lower jaw—had sent them next door, saying that not even Heyes was here this early in the day. The entrance to the church had proven slightly difficult to find, being low, and tucked into a narrow access corridor beside the bar. Walker had to bow her head slightly to enter; Failt trotted in behind her. The room beyond was not big, but was dimly lit, and Walker had to peer round to get a sense of the space. Failt sniffed at the air, sending his little tentacles quivering. "Tastes funny. Smells funny, too."

Carefully, Walker breathed in. The smell was heavy, a little cloying, but spicy and not unpleasant. "It's called incense," she said. "The people who pray here use it."

"Why?"

"I honestly have no idea. I rather like it, though." She glanced at the child. "Do you not like it, Failt?"

"Not so bad. Tastes of long time passing and being patient. Tastes of centuries."

Walker smiled. At times, her little stowaway was quite the poet. "Let's go in and see if there's anyone here," she said.

They walked slowly up the aisle towards the altar, passing through the middle of two blocks of wooden chairs, set in rows. As Walker's eyes adjusted to the low light, she began to pick out more of her surroundings: the metallic walls of the space were covered in hangings, of all things, depicting what Walker assumed were scenes from the Bible. She noticed that they got more and more unpleasant as they progressed: a whipping, a crowning with thorns, a crucifixion. Above the altar, too, hung a wooden crucifix. The simple figure nailed on it was made of dark metal. Nothing valuable, Walker assumed, not a precious metal; surely the door to the church wouldn't be open in that case, or the crucifix would be long gone. Or perhaps the great cross held some power over people that she couldn't understand.

The altar was plain: a big wooden table covered with a large cloth woven in a complex pattern of oranges, yellows, and browns. To one side of the altar, on a small table of its own, stood a statue of a woman in a white dress with a blue cloak and bright red lips. Her arms were outstretched, as if she was waiting to embrace someone, and there were wooden flowers in garish colours all around her feet.

In one of the seats at the front, on the left hand side, sat a big woman dressed in black, with a shock of short white hair. Her eyes were closed, her head was tilted back, and she was snoring magnificently. Walker nudged Failt, who whiffled softly with laughter. At the sound, the woman sat up, abruptly. She stared at them, her eyes wide and her face white. "Who the hell are you?"

Walker held up her hand placatingly. "A visitor."

"Well, bully for you." The woman ran her hand through her shock of thick white hair. "What the hell do you want?"

"I'm looking for Heyes," Walker said. "Are we in the right place?"

The woman closed her eyes again. "Jesus Christ," she muttered. "Thought you'd come about the lighting bills."

"No, but I have a few questions. Is Heyes here?"

The woman folded her arms and leaned back. "Why?" she said. "What's your trouble?"

Walker frowned. "Why do you assume we're in trouble?"

"People don't come to church unless they're in trouble. So what's yours? Apart from the obvious, I mean."

"Does everyone in this bloody place trade in insults?"

"On Shuloma we trade in anything and everything *except* insults. The insults come for free." The woman eyed her thoughtfully. "But I wasn't intending to insult you."

"Then what the hell did you mean?"

She sat up suddenly—a surprisingly quick movement for someone so bulky. "Forget I said anything. Apologies if you were offended. People tend to come here when they're in difficulty."

"I'm not in any difficulty."

The woman gave a throaty laugh. "You must be the only person on Shuloma who isn't. I know within the Expansion people live very orderly lives, but it's more chaotic out here in the Reach."

"Look, I need information, that's all. Heyes can help me." Walker reached into her pocket and drew out a datapin. "I have money," she said. "I can pay. Local scrip, or Expansion units. Just tell me where to find Heyes."

The woman nodded at the datapin. "I hope you've not been waving that about," she said. "There are people round here who'd love to get their hands on that."

"I know how to take care of myself. But do you know where Heyes is? If you don't—I'll make a donation to the flowers or something and be on my way."

Failt tugged at her arm. "Missus," the child said. "Think we're here. Think we've found what we're looking for."

The woman smiled down at the Vetch child. She looked kindly. "That's right," she said. She gave Walker a slight, mocking smile. "Apologies. I thought I'd been clear. I'm Heyes."

"You're the priest?"

Heyes sighed. "I'm the priest. For my sins. So," she said, looking at Walker so sharply, so intently, that Walker almost felt her innermost secrets had been scrutinised, "what's your trouble?"

* * *

IT WAS QUIET out on the water that afternoon. Andrei Gusev had taken his boat out to his usual spot. Now he sat upon his canvas chair and contemplated the deep green water, the wide blue sky, and the startling beauty of the cityscape ahead. Sitting so quietly, so pensively, rod in hand, he resembled a rather dapper garden gnome—but his brain was ticking over, piecing together all the parts of the puzzle that had presented itself to him since his retirement. Below the surface of the water, dark shapes swirled, and he watched their shapes twist and their tails flick in their beautiful, impenetrable dance. He felt the rod pull: something had bitten—but he ignored the tug on the wire and let it go. Life, he thought, was short, and very few things deserved a second chance.

Rachmaninov's *Vespers*. That was what one wanted to listen to if one was about to shuffle off. Unadorned beauty. And yet one's heart was wrung, too. These chants—so lovely, so timeless—they had been the last songs of an entire tradition. Within a matter of months, the churches were closing, the icons smashed, and the music forbidden... To see one's works become obsolete while one still lived, thought Gusev, surely there was no crueller fate. Perhaps it was better not to outlive one's enemies. Still, the parting was bittersweet, and one would like to have seen them brought to justice, for their terrible, terrible crimes...

Gusev studied the patterns made by the fish and contemplated the passing of things. Behind him, the boards of the old boat creaked.

His time had come.

"Well," said Gusev. "Here we are."

There was no answer.

"One had hoped—" Gusev continued, "one had *hoped*—that this day would never come. One had hoped that there would be a few quiet years, at the very least." But in his heart he had always known that whatever one's hopes, in his line of business the reality was that the end would come suddenly, out of the blue. The best one could hope for, really, was that it would not be painful. That someone would show mercy.

Gusev was not expecting that. He felt the slight prick against the back of his neck as one might feel a tick, or the tug of a fish biting suddenly upon the line. With great relief, he realised that it was over and that it wasn't going to be painful at all. In fact, it was almost what one would call merciful. He almost felt grateful.

Gusev was ready. He had been ready for some time now, at least since his last meeting with Walker, and his subsequent realization of all that his opponents had done. He could not be suffered to live. But he had had a little time to plan: to take care of some of his legacy. Drowsiness began to overtake him, and he pressed his thumb against his handheld. He had written the message some hours earlier. It said: *Get out now.* As his eyes darkened he wondered, *Should I have said more? Warned more? Will it be enough?*

It was too late now. Gusev's days were over. His eyes closed and he knew no more. The people on his boat had not quite finished their task yet, but it was quickly done. Gusev's body was weighted and cast over the side of his beloved boat, and with barely a ripple broke the surface of the water. And slowly it sank, swirling and twisting down through the depths of the green sea, while all around his senseless body the sharks and the minnows continued their eternal dance.

CHAPTER SEVEN

UNDER HEYES' MOCKING eyes, Walker was beginning to feel extremely foolish. Now she registered the dark clothing, the silver crucifix on a chain around the other woman's neck... "I didn't know that the Catholic Church even allowed women to become priests."

"Well, they do. Have done for the best part of a century, in fact." Heyes gave a slight laugh. "Permitted since the Fourth Vatican Council. The Holy Mother Church is nothing if not capable of extending and continuing her life. Priests are her life blood. She wouldn't allow that flow to dry up. The quakes don't come often to the Church, but when they do they're huge. They keep her going for another millennium. Now a female *pope*...." Heyes snorted. "Let's say I'm not holding my breath."

Walker was beginning to regroup. "If you're Heyes—and I've no reason to doubt that you are—then I hope you're going to be able to help me."

"Are you sure you're not in some trouble?"

"If I am," said Walker, "that's my own business."

Heyes looked her up and down. Again, Walker had the uncomfortable feeling that the priest was somehow seeing more about her than she wanted revealed. Walker shook herself. Probably a trick they learned in seminary to get people to confess. She should be taking notes.

Suddenly Heyes shifted her weight forwards and with a great sigh heaved herself up from her seat. "Come into my office," she said, and headed off, with a lumbering, swaying gait, towards a little door behind the statue of the woman in blue and white.

Walker nodded to Failt, and they followed Heyes through the door into the cramped room behind it. There were two old armchairs—beaten-up and disgorging stuffing—into one of which Heyes flopped with a comfortable *oof*. Walker lowered herself carefully into the other chair, not entirely trusting that it would survive the strain. Failt took up his station at her elbow, like a faithful dog.

There was a little wooden bureau at the far end of the room, into which it was surely not possible to stuff more paper. A battered old companel stood to one side. Standing on top of the bureau were various plaster of Paris statuettes of quite remarkable hideousness and garishness, including one of a man in a red robe whose heart was visible. Between the two chairs stood a low table. There were one or two books—one was a Bible, Walker assumed— and there were also a few objects that Walker didn't recognise—tools of Heyes' trade, presumably. There was a plastic bottle of water in the shape of a woman, with a blue screw top in the form of a crown. There was also a bottle of whisky—Walker recognised one of those when she saw them, and she recognised the quiver in Heyes' hand, and the relish (and relief) with which the priest opened the bottle.

"Do you get much business here on Shuloma?" said Walker. She shook her head when Heyes offered the bottle.

"Enough to keep me in necessities." Heyes gave a crooked smile and put the bottle down again.

"I didn't think the Church's reach came so far out from the Expansion."

"The Church has always been first into new territories, for better or worse." Heyes frowned. "Mostly worse. Yes, we Catholics get about. I believe there has been a mission to Vetch territory in recent years."

"And how long have you been the Church's representative here?"

"Well," said Heyes, leaning back even more comfortably. "There's a story. A long one. But the upshot is that my services are no longer retained by the one holy catholic and apostolic Church. But you know how it is. You can kick the girl out of church, but you can't kick the church out of the girl."

Walker frowned. "I don't quite understand what you mean."

"I was booted. Defrocked. Technically, I'm not a priest any longer."

Walker glanced back over her shoulder at the little church. "Then what's all that back there? Who's footing the bill for that?"

"Local donations. Even somewhere like here, people like to know there's something constant. *Especially* somewhere like here. There are always people in need of comfort. If they want the sacraments, I'm happy to help. When people are facing death, or want to confess—or both—they don't really care whether I'm officially sanctioned by the Church or not."

"And what does the Church think about that?"

"D'you know," said Heyes, "I've never asked." She filled her glass again. "Now you know about me. So who the hell are you?" She glanced past Walker to Failt. "And why are you travelling with such an interesting companion?"

"Live-in-peace-and-harmony," said Failt, in his singsong voice. "We're looking for the place where they live-in-peace-and-harmony."

Walker did not miss the very sharp look that Heyes gave the Vetch. It would be a mistake, she thought, to dismiss this woman as nothing more than a drunk—as one of the Yershovs of this world, hapless and easy to control.

"Well," said Heyes cheerfully. "That sounds like a very nice place. But I don't know why you think I might know where it is. If I did, do you think I'd be here on Shuloma Station, rather than... What did you call it?"

"Live-in-peace-and-harmony."

"We've come from Shard's World," said Walker. "I was told that you ran an underground railroad there—"

Heyes whistled. "Well, that takes me back."

"You helped people to escape from their owners, and you sent them on to a place where people could live peacefully and be free."

Heyes stared into her glass and ran her finger around the rim. "That's an interesting story," she said. "I wonder what makes you think it's true."

"You're not forgotten on Shard's World," said Walker. "Particularly by the people who ended up out of pocket."

A slow, satisfied smile spread across the priest's round face. "Good," she said. "Good."

Walker leaned forwards. "I'm looking for a place like that," she said. "I've heard that there is a colony world where humans are living..." She hesitated. Should she mention the Weird? She was used to holding her cards close to her chest—by temperament, training, and employment—but looking at Heyes she began to wonder whether this strategy would serve her best. The priest was old and tired, and more than a little drunk, but there was something honest about her. Something that made Walker believe she could be trusted.

Quietly, she began to explain her mission in full: the nature of the Weird threat; the rumour that had reached the Bureau of a world were humans lived in peace with the Weird without being assimilated; the attack on Braun's World; her flight on the *Baba Yaga*, and the path she had followed here to Shuloma Station. "You're my only lead," she confessed. "If this world exists, I have to find it. Otherwise..." She sighed. "Who knows what the Weird can do? What the Bureau might do in response? There's been terrible slaughter already. If you know anything— please, help me."

Heyes had listened to her story attentively, but in silence. When Walker finished, the priest swirled round the last few drops of whisky in her glass, and then drained the contents. "I did run an underground railroad from Shard's World," she said. "A long time ago. I helped slaves escape from there and I sent them to a world on the very edge of the Reach." She smiled at Failt. "So my reputation hangs around on Shard, eh? I suppose I should be glad about that."

"Live-in-peace-and-harmony," said the child. "That true too?"

"I don't know," said Heyes. "I never went there myself. I just sent people on their way."

Walker said, "Is this the reason you were thrown out? Defrocked? Whatever it is that gets done to you?"

"Very perspicacious, Ms Walker. Yes, my activities were discovered by my superiors in my order, back in the Expansion. They weren't particularly pleased. Part of their income came from donations that—I found out later—could be traced back to some powerful business interests operating on Shard's World. My mission there was closed, and I was thrown out of the priesthood."

"And the world you sent people to?" Walker urged. "Where is that? Can you send me there?"

Heyes shook her head. "I don't think it's the world you're looking for."

"But it might be—it's my only lead!" Walker could hear desperation creeping into her voice. "I can make a donation—anything you want. I have money— local, or Expansion. Whatever you want—" She stopped speaking when she realised that Heyes had stopped listening. The priest had her eyes fixed on the door behind Walker, and her hand was half-raised.

"Viola," she said. "Is that you?"

The door opened, and the gnarled old alien from the Crossed Keys came in. "Mother," she said. "Came to warn you—someone's been creeping round asking for you."

Heyes gestured at Failt and Walker. "If you mean this fine young gentleman and his associate, they've found me, and they're no trouble. In fact, I think they're leaving."

Walker opened her mouth to protest, but the alien spoke first. "Not them, Mother. Someone else. Someone coming looking for you. Don't like the look of them. Kept them in the bar."

"Well," said Heyes. "I'm not sure I like the sound of that."

Walker stood up. "I'll come with you," she said. "I might be able to help. If you're in trouble, that is."

Heyes eyed her thoughtfully, then nodded. "All right. Let's go and see who it is."

AMBER HAD ROOMS on red level, section eight. She said that it was only a short walk, but Maria's head was swimming—hunger, she thought, and the shock of their recent near miss, and, of course, grief. She gritted her teeth, and put one foot in front of the other, and hoped that soon she would be able to sit down. Jenny hung on her mother's arm, and didn't say a word the whole time they were walking. Every so often, Maria looked down at her daughter's tired, pale, drawn face, and almost wished that her little girl was still complaining. But Jenny kept on walking, doggedly, showing something of her daddy's grit and persistence.

"Nearly there," Amber said. Her voice was low and mellifluous, but Maria still jumped at the sound. She realised she had fallen into a sort of doze while walking. Jenny was a solid weight at her side. "Do you hear that, sweetheart?" Maria said softly.

"We're nearly there. We'll sit down soon and have something to eat and drink, and then we can rest. Amber is looking after us now."

They went along one more walkway, then through a small but lively interchange, and then Amber led them down a narrow access passage lined with little hatches beyond which, Maria assumed, various residents of the station had their living quarters. She struggled to think of these odd gunmetal rooms without gardens or sunsets as 'homes.' But people did live here—lived out their lives—and some were even born here, she guessed, and thought of the station as home in the same way that she had thought of the little houses she and Kit and Jenny had shared on Fleet bases around the Expansion... And who was she to judge? Home was where you could be happy and at peace, with the people that you loved most. Whether she would ever find that again, she did not know. She and Kit and Jenny would never be together again.

"We're here," said Amber. She had stopped outside a little hatch, which clanked open when she pressed her hand against the door panel. They were greeted by a rush of warm air, perfumed heavily with roses. Maria took Jenny's hand and followed Amber inside.

"Lights," said their protector. "Low."

An orange haze filled the room. Maria squinted through it, discerning a warm and comfortable room beyond. Her spirits rose, a little. Yes, she could rest here. She could close her eyes and they could both sleep and perhaps, even, forget for a while...

"Come in," said Amber, leading them inside. She gestured to a low wide sofa which stood along one of the walls, as big as a bed. "Sit down. I'll get you both something to drink."

"I'm hungry," said Jenny.

"Jenny!" Maria said, embarrassed. "I'm sorry," she said to Amber. "We've not really eaten for a few days."

But Amber only smiled. "I'll get you both something to eat too."

She was as good as her word. Maria slumped back on the sofa, Jenny curled up under her arm. From a corner of the room, she heard the clank of dishes and the rush of water. Soon Amber returned with cups filled with a hot tea, and steaming bowls.

"Some soup," she said. "Nothing special—just proteins and vegetables. But filling and warming."

"It's great," said Maria, digging in. It might have been her hunger, but she thought it tasted fantastic: a good savoury flavour with a little spice. Jenny was enjoying it too. They both tore through what they had (and seconds) and, when they were done, Jenny curled up in the crook of Maria's arm. Maria stroked the little girl's hair for a while, and slowly Jenny's breathing began to slow, and she snuffled her way into sleep.

"I can't begin to say how grateful I am," Maria said softly. "I don't know what we would have done if you hadn't turned up when you did."

Amber, who was sitting in a chair opposite, cradling a mug of tea, shook her head. "No need to thank me. I saw what was happening and I knew I could do something. Shuloma's not a bad place to live on the whole, but there are always some people trying to make a quick buck out of others, whatever the consequences. It's the price we pay for living outside the Expansion."

For being free, Maria thought. That was what Reach-people thought, wasn't it? That living outside of the rules and regulations that controlled everyday life in the Expansion was what made them free...

"You have to take care," Amber went on. "And sometimes we need someone else to look out for us—" She stopped. Maria's mouth had opened in a jaw-cracking yawn.

"I'm so sorry!" Maria said. "It's been a long day... An awful day... I can't even begin to tell you."

Amber smiled and her gold teeth shone in the dim light. "Don't worry about it. You had a shock—and I think there's another story behind all this. But that's for the morning." She looked at the child leaning against her mother. "She's deep asleep, and I think you will be too, soon."

Maria gave another huge yawn. Her eyes were drooping, and there was a warm fuzz working its ways through her limbs. Her arms and legs felt heavy.

"Lie down beside your girl," said Amber. Her voice was very soft. *Yes*, thought Maria, *if I could lie down for a while, everything would feel so much better...* "You don't have to worry," Amber was saying. "Sleep now. We'll talk again in the morning..."

Yes, thought Maria. *You're right. I should do what you say. I should sleep. You're right. You're right. I'll do what you say...*

ALTHOUGH GUSEV HAD only resigned a few weeks ago, Grant had installed herself in his office within days. This was the first time that Kinsella had been summoned to see the new power in the Bureau in her lair—and that in itself was a change that spoke volumes. He had been in and out of Andrei's office almost every day.

The room in which Grant sat was nothing like the one in which Kinsella had spent so many hours with colleagues, strategizing, analysing, making and refining plans, while their patron watched over them with a sharp, amused eye. The room had looked like a professor's study, at an old, prestigious university: shabby armchairs that sagged comfortably under one; the shelves weighted with those rarest and most precious of artefacts, genuine paper books; and a glass or two of something warming to help heat up the debate.

Grant's space was completely different. The walls, once cluttered with portraits and bookcases, were now white and blank, except for one covered with viewscreens. Twelve in total, four by three, bringing Grant news and information from across the Expansion. The sound had at least been lowered to no more than a background hum, although Kinsella doubted that this was in deference to his presence. Andrei's single viewscreen, propped on a wooden chair behind his desk, had been tuned to play classical music, and Kinsella had never seen it showing pictures. Yet somehow Andrei had managed to keep abreast of everything significant happening within the Bureau and across the Expansion.

Andrei's big faux-wood desk was gone too: Grant had replaced it with something clear—Glass? Perspex? The comfortable chairs were now moulded plastic, except for the one behind the desk, in leather and chrome. This was a wholly functional space: the space of a person who, it seemed to Kinsella, had no time for the finer things in life, and had pared down to what was considered essential. Kinsella wondered, if he asked for a glass of water, whether Grant would be able to supply it.

At a gesture from Grant, Kinsella perched on the edge of one of the new chairs. Grant continued working at her personal viewscreen, which was the only piece of equipment on her desk. After a few minutes, she closed the lid, firmly, and turned a cold eye on Kinsella.

"Where's Larsen?"

"What?" said Kinsella, caught completely off-guard.

"Kay Larsen has disappeared. I want to know where she is and where's she heading. I assume that you know and I'd like you tell me where she is and why she left."

Kinsella gaped like a fish. "Why would I...? What makes you think that I'd...? Kay's *gone*?"

"Nice try, but I'm not buying it."

"She's *gone*? When? How?"

Grant rested one hand upon the lid of the viewscreen. "I strongly suggest that you drop the pretence—"

Kinsella regrouped, slightly. "If Kay Larsen has decided to go AWOL, I swear I know nothing about it. Why would she tell *me*?"

"You were lovers, yes?"

"A long time ago!"

"Her and Walker—you get about, don't you, Kinsella?"

"Neither of them were exactly what you could call monogamous—"

"You had a private meeting with Larsen at the end of last week—"

Kinsella shifted uncomfortably in his uncomfortable seat. "I consulted my doctor about migraines."

Grant slammed her other hand down flat against the desk. "Don't treat me like an idiot! Delia Walker is gone, and now Kay Larsen is gone, and behind them they've left at least one corpse."

Kinsella stared at her. "A corpse?"

Grant folded her hands in front of her. "We've been keeping this as quiet as we possibly could." She regarded him coldly. "Andrei Gusev's body washed up on the beach at Merida Island yesterday."

For a moment the world seemed to sway around Kinsella, as if he had unexpectedly gone into phase and entered the void. "Andrei..."

"He had been missing since the start of the week. Had you not tried to reach him?"

He had in fact tried several times over the past week. "I thought he was fishing... Taking a break... I didn't *think*..." For a moment, he found himself disbelieving Grant, as if she was playing some kind of baroque trick on him. It was much easier to believe that than that Andrei Gusev was dead. Andrei was going to live forever, surely... But then Kinsella would not have believed a month ago that this room could be as different as it was now. Things changed, it seemed, and rapidly.

"I realise this is hard to believe," Grant was saying, "but I'm not in the custom of lying about such matters. Andrei Gusev is dead, and Kay Larsen is missing. It is natural for us to connect these two events."

"You surely can't believe Kay has anything to do with Andrei's death?"

"You have to admit it looks suspicious."

"No, actually, I don't! Do you know that it's murder?"

"Gusev didn't strike me as the kind of man to commit suicide."

"I mean—a heart attack or something. He took good care of himself, but he liked a drink and he liked a good dinner. If he'd had a heart attack, he could have fallen over the edge of the boat and drowned..."

"He could, but there's been a post mortem. Do you think I'd leap to conclusions?"

Kinsella had to admit that she wasn't the type. He doubted she'd done anything spontaneous in her life.

"Gusev didn't drown," Grant said. "He was dead when he went into the water. Poisoned. If he committed suicide, he managed to haul his own body over the side of the boat."

Murder, then. "But Andrei was a man with many enemies." *Not Kay...* Kinsella put his hands to head. He could not believe this of Kay Larsen, whom he had known for so long, and whom he had once loved. Yet he was sure, absolutely sure, that it was Kay who had told their superiors about Delia's pregnancy. "This is a nightmare..."

"If you know anything," Grant said quietly, "now is the time to tell me." Her voice grew gentler, coaxing. "Come on, Mark. What was the plan? Was there an inheritance? Andrei had no children. Were you and Larsen and Walker the beneficiaries? The island alone would have put all three of you into comfortable retirement. Did you know that you were all on the way out here at the Bureau and decide to get out? Money would come in handy if you were trying to get away—"

"What?" Kinsella stared at her. "Don't be ridiculous! We all loved Andrei!" He looked around the room; white and empty now as a ghost. "We *all* loved him," he repeated. But the seed of doubt had been sown. Larsen had betrayed Walker to Grant. What else was she prepared to do? Had he really misjudged her so badly? Had he misjudged both of them? They were gone, Andrei was dead, and he was the one sitting in Grant's office, under suspicion. Had he been played for a fool?

"Well," said Grant, "we'll find out the reason in due course. Murderers very rarely get away with their crimes. In the meantime, we are treating Walker and Larsen as rogue, and—given their seniority in the past—that makes them a threat to the Expansion. Which leaves me with a mission to assign."

"A mission?"

"One that someone whose loyalty had recently come under scrutiny might well choose to take on— if he had any sense."

Kinsella felt the net closing around him. Wearily, he said, "What do I have to do?"

"Find Walker. Find Larsen. Track them down and bring them back."

Kinsella straightened up in the uncomfortable seat and stared right back at her. "Dead or alive?"

Grant's eyes widened. "Alive is more useful. Dead is... tidier."

Kinsella looked round the room. "And you like things tidy, don't you, Commander?"

Grant smiled. "I like things orderly." She opened up her viewscreen once again. "I'll arrange for a ship to be put at your disposal. Good luck, and happy hunting."

*   *   *

WALKER AND FAILT followed Heyes and Viola back into the Crossed Keys. "At the back," said Viola quietly. "In the far booth."

Walker led the way, wishing, not for the first time, that she had brought some kind of weapon with her. But her fears dissipated when she reached the booth. Slumped over a glass, head in hands, was Yershov.

"For Christ's sake," muttered Walker, then glanced at Heyes. "Sorry."

"Don't mind me," said the priest. "Do you know this, er, gentleman?"

"He's my pilot."

Yershov looked up glassily. "I'm my own pilot," he said. "My own man."

"Yes, yes," Walker said, impatiently. She was conscious of Heyes, watching them with curiosity. "What's brought you here, Yershov? I thought I told you to stay by the ship."

"Someone down there came to speak to me. Said that someone had been asking questions about the *Baba Yaga* and the visitors from the Expansion. I came," Yershov said, with considerable hostility, "to *warn* you."

Walker frowned. Had someone been sent after her? All the more reason to get information from Heyes about her planet of refugees and be on their way.

"The *Baba Yaga*?" Heyes asked.

"That's the name of our ship," said Walker.

"*My* ship," Yershov muttered.

Heyes smiled at him. "A good name."

Yershov scowled back at her and said nothing.

"Why?" said Walker. She had assumed it was some kind of nonsense that Yershov had dredged up from somewhere. "Why's it a good name?"

"You've never heard of Baba Yaga?" Heyes laughed. "The old witch who lives in the forest in a hut that runs about on chicken legs, and who flies about on a mortar and pestle?

Good God, Walker thought, it really was some kind of nonsense that Yershov had dredged up from somewhere. "That sounds like a children's story."

"But no less truthful for that," said Heyes. "The wise woman, the arch-crone, the goddess of wisdom and death. In some versions of the legend she has iron teeth." Heyes looked wistful. "I rather liked that. Iron teeth. Anyway, you're wise not to cross her. You're wise to stay on the right side of her."

"I'll bear that in mind," said Walker dryly. "All right, now we know that there's nobody here to kill any of us, can we get back to business? I was trying to get your help. This place where you sent your refugees from Shard's World—can you send me there?"

There was a long pause, but eventually Heyes shook her head. "I'm sorry."

"You've got to understand," said Walker, "I'm running out of options."

"It was years ago, all of this—I've no idea whether there's anyone still there. And I never heard anything on the lines of what you're describing. I've heard of the Weird and..." Heyes shook her head again. "No. There was nothing like that."

"If you're afraid I'll betray your people there, the people that you saved—believe me when I say I'm good at keeping a secret. I won't give them away."

"I can't," said Heyes. "For many reasons, but

even more so given your condition—" She stopped herself. "I'm sorry," she said quietly, "I shouldn't have said that."

Walker glanced hurriedly at Yershov, but he seemed not to have heard. "Please," she said. "I've given up everything to find this place. If you think I can simply go back to the Expansion—I can't. There's nothing left for me there."

"There's nothing in the Reach for you either," said Heyes gently. "This is not the same place as your Expansion. This is a wilder world, and sometimes it can be a crueller one. Is that what you want for—is that what you want?"

No, of course Walker didn't want that, but she didn't want the consumption of all humankind either. Somebody had to take this chance, to find out whether there was a way that humans and Weird could live together, or else there would be no more humans, never mind one baby. Somebody had to do this—and who else was fool enough or desperate enough to try?

"Consider your options," said Heyes softly. "Consider whether you can go home."

Walker stood up. "Thank you for your time," she said stiffly. "Can I make that donation?"

The priest sighed. "I think you should save what money you have," she said. "Good luck. Take care of yourself." She glanced at Failt. "Stay close to that one. He's a keeper."

They left the bar. Walker strode off back to the dropchute, Failt at her elbow and Yershov trailing behind. "What did she mean," said Yershov, after a few minutes, "by 'your condition'?"

Failt shot the pilot a scornful look. "You stupid?

The missus is going to be a mama! Soon there'll be a baby!"

"Failt, no!" Walker raised her hand to quieten the child, but it was too late. Yershov had pulled up short, and was staring at Walker in horror. Failt turned to Walker in dismay. "Missus Dee!" he cried. "Missus Dee, I'm sorry!"

"It's all right, Failt," Walker said. She turned to the old pilot. "This isn't going to be a problem, is it?"

"A *problem?* Are you *mad*, woman?"

"I assure you I am quite sane."

"A *baby?* Out here? Don't you understand what kind of place this is?"

"That's my problem."

"Not if you're flying on my ship!"

"A ship which I've hired."

"I don't need your damned money!"

"Yes, you do," said Walker coldly. "And you certainly need my drugs."

For a moment, she thought Yershov was going to hit her. But he turned away, cursing under his breath, and strode on. Failt tugged at Walker's arm. "Missus," he said, awkwardly. "I'm so sorry. Thought we all knew."

She patted his arm. "It's all right. It wasn't your fault." She frowned. She didn't think she was showing yet and, besides, how would a Vetch child know about human pregnancy? "How *did* you know?"

"There's mamas on Shard," Failt said. His tentacles twitched. "They have a smell."

A smell. Walker shook her head and decided not to press further. She followed Yershov towards the dropchute. That explained Failt, she supposed.

But it didn't explain Heyes. And Heyes had definitely known.

How?

IT WAS SURELY testament to the great sums of money that Merriman Fredricks paid his bodyguards that they noticed the black-clad figures across the street at all. They were not amateurs and they really were extremely well-paid. Even so, they noticed the figures far too late to be able to do something about them. However professional and well-remunerated, they were well out of their league. Both men lay dead before they could raise the alarm.

Which left Fredricks, sitting in his counting house, completely vulnerable. An easy target, in fact, and the people coming to visit him today took full advantage of the opportunity. There were four of them altogether. Three of them stayed in the great vestibule to tidy away the bodies. The fourth strolled upstairs, completely at her ease, and went into Fredricks' office.

The man known as Fredricks looked up from his accounts. There was a woman in his office, standing with her hand resting on the eagle's cage. "That's a nice necklace," she said.

"Who the hell are you?" said Fredricks.

Quite some time passed between this and the moment when Fredricks, at last, fell face down dead, blood pooling quietly across the papers on his desk. Three minutes after Fredricks died, the four-person team was lost in the murk that hovered permanently over the sad little city of Roby. About an hour later, they were in flight and readying to enter the void, taking full advantage of the lax border controls at Roby's main spaceport.

It's a sad fact that people like Merriman Fredricks tend not to have warm personal friendships, and as such, it was another two days before his body was found. He missed a meeting with a fellow scoundrel across the city and, since the scoundrel had been expecting to shell out a large amount of protection money to Fredricks, it seemed unlikely that the slaver would miss the meeting—and, more importantly, he didn't want to find himself in the frame for whatever had happened to Fredricks. So he raised the alarm. The authorities—such as they were on Shard's World—sighed, pulled on their uniforms (they were all part-timers), took a nose around his offices, sighed again, arranged a clean-up, and moved on to the next thankless, underpaid task. Fredricks' body lay in the morgue for a couple of weeks, and then, unclaimed, went to the incinerator.

Perhaps someone, somewhere, would mourn him—he must, after all, have had a mother, although perhaps she had not regretted the day he left home. On Shard's World tears were few and far between, and the best that his business associates could say of him was that he never cheated you for the sake of it. As for all the money—who knew where it went? No doubt someone, somewhere, was getting rich.

CHAPTER EIGHT

DESPITE HER EXHAUSTION, Maria spent a restless night tossing and turning under the coverlet on the big sofa. She could not get comfortable. She woke, feeling terribly hot and thirsty, and looked around. A single lamp, casting a small amount of yellow light, glowed in one corner of the room. Jenny was fast asleep beside her. Amber was nowhere to be seen, although she could hear the other woman's breathing from beyond a small door. Carefully, not wanting to wake anyone, Maria slipped round Jenny and then picked her away over to the little kitchen space where Amber had cooked their supper, and got a glass of water. Then she settled herself in the armchair where Amber had sat the night before, and fell into a deep sleep.

Her dreams were vivid, almost hallucinatory. She dreamed of Kit, on their wedding day, a handsome young sergeant whose courage under fire had won him commendations. He stood at the desk of the registry office, paper-white with nerves at the sight of his wife-to-be. There was a strong smell of roses which, even in her dream, Maria thought was odd, as her bouquet had been violets (after her dead mother), purple and pretty and synthetic. Real flowers had been well beyond their means. Before she could reach Kit the dream shifted, becoming odder and less comfortable. She relived their flight from their little home; the escape from Braun's World; the sight of the planet on fire behind them. At one point she thought she heard a woman speaking—"*No, no idea...*"—and a man's voice, rumbling indistinctly in the background. Waking, she realized her arms felt empty, so she slipped back onto the sofa next to Jenny, pulling the little girl closer to her, and she fell back into a deep sleep which lasted the rest of the night, and was undisturbed except, briefly, by the woman's voice again: "*On the run...*"

Maria woke suddenly, with a very dry throat. Jenny was still asleep beside her, so she shifted round her until she was free to stand, moved the little girl more comfortably back onto the sofa, stood up and stretched.

The lamp was still burning. There was no sign of Amber. Maria got up and rattled round the kitchen for a while. She drank some more water, but couldn't find any food. She sighed, deeply, and once again thought she caught a scent of some perfume; something she couldn't quite name, but which seemed familiar. The scent seemed to be coming from beyond the other door. Maria stepped closer: there were voices, in quiet conversation. Amber must be awake. She would offer to make breakfast, as a gesture. Padding across the room, she tapped on the door to give advance warning, before pushing the door open and going through.

"Could I make some breakfast...?" she began, but she stopped when she saw what lay beyond the door.

The room was entirely dominated by the bed, to the extent that there was hardly room for a person to get round on either side. Amber was there, lying under crumpled bright orange sheets. Her shoulders were bare and one arm was flung behind her head. She was not alone. Her companion was a man in his forties, unshaven and with lanky brown hair. His most distinguishing feature, however, was the little scar that cut through his left eyebrow. Maria gasped. It was one of the men from the previous night; one of the three who had tried to assault her. Springer. He looked at her for a moment or two, and then he began to laugh.

Amber seemed completely unconcerned at being found like this. "Ah," she said. "So you've discovered my little secret." She stretched, lazily, like a cat in sunlight. "I'd have liked a day or two more to bed you in properly, but I suppose there's no real need. It's all done."

Springer was rubbing her hand. "You always get the job done," he said. "There'll never be another like you, Amber. But this one might have a few years in her."

Maria stood frozen in the doorway. Her tongue was completely dry in her mouth.

Amber smiled lazily, her golden smile glinting. "I hope you slept well. You, and the little girl. How is she? Still sleeping, I should think. She'll sleep for a while yet."

Maria tried to pull back, to run, but something seemed to be stopping her from moving. She stared at Amber, who was rising now from the bed, wrapping a robe around her, and moving closer and closer. Maria couldn't move, couldn't speak, she couldn't do anything at all, apart from stare at the woman coming towards her. The smell of roses was now overpoweringly strong.

IT WAS NOT that Kinsella deliberately delayed leaving Hennessy's World in pursuit of his former colleagues, not least because he did not want to place himself under further suspicion, but still almost a week passed between his meeting with Grant and his eventual departure. It was true that he did not want the mission—who would want to have to confront two former colleagues (both ex-lovers) about their possible treachery, with their potential summary executions hanging in the air? But Kinsella was trying not to think about where this journey might end. He justified his delay to himself as being solid preparation for a difficult and potentially dangerous journey: he had no intention of setting out blindly towards Satan's Reach; any operative worth his salt took the time to prepare their missions carefully; only an idiot would set out on a journey to the Reach without a clear plan of action.

An idiot like Delia Walker, for example.

They'd known each other well, Kinsella had thought, as well they might after years of working together under Andrei Gusev. He had loved her too, after a fashion, or perhaps, he admitted to himself now, grudgingly, he had loved the *idea* of her—

confident, cool, undemanding, and a tremendous boost to his self-image. But her most recent actions, never mind her sudden disappearance, had been a complete enigma to him, and the shock of the news of Andrei's death and Kay's disappearance had done a great deal to undermine his sense of himself as a man of good judgement. Still, a part of him hoped that there had been a terrible misunderstanding, that Delia and Kay had not, between them, cooked up this madcap story of a world where the Weird lived harmoniously with humans, not to mention a pregnancy of all things, in order to get away from the Bureau with Andrei Gusev's money. But what else could have driven both women to such desperate actions? He was willing to assume that they both were acting rationally—or thought they were—and so he struggled to find some solid reason for their departure. As he searched through Walker's most recent files to see what he could discover—a clue to where she might have headed, some trace that she might have left as she passed out of Expansion space and into the Reach—he rehearsed a conversation with her in his head, in which she agreed that she had misjudged him, that she had acted in haste, that she agreed it would be all to the good if she returned with him to Hennessy's World and set the record straight...

After the best part of a week sifting through Walker's files, he had to concede that Walker knew her business at least as well as him, and probably better. She had, to all intents and purposes, disappeared into a puff of smoke, round about the same time that an unlicensed freighter, the *Baba Yaga*, had also disappeared from the rundown old St Martin's docks on the far north-west side of the lagoon. Of the *Baba Yaga*, Kinsella could discover a great deal when it came to its history: decades of respectable service hauling cargo around the inner worlds, followed by a sudden and undignified retirement when a fault was discovered in its secondary drive; its purchase by one Sasha Yershov, who, it appeared, had had an equally sudden and undignified retirement from the merchant fleet (Kinsella didn't dig too deeply there). Of the *Baba Yaga*'s movements in recent weeks, Kinsella could find nothing. He had no idea what might have brought Walker and Yershov together, but he suspected the hand of Andrei Gusev in this— and, of course, Andrei was not there to ask, although Kinsella thought he could hear the old man's quiet laughter in his ear. *Struggling again, Mark? Has our dear lady outclassed you again?*

By necessity, Kinsella cast his net more widely, setting up searches for any unusual information traffic in recent weeks. A pattern... He was looking for a pattern... Eventually he found one. A number of internal requests (originator unclear) calling up all files related to a certain Merriman Fredricks.

Kinsella rocked back in his office chair, almost reeling in surprise. Now that was a name from the past, and one that Kinsella could not help but associate with Walker. Their encounter with Fredricks had been the first time Kinsella had understood Walker's hidden depths. Cold depths, which Kinsella personally hoped he would never have to navigate. Fredricks, certainly, had nearly drowned there. But Walker had decided that a live Fredricks in debt to her was more useful than a dead one, however tidy a resolution that was, so she allowed him the unusual distinction of leaving the lower levels of the Bureau's headquarters alive and, largely, intact. There had been some paperwork, all of which Walker handled, and Fredricks had been parcelled off, new identity and all, to a quiet world on the very edge of Expansion jurisdiction. From there he had clearly decided to put as much distance as possible between him and Walker, and the murderers that had been employing him and whom he had betrayed. Fredricks' last known location, according to the search results that Kinsella found, was a mining planet in the Reach called Shard's World. Kinsella nodded to himself. Yes, he thought, that was the place to start.

He notified Grant to tell her that he was ready to leave Hennessy's World, passing over the delay, and requesting that the ship she had promised be made available to him. Arriving at the small secluded spaceport that the Bureau used for its own business, he discovered that not only had Grant been as good as her word, she had excelled herself. The ship was compact, but fast and powerful; not the latest design, but more than adequate for his needs. It was called *The White Horseman*. As Kinsella approached it to board, he found himself almost looking forward to flying it. He was a decent pilot, not flashy but more than competent, and he had not had the opportunity to put in many hours in recent years.

"Kinsella."

He didn't recognise the voice, and something about the tone triggered an old instinct that had him reaching to his side for a weapon that he hadn't carried on a regular basis in years. Turning, he saw a young woman walking towards him, dressed in the familiar—and disliked—dark blue uniform of Fleet Intelligence. She clearly caught the movement of his hand, but she didn't smile, or blink, or in any other way give away what she thought. She simply registered the information and filed it away. When she reached Kinsella, she tapped the identity chip on the back of her hand. "Commander Grant sent me," she said. "But you can check my credentials if you like."

"You know," said Kinsella, "I think I will."

He took out his handheld and ran the scanner over the chip. *Scarlett Conway, Major, Fleet Intelligence. Currently seconded to Commander Grant, senior operations officer, Expansion Information Bureau.*

Scarlett? Good God, what names these children had. The handheld offered him her full service record, which Kinsella downloaded for future light reading. Then he looked at the woman more closely. She was in her late twenties, he guessed; on the tallish side, muscular in a slender way, and obviously extremely fit. Despite her relatively slight build, he decided he wouldn't like to have to arm wrestle her, not after so many years behind a desk. And she had the cool air of one whose eye was on promotion, who was cultivating the right people, and who didn't intend to allow anyone to stand in her way. Particularly not a middle-aged spook whose own patron had recently been found washed up on a beach. That kind of single-mindedness, combined with the cruelty of youth, was, in Kinsella's experience, a potentially deadly combination.

"Well," he said. "Major Conway. What brings you here this fine spring morning?"

"I gather Commander Grant thought you might appreciate some assistance on your mission."

"'Assistance'? For God's sake, I'm not an idiot," Kinsella said through gritted teeth. She was here to watch him. To make sure he didn't jump ship the moment he was out of Expansion space. To make sure that he brought back Larsen and Walker rather than joined them on whatever madcap quest or insane escape attempt they were currently embarked upon.

Conway looked back impassively. "If you have a problem, you should probably take it up with Commander Grant. I'm here at her request."

"Yes, yes, following orders. Jesus Christ!" He turned away, back to his sleek little ship. "Well, you can go back to Grant and tell her where she can stick those orders. I have been loyal to the Bureau and the Expansion for the whole of my adult life. I don't need a minder, particularly one half my age, and I'm certainly not taking one with me."

"I'm afraid that's where you're wrong, Mr Kinsella," Conway said calmly.

He stared at her. "Is that some kind of threat?"

"Do I need to make some kind of threat?"

"You're welcome to try."

"Very well." She folded her arms behind her, then glanced up at his new ship. "It's a very good ship. One of the best. Be a pity to die on it."

Kinsella almost jolted in shock. Jesus, who was this woman? Was this the kind of person Grant was bringing in as a matter of course? "What the hell do you mean?"

"Mr Kinsella," she said patiently, as if he did not have all his wits about him, "do you really think the Commander is going to let you fly off into the wide blue yonder without insurance? No, of course not," she said confidently, and now that she said it,

Kinsella couldn't believe he had thought it either. "This ship," Conway went on, "will phase into the void—but it won't phase out. Not without the right codes. Which I have and you don't. The void is a boring place. I doubt you want spend the rest of your life floating around in it trying to get out. Though you're welcome to try. I doubt it would be a long life. Suicide would surely be a rapidly attractive option."

Furiously, he turned away from her, and strode across the hangar to his now considerably less-than-attractive ship. Conway followed close behind, comfortably matching his pace, only adding to his aggravation. As they made their way up the metal steps outside the ship to the entry hatch, Kinsella found himself wondering: was he angry because Grant did not trust him, or because a potential avenue of escape had now been closed to him? He wasn't entirely sure himself.

THE CREW OF the *Baba Yaga* was sitting at an intersection, watching the station traffic pass them by and trying to decide their next move. Failt was happy exactly where he was: he had found more alien delicacies to nibble on, and as long as Walker kept them coming, he would sit where he was and watch the world go by forever. It was as if he was making up for the lost years of his childhood, Walker thought; years of privation and hard work, with very little to live on. Years stolen from him.

Yershov wanted to return to the Crossed Keys. He had liked the place, despite the unexpected arrival of a Catholic priest, and he saw no reason not to go back and sample more of its wares. Besides, he said, if there were still people hanging around the ship asking questions, did they really want to run into them? No, he said, shaking his head—let them get tired of waiting and go away.

Or else give them plenty of time to settle in and shoot them all on their return, Walker thought, but she didn't have the energy to argue. She was beyond tired; an ache had settled in her bones and all she wanted to do was lie down and sleep... Yershov, looking over at her, cleared his throat. "You all right?"

"I'm fine."

"Not... sick?"

"No," said Walker, shortly. And it was true: she had not been sick at all. She'd been expecting it, but it hadn't happened, as if her body was colluding with her mind to keep her in denial about what was happening to her. But she couldn't remain in denial, could she? She had to make some hard choices. Her body was, after all, on a schedule...

I must be mad. I should go home. But I can't go home, she thought desperately. *There's nothing for me there and it's all gone too far. But where do I go instead? Where do we go, little one? Where can I take you where you will be safe?*

Where else? Onwards. To live-in-peace-and-harmony.

I'll find this place if it kills me, thought Walker. *I'll find this place for you, little minnow. Peace and harmony.*

She rubbed her eyes. Her fingers came away damp.

"Missus," said Failt, tugging at her arm. "Why don't we try the little man again?"

Walker tried to focus. "I'm sorry, Failt, I don't know who you mean."

"The little man. You know." The child rounded his shoulders so that his wiry, hungry little body seemed suddenly plump, and then pulled at two of his tentacles, which bounced up in curls. Walker burst out laughing. For all the world, the Vetch child looked exactly like DeSoto.

"Didn't know you were a mimic along with everything else, Failt."

He sketched a small bow. "Many talents, missus. All yours."

"Well, I think you're probably right. DeSoto might know something..." She sounded doubtful even as she said it. "But I suppose there's nobody else to try." She called over to Yershov. "I'm going to try my contact again," she said. "I think you should go back to the ship and see what's going on."

"Back to the ship?" said Yershov. "Are you insane? I'm going back to that bar."

"Yershov," said Walker, wearily, "I'm tired. Don't piss me off. Not today."

With a low curse, Yershov pulled himself up and followed her and Failt across the intersection. Their way went together for some distance, and all three of them stepped onto the huge moving walkway that connected this sector of the station with the next. They were wide as well as long, with enough space for eight or nine people to stand abreast. An unspoken rule meant that no more than four stood, however, letting those who wanted to skip along more quickly stream past. It was a civilised system, Walker thought. Not something she'd associate with the Reach.

She and her companion stood while people dashed past. As they moved, Walker raised DeSoto on her comm. "When are you available?" she said. "We need to meet."

"*No way!*" the man hissed, loudly and angrily enough that the couple standing in front looked over the shoulders at her in surprise. She baulked at issuing threats in public, so she tried something else. "Fredricks said—"

"*Fredricks!*" he hissed. "*Damn Fredricks! He's left me in a lot of trouble—*"

"Left you? Why? Where's he gone?"

"*To Hell, I should imagine, that double-crossing, double-dealing bastard. Wish I'd had the chance to lay my hands on him before whoever got him...*"

"Hold on a minute. Fredricks is dead?"

"*Dead? Of course he's dead! They've caught up with him at last—whoever it is he pissed off this time—and if you were so thick with him, I don't want anything more to do with you. So sod off, Ms Walker!*"

The line was cut. The couple in front, with one last glance backwards, decided that they were better off walking for a while now.

Dead...

It was not that she had liked Fredricks—quite the opposite—and he had obviously led the kind of life that earned him many enemies. But she had seen him so recently and he had been thriving. A shiver passed up her spine. There was something else: those bodyguards she had seen had clearly been well paid and well able for their task. The villains and vagabonds of Shard were certainly no match for them. But someone more skilled? Someone from the Expansion, perhaps, with the resources of a big organization behind them...? She shuddered. She had thought that if she returned, she would get no more than a slap on the wrist. But perhaps the sudden disappearance of a disgruntled ex-Bureauwoman was not being treated so lightly. Perhaps they thought she was infected—she had never had the scan, after all. Perhaps they were coming after her. Perhaps they were already here, at the *Baba Yaga*...

Jesus Christ, what do I do now?

"Something the matter, missus?"

"What's that?"

"You worried? You uneasy?"

She sighed. She didn't want to frighten him. "No. But I'm shocked to hear about Fredricks, and I'm still wondering what to do next."

But that wasn't the truth, by any means, and the sharp look Failt gave her made her suspect that she wasn't fooling him. Was it coincidence Fredricks had been murdered so soon after their meeting? Or was it time, Walker wondered, to start being more than a little afraid?

The walkway came to an end and the three of them—man, woman, and child—huddled together at the edge of a busy concourse. "All right," said Walker. "Change of plan. We're coming back to the ship with you, Yershov. I want to know more about the people who have been asking questions about us."

He shook his head. "Still think we should lie low for a while."

"Well, I don't agree. But first," she said, "I want to buy a little protection."

Yershov frowned. "Protection?"

"A weapon, Yershov," she said, patiently. "I'm going to buy myself a weapon."

She was armed within the hour. It had cost a substantial chunk of her savings, and it had taken them to a desperate part of the station. "Now," she said, "we'll go back to the ship."

AMBER TOOK MARIA by the arm and led her out of the bedroom and back into the main room. A part of Maria's mind was screaming that she did not want to be touched, that she wanted the younger woman to take her hands off her, but somehow that part of her brain could not gain control, and she did not struggle or even complain when Amber pushed her down onto the cushions beside the still-sleeping Jenny.

She did manage to speak, however. "What have you given me?" She was trembling, desperate to grab Jenny and leave this awful place, but she couldn't make herself move. "What is it, for God's sake?"

Amber eased herself into her big armchair, lazy and satisfied as a cat. "I've not given you anything," she said.

"You must have done!" Maria gasped, forcing herself not to speak through the fog descending upon her brain, but struggling even to form the thought that Amber was dangerous and not to be trusted. "I've been half-asleep since I got here! I thought I must be tired after all that's happened..." For a brief, terrifying moment, Maria couldn't remember anything that had happened before meeting Amber. Nothing at all. It was as if this was where the world had begun—and this was where, inevitably, it would end. She felt Jenny against her. Maria glanced down at the girl, and she thought, *Oh, Kit—what have I done? Oh, my darling Kit—I've let you down!* "You slipped me something, didn't you?"

Amber smiled and her gold teeth glinted. "I

promise I've not given you anything," she said. "You slept because you were tired. You'd had a bad day, I think."

The part of Maria's mind that still felt under her control cried, *He's dead! My husband is dead! What kind of person are you, to take advantage of someone like me?*

"Springer saw you wandering about. So we decided... Well, we decided you both needed someone to take care of you. You came back here, you ate some food, and you felt safe and you fell asleep!"

Maria pinched herself on the arm, hard. It cleared her head for a moment. "But I felt something!" she said. "I believed I could trust you—no, it was something more than that. I felt like I could only be safe if you were there. That I had to come with you, and do what you said. You must have drugged me!"

"That wasn't a drug," Amber said. "At least, not one taken by you." She shifted in her seat, and for a moment Maria thought she glimpsed a different woman; someone darker and harder and older. Someone who was not as in control of herself as she might like.

"What do you mean?"

The door into the bedroom creaked open, and Springer came out. "She means that she's the one taking the drug." He came to stand behind the armchair, one hand on the back of the chair, one hand on Amber's shoulder. She didn't try to shake him off. "It's a clever thing. Makes her quite irresistible."

Maria understood. "To clients, you mean, don't you? You're her pimp. You've got her on some kind of drug, and she uses it to hook clients to make you money."

Springer smiled. "Not quite as innocent as you look, are you?"

"I learn quickly. But what do you want with me? I'm no Amber!" She laughed bitterly. "You'll need more than some clever drug to make me irresistible." She was starting to feel stronger now, as if the explanation was somehow stopping Amber's effect on her. She reached out and clutched Jenny's hand. Perhaps she would be able to get them both away...

"Maybe so," said Amber, "but as I said, I haven't given *you* anything."

Maria didn't miss the stress. She looked down at Jenny, still in a deep unmoving sleep, and a dark hollow opened within her. "Jenny," she whispered. She shook the little girl, who rocked senselessly to and fro against her. "Oh, my God, Jenny! Wake up! Wake *up!*" But the little girl didn't move. Maria looked up at Amber and Springer, helpless and furious. "What have you *done* to her?"

Springer tapped Amber on the shoulder, and she slid out of the chair. He stepped round to sit, the very picture of ease. Amber sat down again, at his feet. "It's nothing dangerous," Springer said, in a lazy voice. "At least, it's not dangerous as long as she keeps getting a regular dose of it. But if she misses a dose or two... Well, that's not so pleasant. You'd be well advised not to test my word on this."

"Why?" said Maria, aghast. "She's a little girl— she's not even five years old! Why would you do something like this? What kind of people *are* you?"

Springer looked almost bored by her outburst. "You know, in many ways, you might decide that this is for the best."

"The *best*? You've given my daughter some kind

of drug—addicted her! How can that be for the best? You're a *maniac!*"

Springer leaned forward, his eyes flashing. "Now you listen to me! When we met you, you were in trouble—"

"Trouble you'd manufactured!"

"You were lucky we got there first! It was only a matter of time before someone else got to you. There are bad people on this station—people who wouldn't think twice about murdering you for that pretty wedding ring on your finger and that cute little pendant round your neck. I don't want you dead. You're no use to me dead." He held up his hands. "I'm offering you sanctuary. You and the girl. Work for me, and I'll protect you. But there's no such thing as a free lunch, and I want people I can depend on. Not people who are looking to get away the first opportunity that comes up. This way, you need me."

"You're sick."

Springer laughed. But Amber, at his feet, whispered, "Yes." There was something in the tone of her voice that made Maria take a closer look at her.

The light in the room was dim, but even so Maria could see the change. Her skin, which had been fresh and youthful, now had a frail and papery look. Her shoulders were slumped, as if her spine was brittle and could hardly bear the strain of holding up the weight of her body. Her dark hair seemed to be threaded with thick wiry strands of grey. Twenty minutes ago a young woman had been sitting in this room. Now an old woman was here.

"The drug is potent," Amber said, "but the side effects are cruel. And these episodes"—she gestured at herself with a trembling hand—"become longer and more frequent." Her quivering hand reached out to Maria, who recoiled as if pulling away from a claw. "Every day I grow weaker! I need someone to look after me! I need someone to care for me!"

"Think of this," said Springer, "as finding your calling in life. Your vocation. Looking after Amber will be a kindness."

"My *vocation?* You're *evil!*" Maria turned to Amber. "You lied to me! You drugged my daughter! Do you think I'll help you now?"

"You've no choice," Amber croaked. "The little girl will die if she doesn't get her medicine! You'll do what I say for her sake, and one day she'll grow up and she'll be pretty, and she'll know what it's like to have power over everyone she meets..."

Maria grabbed hold of Jenny. The child flopped in her arms, like a doll.

"She'll die," said Amber. She had started to crawl towards Maria, on her hands and knees. "Away from here—she'll die."

"I'll take that chance!"

"It's painful," said Amber. She had reached them now. She was trying to stand up. "You'll see her gasp and choke and writhe."

"You're lying."

"Better stay here," she crooned, stretching out her hand. "Stay with me! Help me!"

Desperation lent Maria strength. Using Jenny's body weight, she shoved the other woman back, hard, towards the chair. Amber went toppling down onto Springer, and Maria dragged Jenny over to the door, scrabbling to open the door panel. She threw herself out of Amber's lair into the corridor beyond, and had only gone a few steps when she heard Springer's voice calling out behind her. "You won't go far! You can't go far! And you'll see that little one suffer if you do!"

Maria looked back over her shoulder. Springer was coming through the door and heading towards her, unencumbered.

Clumsily, staggering under the weight of her limp, lifeless daughter, Maria tried to run for it. She heard quick footsteps on the metal behind her, giving chase, and rapidly catching up. She tried to speed up, but Jenny was dead weight in her arms. She reached the end of the access corridor. Struggling forwards, heading towards the nearest intersection, she crashed straight into a woman coming that way, nearly sending her flying.

"Hey! Watch where you're going!"

Maria grabbed the woman's arm. She must look mad, she thought, her hair flying everywhere and the unconscious child in her arms. She didn't have time to worry about this, though; nor did she have time to wonder at a human woman travelling with a Vetch child. She held onto the woman's arm and begged, "Please, help us! For the love of God, help us! Before they kill us!"

CHAPTER NINE

THE WOMAN WAS carrying a small child in her arms, and the weight of them both together nearly sent Walker flying. Walker struggled to regain her balance and pulled back to get a good look, reaching for her new weapon. "Hey!" she said. "Watch where you're going!"

The woman grabbed her arm, stopping her reaching for her gun. Walker was starting not to like this encounter. "Please," said the woman. "Please, help us! For the love of God, help us! Before they kill us!"

Gently, but firmly, Walker made the woman release her grip, and quickly she took stock of the situation unfolding around her. The woman and her child had come running out of a nearby access corridor, from which a mean-looking bastard with a scar down one eyebrow was now emerging. He had his eye on the woman and child, and was advancing towards them.

"I don't like the look of him," Yershov muttered. "No-one should be chasing a woman and a babby." He stepped forwards.

Gallantry could be found in the unlikeliest of places, thought Walker, but given that she agreed with his assessment of the situation, she didn't complain. And Yershov had even more surprises up his sleeve. He stepped forwards and put himself between the woman and child and the man.

"Who the hell are you?" said the man.

"I'm the one telling you to get back where you came from," Yershov said.

"Get out of my way, old man."

"I'm not going anywhere," said Yershov. There were red spots forming on his unshaven cheeks. Walker was starting to wonder exactly how much he had managed to get down him in that booth at the Crossed Keys.

The man stepped towards them. "She's ours. I want her back."

"Oh, God," said the woman. She was pale with terror and shaking. "God, don't let him take us! Please—he's hurt Jenny already; drugged her!"

The man moved in closer. Yershov leaned forwards and spat in his face. *Christ*, thought Walker. *What a time for him to discover his inner gentleman.*

Things escalated quickly. Walker pushed the woman and child behind her, Failt too, and reached for her weapon. There was no chance of a clear shot—not while Yershov, their unexpected and frankly pretty unconvincing white knight, was wrestling with their assailant—and while it was tempting to put the pilot out of his misery, he was coming in handy. So Walker bided her time and waited until she had a clear shot.

Then the other woman appeared.

Walker struggled to describe her, afterwards. She had an impression of beauty, and grace, and long dark hair. There was a strong scent of flowers—roses, Walker thought, remembering the bouquets her grandmother had placed in every room of her childhood home, grown and bought at great expense. She realised that something was happening to her—that mind was clouding—and she shook her head to try to get back her usual clarity. Behind her, the woman with the child gave a low, panicked moan. Walker found herself lowering her weapon: she watched as her arm went down, almost of its own volition. *What the hell is happening here...?*

Then the voice came, sweet and low. "Stop this. You. Let him go. Move away."

There was a moment where Walker saw Yershov struggle against the command. But then he obeyed—dropping his arms and moving backwards. The scarred man picked himself up from the floor and started to smile.

"What the hell are you doing, Yershov?" Walker hissed, but the woman had started speaking again. Walker found herself straining to hear as much of her voice as possible. She seemed almost to *crave* it...

"We don't mean you any harm," said the young woman. "Maria seems to think we mean her harm—but we are her friends!" She opened her arm. "Will you come back to us, Maria? Will you let us look after you—and Jenny?"

Walker was dimly aware that the woman behind her—Maria—was still moaning, but she couldn't make out any words and wasn't even sure whether Maria was saying anything. Distantly, though, she heard Failt tug on her arm and speak to her: *Missus! Missus Dee! What you doing? What's happening?* She brushed the child away. She didn't want to listen to him. She was sick of his chattering. She wanted to hear what this young woman was going to say next. It was, she thought later, like waiting to hear the voice of a goddess.

"My name is Amber," she said. Beside Walker, Yershov sighed in happiness to hear her speak again. "There has been a misunderstanding." She gestured back towards the access corridor with a long, beautiful hand. "My home is very close. Perhaps you would be willing to come back with me there? We can talk together—explain to you what is happening, and you can see for yourselves that Maria and Jenny are safe with us. Maria," she said, and her voice became regretful, almost hurt, "how could you think that we would harm you? We wouldn't dream of it!"

Maria, it seemed, had no reply to this. Her mouth was open, but no sound came out. Yes, thought Walker, there must have been a mistake. Maria was hysterical, obviously. Amber would not—*could* not—mean anyone any harm...

"Will you come back with me?" said Amber.

"Yes!" cried Yershov. "Yes, we'll come with you!"

The woman granted him a golden smile. "Good," she said. "I'm so glad. We'll take care of you." She stretched out her hand, palm open, gesturing them to come towards her, reeling them in. And then, suddenly, she shrieked in pain. She turned round and saw Failt. "What the fuck?" Her voice was now harsh and unlovely. "You fucking piece of Vetch shit! You fucking *bit* me!"

"Sorry," Failt said, without a hint of remorse. He turned to look up at Walker. "Didn't like the sound of her voice." His tentacles quivered. "She smells funny too. Made everyone go funny. Promise I won't bite again."

"I'm glad to hear that," Walker said. "But thank you nonetheless. I think you broke her spell." She turned to Amber, whose furious face no longer seemed so perfectly beautiful, and she raised her weapon. "I think you'd better go," Walker said. She nodded at the man with the scar. "And take him with you."

Slowly, Amber backed away, the man retreating with her. Yershov aimed a kick in his direction, and he lunged at Yershov, but the pilot was ready for it, blocked the blow, shoved the man to the ground, and began to kick, nastily. Amber, seeing her champion was down, turned to run down the access corridor.

"Get down, Yershov," Walker commanded and, astonishingly, the pilot did what he was told. Walker fired, hitting Amber in the back. Yershov moved away from the man with the scar, and Walker went over to him, pulled him up from the ground, and covered his mouth. She dragged him down the access corridor, and shot him too.

When she came out, Yershov was still standing where she had left him. He stared over at her as she put away her weapon. "Christ," he said. "You're cold."

"You're not the sweetest person I've ever met, either," Walker said. "Perhaps this will remind you to stay on the right side of me." She looked back down the access corridor at Amber's body, and was shocked at what she saw. The young woman's body was completely changed from the goddess that had confronted them. It was as if she decayed all at once. The hair had greyed, and turned wispy. Her skin, which had seemed so fresh, so lustrous, was as frail as parchment. On the face, it was falling into the skull. Walker turned away, revolted.

Maria spoke. "You killed her," she said.

Walker looked over at her. Maria was sitting on the floor, her arms cradling her little girl. The child had finally woken, but she looked very drowsy. She looked like she had been drugged. What was going on here? "Yes," she said. "I killed both of them. Is that a problem?"

"No," said Maria. "No, that's not a problem, although I wish I'd got to do it myself. To both of them." She looked thoughtfully at Walker, and then pointed to her jacket, at the slight bulge where the weapon sat concealed. "Will you show me how to use that?"

Walker studied her for a moment, and then looked at the child in her arms. Was this someone else to take care of? A few months ago, Walker had barely given thought to children. She barely saw any. Now they were everywhere.

Walker sighed. "Yes," she said. "I think I probably should."

THE *WHITE HORSEMAN* came out of phase close to Shard's World, landing on a damp morning at the spaceport outside Roby. Conway had taken the pilot's sling, plotting the course from Hennessy's World through the void. Kinsella had watched closely, but there was no chance of learning whether what she had said about the access codes was true and, in truth, he hadn't expected it. He wasn't entirely convinced that Conway's claim was true. Surely Grant wasn't so callous as to condemn a man to the perpetual grey of the void?

There had been little conversation between Kinsella and Conway during the flight: enough for Kinsella to assist operations, and to establish who was to take which cabin. Once the ship was down, however, Kinsella suggested that Conway abandon her uniform. They were, he pointed out, no longer within Expansion jurisdiction, and the uniform might make people uncooperative, at best. After some thought, she agreed, and changed into civvies. Kinsella himself dressed comfortably and practically for what he assumed would be a day of moving around a wet city, although he tucked a small but compact laser within reach. Conway, he assumed, was armed to the teeth.

Outside, the early morning was wretched. The rain was not being kind to the city of Roby, which seemed to be covered in a thin layer of grease. The city-bound shuttle trundled dispiritedly through a sad landscape and several ill-kept stations before depositing them in the city's centre. Fredricks' offices were easily located in one of the buildings crumbling around the main square. The main doors were closed, but unguarded, and opened at once when pushed.

"Strange," said Kinsella.

"What's strange?" Conway said.

"I would have thought someone like Fredricks would have guards out front."

Conway shrugged. "Easier for us," she said, and went inside.

They passed through a deserted vestibule and towards a big flight of stairs. There were no lights on, although the morning had started out gloomy and was, if anything, getting darker as the rain clouds rolled in. There were no sounds either, no voices coming from far rooms in the ruined mansion, only their own footsteps thudding dully against the thinly-carpeted floor. At the end of the corridor they came to a big door. Kinsella went through first, with Conway following close behind. He looked round the dingy room with distaste. If this had once been the hub of Fredricks' business operations, everything he'd owned was now gone. All that was left was a couple of broken chairs and a pervasive smell of damp. A window had been broken at some point, and then it had rained steadily for several days. Kinsella sighed. "I guess we're too late," he said.

Conway nodded, but was unperturbed. "A search of the room might reveal something."

"Search?" Kinsella looked around. "There's nothing left here *to* search! If Fredricks knew where Walker was heading, that information has gone with him."

"Nevertheless, I believe we should take a look around."

Kinsella, dutifully, poked about the room. A few bits of rubbish, either discarded or blown in through the window. Some scraps of paper that revealed little. Conway, meanwhile, had gone over to the door, and was standing there, arms folded, looking down the corridor. Almost as if she was waiting for someone...

Kinsella heard footsteps coming up the stairs. Kinsella's hand went straight to his weapon, but Conway seemed untroubled. She pushed the door open, and two men came in. They greeted Conway cordially, as if expecting to find her here, giving overly smart salutes that, to Kinsella's eye, bordered on the insubordinate. Conway seemed unsurprised by their arrival. Kinsella, by the window, looked down into the square. There were two more of them outside, two women, standing on the pavement by the entrance to the building. A team of four, all the way from Hennessy's World, presumably, clearly military of some kind, and Conway had been expecting them. Who the hell were they?

Pretending to be examining a soggy cardboard box on the windowsill, Kinsella listened to the quiet exchanges between Conway and the two men. A cold chill passed through him. He knew them, he realised; they haunted your dreams, and when they stepped out into the real world, turned your life into a nightmare. Crimopaths: people who had killed without conscience, remorselessly, and repeatedly. Most of them were telepaths, or low-level psychics, who'd struggled with their abilities. The Bureau had identified them, experimented on them, to augment their abilities, to burn out what little moral compunction they had. To use them to do the Bureau's dirty work. It was an experiment best forgotten.

But here they were, and Conway had been expecting them.

"Thank you," Conway said calmly to the leader. "Perhaps you might wait for us outside. I believe Mr Kinsella wishes to speak to me in private."

The man nodded. Smiling almost pleasantly at Kinsella, he quit the room, taking his colleague with him.

Kinsella crossed the room. "Conway, what the hell is going on here?"

"Come now, Mr Kinsella. I'm sure you know that already. These are our new travelling companions."

"Don't you know what they are? They're crimopaths!"

She looked back at him patiently. "I know that. Of course I know that."

"But you obviously don't understand what that means? Now I'll admit they're a perfect fit for the Reach, but I don't want to go near them." Conway, he thought, was not reacting as someone should who had just been told that four cold-blooded killers had arrived to take up residence in her life. "And you were *expecting* these people?"

"I'll be perfectly honest, Mr Kinsella, and say that I wasn't expecting four of them. Three at the very most." She rubbed her cheek. "Still, I suppose they'll come in useful."

"Three? Well, I suppose *three* of them would have been perfectly reasonable! Have you taken leave of your senses? You must send these people back to where they came from—"

She lifted her hand and he remembered that, although dressed casually, she was a Fleet major, and much younger and fitter than him. "Mr Kinsella," she said, "whatever you may think, I do know my business, and I do not take unnecessary risks. I understand crimopaths and have extensive experience of working alongside them. I know better than anyone that it would be an act of self-destructive madness to travel with these people if one did not have a means to control them."

"I don't care what your experience of them is— and, to be honest, I don't want to know. But you're deluding yourself if you think you can control these people. They're uncontrollable by definition. That's why their use was phased out and the whole lot of them were locked in a prison deep beneath the ocean."

"With great respect, you are behind the times," Conway said. "Fleet Intelligence has been working for years on means to harness their unique capabilities to the service of the Expansion."

"People don't learn, do they? Fleet Intelligence *made* these monsters in the first place."

"And now we can control them." She walked over to the window, gesturing to Kinsella to follow her, and then reached down to touch the handheld strapped to her side. "Watch," she said.

Kinsella looked down onto the street below. Conway pressed a button on her handheld, and the nearest of the crimopaths jerked suddenly, then fell to the ground, hands clutched to his head. The brief scene that unfolded was one of the most disturbing Kinsella had ever witnessed in his long career as a spook. The crimopath was clearly in pain, but he was not distressed—he simply grunted and shook as if the pain was something almost external to him. At one point, he even seemed to be amused by it—his own agony a source of perverse pleasure. His colleagues, meanwhile, stood and watched as if he were some kind of specimen. One even walked round, to see the display from all angles, her head cocked in interest. Otherwise, there was no emotional response that Kinsella could see: they simply observed. If Conway could do this to all of them—and he assumed that she could—the thought that this might happen to them didn't distress them either. It merely... pacified them.

Kinsella was revolted. "All right," he whispered.

"You've made your point. Whatever you're doing, stop it."

Conway let the show continue for a few seconds longer, then pressed the button on her handheld again. "Pain is a useful motivator with individuals like this," she said. "While they don't react with fear—they don't feel fear, of course—the experience is not particularly pleasant and, in general, they try to avoid it. It therefore becomes a means of controlling their behaviour—preventing them from acting upon their worst impulses, or else acting them out in ways which can be used."

Kinsella put his back to the window. He thought, for a moment, that he was going to be sick, but he swallowed a few times and got himself back under control. "So who controls you, Conway?"

She turned an impassive eye upon him. "Nobody controls me, Mr Kinsella. But as I've explained to you already, I obey my orders." She looked around the room. "Superiors change. One is seconded to a new organisation, and finds oneself with a new commander. But the chain of command remains intact." She looked round the room. "We can go now. We've got what we came for. Those people out there—who you are so eager to send on their way— have been able to tell me that Delia Walker went to Shuloma Station in search of someone called Heyes. We'll find her there, or, if she has left, we can follow the lead from Shuloma."

At the thought of bringing these people anywhere near Delia, Kinsella almost threw up again. "You're very sure of that."

Conway made for the door. "My team excels at what it does."

* * *

MARIA LOOKED AT the woman who had saved her life. She had short dark hair, almost black, although there were hints of chestnut in it, and a few grey strands. Her hair was cut in a short bob, neat and business-like. She was kneeling down next to her, reaching for Jenny's hand. Jenny looked up at her sleepily. "Are you going to help us find my daddy?" said the little girl.

"I'm not sure," said the woman, and glanced at Maria, who shook her head. "Let's get to know each other better first."

"Monkey, too," said the little girl, closing her eyes again. "I miss Monkey."

"Well, we'll see about that." The woman turned to Maria. "Perhaps you could tell me something about yourself. What the hell was that all about? Who were those two?"

Maria was desperate to trust this woman—she wanted to trust her so much—but Amber, after all, had seemed so wonderful, like a guardian angel who had appeared out of nowhere, and who had turned out to be the Devil in disguise. She shook her head.

The woman frowned. "I'm Walker. Delia Walker. That one over there is Yershov, and this little one here who saved all our lives is Failt."

Maria took in the little creature standing nearby, with its ugly face and horrible tentacles. She tried not to shudder at the sight. "He's Vetch, isn't he?"

"He's Vetch, and he's friendly. Okay—you know who we are. Can you tell me something about yourself?"

Maria grasped Jenny into a hug and shook her head.

"Okay," said Walker. "You don't have to tell me anything. You can go on your way if you want—although it seems to me that you're not flourishing right now, and that you could probably do with a friend."

Maria retrieved Jenny's hand from Walker. She'd had a friend. Kit. The only friend she had ever wanted. Kit and Maria, together forever...

"I'm not going to press you," Walker said. She had taken the hint and withdrawn slightly, and was now sitting hunched on her heels. "We can sit here for a while until you get your breath back. Then you can go on your way. Wherever it is that you're going."

But Maria was going nowhere. She and Jenny were stuck on this hellhole, and she didn't know what to do or where to go, and she couldn't tell any more who was going to help her and who was going to harm her...

Walker was speaking again. "You know, your little girl doesn't look very well." Her voice was neutral, almost analytical in tone. "I imagine you've noticed that already."

Maria began to cry.

"What's wrong with her?" said Walker.

Between sobs, Maria explained. "That woman... The one you shot... She and the man gave Jenny some kind of drug... They wanted to trap me into taking care of her... I don't know what it is they've given her!"

Yershov, standing nearby, muttered, "Filthy bastards."

"I agree," said Walker. "Thank you for trusting me—Maria, yes? Maria and Jenny?"

Maria nodded.

"It sounds like you've had a hell of a time, and I'm not surprised you're not ready to trust us. But we're passing through, and we don't want anything from you. All we want to do is help you, or find someone who can help you. Do you know anyone here? Is there anywhere that we can take you?"

Maria shook her head. "We only just arrived. Kit brought us here. Found us a safe place. But it wasn't safe. We had to go, without Kit. And then, and then..."

"Who's Kit?" asked Walker.

"My husband..."

Walker studied her closely, her eyes narrowing as if appraising Maria's situation. After a moment or two, she sighed. "I see. So you're alone now. I'm sorry. But we're not staying, I'm afraid—not for much longer. We're going back to our ship and leaving soon."

"Is that right, missus? Where we going now?" asked the Vetch child. He talked to Walker as if she were his superior. No, that wasn't quite right, Maria thought. He talked to Walker almost as if she was his owner and he was her dog. She eyed the Vetch child cautiously. Her father had been in the Vetch war and had nothing good to say about them. But this little one hadn't been born then, had he? And he had saved her life. The world was turned utterly upside-down, Maria thought. Very little of what happened to her now made much sense.

"There's nothing for us here, Failt," Walker said. She sounded unhappy about that, Maria thought, and wondered why. Who wouldn't want to leave this place if they could? Perhaps if Maria asked, Walker might take them with her. Take them somewhere safe... She shook herself. She had trusted Amber too easily. She wasn't going to make that mistake again. She had to look out for herself now, for Jenny's sake, rather than always being on the look-out for a new protector. Even Kit hadn't been able to protect her entirely, in the end.

"We may as well go onwards," Walker went on. "But we don't have to go at once, and we should make sure that these two are safe." She stood up and looked around, as if thinking of a plan.

"They could come with us," said Failt. "The mama and her little one both."

Yershov looked like he might be persuaded, but Walker shook her head, and she was definitely the one in charge here.

"I don't think that's a good idea," Walker said, "not least because Jenny needs to see a doctor. Anyway, I've had an idea. Maria—if it's okay with you, we're going to take you to someone that we know who lives here. She's kind, and she's got a history of looking after people who are in trouble— really looking after them, I mean, not exploiting them. I think she'll be able to help you, or be able to send you to someone who can."

The Vetch child chuckled. "Not sure Heyes'll be glad to see us again!"

"We won't stay long." Walker glanced at Yershov. "You might even get a drink in at the Crossed Keys."

Turning to Maria, Walker offered her hand, but Maria shook her head, wrapping her arms more tightly around Jenny. "I'm not going anywhere with you. Not unless you tell me where and how you know this person. Amber said she was going to help me. And look what she's done."

Walker looked distinctly uncomfortable. She patted Maria on the arm. "Yes, of course, that's very sensible. All right, this person is a priest—"

"A *priest?*"

"Well, she *was* a priest. She used to help people get away from trouble to a safe place. I don't think she does that any longer, but she might be able to get you away from here. And if it needs money..." Walker sighed. "I have money. I'll help."

The Vetch child, Failt, muttered, "Won't be much left, soon, the way we're spending."

"Why would you do this?" said Maria. "What's in it for you?"

"There's nothing in this for me," said Walker. She was looking at Jenny. "Except that one day I might need a friend, and I hope that if that day comes, then there'll be someone willing to do the same for me." She shrugged. "Call it karma."

"I don't believe in karma," said Maria. "I don't believe in God either, Catholic or otherwise."

"Nor do I," said Walker. "But we live in hope." Again she offered Maria her hand. "Will you let me help you?"

She looked so tired and sad—so far away from the confidence and glamour that Amber had exuded— that Maria found herself saying 'yes' just to make the woman feel better. And indeed Walker did give a small smile, and said, almost to herself, "Well, at least I'll have managed to help *someone*..."

They began to make their way back across the station. They had not been travelling for long when Maria realised that something in her pocket was vibrating. She put her hand inside her pocket and found—

The datapin. Kit's last gift, the reason she and Jenny were here, alone, the reason Kit had died. Its owner had come to collect.

Suddenly, someone stepped forwards from a nearby access corridor. A woman in her forties, who looked like she had been on a long, tiring journey. "Walker," she said.

At the sight of her, Walker was transformed. Gone was the unhappy woman who a moment ago had been pleading to Maria to allow her to save her life. Here once again was the fighter; who had shot someone in the back as they tried to run away, and then dragged a man into a corridor and killed him in cold blood. "*You!*" she said, reaching for her weapon.

The woman had her hands up. "Delia," she said, "please, listen to me. I know you think you've got no reason to trust me, but you've not got the whole story."

Maria saw Walker's hand clench, ready to fire. But this was who she had been waiting for. This was the person Kit had said would come find them... "Don't shoot her!" Maria cried. "I know her! At least, I think I do!"

Walker turned to her. "You *know* her? How the hell do you know her? Larsen, is this true?"

"I hesitate to say this," said Kay Larsen, "but I've never set eyes on you in my life."

"You saved our lives," Maria said. "I'm Kit's wife. It was you, wasn't it?"

Walker lowered her weapon and looked between them. "What's going on here? Larsen?"

Maria walked past her towards Larsen. "Kit was in contact with you from the start. You got us the ship. You gave us the codes. You helped us get away."

Walker's weapon lay uneasily in her hands. "Helped you get away from where?" She glanced over at Larsen. "I'm not sure I like what I'm hearing here."

Maria turned to her. "My husband, Kit, was a junior officer in the Fleet. We were stationed on Braun's World—"

Walker's weapon came up. She pushed Failt behind her and stared at Maria in horror.

"We ran away," said Maria. "And I think that this woman—Larsen?—I think that she helped us escape." She turned to Larsen. "It was you, wasn't it? We spoke to each other."

Larsen looked uncomfortable.

"There's no point in denying it," said Maria. "I have the datapin. Kit said it would activate when the person who should get it was nearby. And it did, just now. I'd almost forgotten about it. Isn't that crazy? The whole reason I'm in this mess, and I'd almost forgotten about it. Then it began to buzz, and you turned up. I'm supposed to hand it over to you, aren't I? That's what Kit wanted." She made a move towards Larsen.

Walker pointed the weapon at her. "If you were on Braun's World, you could be infected."

"I don't think I am," said Maria. "Kit said we couldn't be, and I believe him." She looked at Larsen. "Although I would never have thought that Kit would go AWOL, and he did."

"How can you be sure you're not infected?" said Walker. She looked at Larsen. "You should have known better than to have helped someone leave.

For Christ's sake, Kay, they wiped out everyone there!"

"She can't be infected," said Larsen, flatly. "This is what I'm trying to tell you. She *can't* be."

Walker looked at her narrowly. "What do you mean?"

Larsen sighed. "I assume you have a ship, Delia?"

"I do, but you can go to Hell if you think you're getting anywhere near it."

"I'm done with all this," said Larsen, simply. "I've come too far and there's too much at stake. I betrayed you, yes—but there were good reasons, and you need to hear them. The datapin Maria is carrying can substantiate what I say—at least, I hope it can. But you need to back off, Delia. Gung ho doesn't suit you, you know. You're not the kind to go in all guns blazing. You have people for that." She nodded at the weapon irritably. "For heaven's sake, will you put the damn thing away?"

Slowly, Walker tucked the weapon away under her jacket. "All right," she said. "Truce. I'll listen—for a little while. Get talking."

Larsen shook her head. "Not here," she said. "We need to get away from here. What I'm going to tell you—we should be in private." She turned to Maria. "You should come too," she said, looking at her with compassion. "You should hear this. The reason why your husband went AWOL. The reason he died."

CHAPTER TEN

"SO THIS IS your ship?" Larsen ran her finger along the wall on the flight deck and examined her fingertip with some distaste. "I imagined you in something considerably sleeker, Delia. You always preferred the finer things in life."

"Needs must when you find yourself betrayed by your friends," said Walker. She found herself almost feeling defensive of the *Baba Yaga*, which had served her well so far. "Anyway, it's done the job. It got me off Hennessy's World, and it's got me this far." She settled back in her sling. "You said you had a story to tell, Kay. Or were you just trying to save your skin?"

Larsen leaned back wearily against the wall. "I'm tired of games. Really, I'm done."

"Then *why did you betray me to Latimer?*" Walker's voice almost shook as she remembered that day: the conversation with Kay, confirming the pregnancy, and her sudden and world-shattering dismissal. The sense of dislocation, of being at sea. She was not sure that she had quite recovered from the shock yet. "I came to you for help. I trusted you."

Larsen nodded. "I know."

"You were my *doctor*. But you must have been on the line to Latimer before I was back at my desk."

"I was," said Larsen, simply. Walker shook her head in disgust. "And I'm sorry," Larsen went on. "But I had to make sure they kept their trust in me, and the best way to do that was to... Well, to sacrifice you. You were collateral damage, Delia. I'm sorry, but that's the truth."

"Collateral damage. Tell me again why I shouldn't shoot you?"

Maria, who had been listening quietly, intervened. "I don't know what has happened between you, but I do know that Ms Larsen has helped me and Jenny. We would have died on Braun's World without her help."

Larsen gave a small smile. "That's generous of you. I told your husband to abandon you, you know."

"I know," said Maria. "But once you knew we were there, you didn't abandon us. You tried to help. I'm sure that must have put you at risk." She turned to Walker. "Yours isn't the only story here, Ms Walker. I'm grateful to you—God knows I'm grateful—but I have a right to know why Kit brought me and Jenny here. I have a right to know why he died."

"Will you let me explain, Delia?"

Suddenly Walker, too, felt tired of games. "All right," she said. "But for your sake, Kay, you'd better make this good."

"Oh, it's a good story," said Larsen grimly. She

looked around. "Are you sure this is a safe space, though? Private?"

"Yes."

"What about your pilot?"

"He'll be asleep for a while yet."

"And the Vetch child?"

"Will not betray me. You're safe to speak, Kay," Walker said, with the authority of twenty years' service in the Bureau.

Larsen smiled. "If you say it, then I'm prepared to believe it." She took a deep breath. "All right, here goes. You asked how I knew that Maria and Jenny couldn't be infected by the Weird. It's simple enough: there was no Weird portal on Braun's World."

Walker stared at her in confusion. "I don't understand..."

"The Weird never opened a portal on Braun's World," said Larsen. "They were never there. The footage that we saw in the Bureau—it was faked. Correction," said Larsen, seeing the question forming on Walker's lips, "the footage was real; it was the attack on Cassandra, last year. The images you saw had been doctored to look like Braun's World. Different sky, different buildings. I'll give them their due," Larsen said bitterly, "they did a bang-up job. Real attention to detail."

At first, Walker couldn't quite begin to put together all the pieces of this. "There was no Weird portal," she said.

"That's right."

"And what we saw in the Bureau that night—"

"All faked."

"So what about the bombardment of Braun's World? Did that happen?"

"Oh, that happened," said Maria, softly. "I saw it."

"Dear God," said Walker.

"I see you're starting to understand," said Larsen. "You had them on the run, Delia. The hawks, the fighters, the ones who want to tear a hole into the void and send all the firepower we've got in there to finish the Weird for good. You and Andrei were about to see them off. But they weren't going to surrender power easily. So they changed the rules of the game. They needed people to be scared of the Weird. But the Weird don't appear on demand. So they had to be conjured. They faked the news of the portal opening on Braun's World—"

And they murdered the whole population of the planet to cover up what they had done. "Jesus Christ."

Larsen gave her a tight smile. "Do you see the quandary I was in when, you told me your news? I had to make some very quick, very hard decisions."

"Who's involved?" said Walker. "Grant? Latimer? Does it go all the way up to the Council?"

"I don't know how high this goes," Larsen admitted. "They were onto me and I had to get out. But I'm guessing it goes pretty high."

Walker sat for a while and contemplated Larsen's story. A crime like this—would someone really murder so many people for no better reason than to oust their enemies within the Bureau? To secure their power base? The more she thought about it, the more she could believe it. The Weird were terrifying: hideously alien and utterly inscrutable. She had seen the terror lurking behind the eyes of many of her colleagues; the fear that here, at last, was an enemy that could not be defeated. Perhaps it was that fear that had driven them. Slowly, she said, "Do you have any proof, Kay?"

"No," said Larsen. She looked at Maria. "But I'm hoping *you* do."

Maria pulled out the datapin that Kit had entrusted to her, a few short days and a lifetime ago. Walker took the pin and inserted it into place on the companel. A passcode was required, which Larsen gave. There was a large number of video files. Walker picked one at random. It made for uncomfortable viewing.

The scene was a city street. The vidcam recording the scene was obviously hidden: every so often the image would suddenly go out-of-focus, or show the inside of the camera-person's jacket. But there was enough to see what was going on. In the background, a siren was blaring, and a repeated warning blared out across the street to tell people that a curfew was now in force, and that citizens should return to their homes. A large crowd had gathered to protest this infringement of their liberties, and the security forces were attempting to contain them. Eventually, they opened fire. After a few seconds, the recording cut out.

Larsen took it back to the beginning, and froze the image to show the city street. "This is the centre of Elliston," said Larsen. "That's the second biggest city on Braun's World's main continent. There was footage from there in the Bureau, Delia—do you remember? Showing the Sleer and the Flyers arriving and beginning their assault."

Walker nodded. She remembered. She could hardly forget. "So there's been a riot on Braun's World. What does that prove?"

"It's to do with the dates, isn't it?" said Maria, suddenly. "I bet if we checked the footage you saw, you'd find that this is happening *after* the Weird were supposed to have attacked. After Elliston was laid waste by the Weird."

Larsen nodded. "That's it exactly, Maria. It seems that the people on Braun's World got wind of what was planned for them. They protested, and they were murdered for those pains." She frowned. "Perhaps they were the lucky ones. They didn't have to die in the bombardment."

Slowly, painstakingly, they worked their way through more of the files. The story was the same across Braun's World. Larsen pulled out another datapin, and fired up the footage of the Weird assault Walker had seen back at the Bureau. "It'll take some work," Larsen said, "but I'm sure we can prove that the recordings don't match up. That the dates and the times are wrong."

"So this is why Kit died," Maria said softly. She rubbed her eyes. "I'm glad it was for something that mattered." A new edge entered her voice. "Who could do such a thing? Tell a lie like this? They can't be allowed to get away with it."

"Delia, I'm sorry," said Larsen softly. "I threw you to the wolves. But I think we're still on the same side?"

Walker stared at the images on the viewscreen. It was hard to let go of anger. But it was a relief too— and a relief to know that her judgement hadn't been impaired. She had been right to trust Larsen. But she hadn't known the extent to which the parameters had changed. "I understand. Desperate times, desperate measures. You're here now."

"And we should probably get away," Larsen said. "I don't know if I'm being followed, but my absence has surely been discovered by now. They'll be sending somebody after me. They want me dead, and they'll come after anyone with whom they think I might have shared this information. That means you now, Delia."

"I imagine they think I'm part of it already," Walker said. "I disappear, then you disappear. That's bound to raise suspicion."

"What about me and Jenny?" said Maria. "Are we still not safe? I thought that if we handed over the datapin, then perhaps we would be safe... But we'll never be safe again, will we? Whoever did all this"—she swept her hand toward the viewscreen—"they wouldn't think twice about killing me and Jenny, would they?"

"No," said Walker.

"So what shall we do?" asked Larsen. "Where were you going next, Delia? Are you any closer to finding this mythical colony world?"

Walker sat in thought for a while. "I think I know someone who knows where it is, but she's proving unwilling to provide further information."

Larsen laughed. "It must be a while since that happened to you."

"I lack the resources I once had." Walker leaned back in her sling and stared at the ancient control panel. They had to go—and soon. The Bureau—or whoever controlled it now—would be pouring resources into finding Larsen, and the evidence she had that the destruction on Braun's World had not been caused by the Weird. They needed a bolthole—and a mysterious planet where the Weird flourished would be ideal. If only she could persuade Heyes that it was in her interests to talk...

Slowly, Walker began to smile. "I think that I have an idea."

THE CRIMOPATHS LOST no time settling in on the *White Horseman,* assigning themselves quarters and making themselves comfortable in the small rec room. When the ship left Shard's World, Kinsella felt a terrible claustrophobia engulf him. Wherever he went, he seemed to feel the eyes of the crimopaths upon him, studying him, observing him. Even locked away in his quarters he did not feel safe, fearing to fall asleep in case, waking, he found one of them looming over him or, worse, simply sitting by his bedside, watching. Struggling to rest, he could only feel a cold, bitter anger towards Grant, putting him into such a small space with these unpredictable animals. Whatever Conway thought, Kinsella did not believe that they could be controlled.

He abandoned attempts at sleep, and went in search of Conway. She was alone in the rec room, eating a solitary, functional, and industrial meal. "We need to think about our next move," he said. "Fredricks was my best lead." His only lead, in fact, but he didn't need to make himself seem incompetent. "The ship's computer has accessed his files on Shard—those, at least, survived—and it's going through them. But it's going to be a slow job and I'm not sure how long it will take. But at some point we'll find something to give us a clue where Walker was heading next."

Conway cut her slab of protein into neat cubes. "We know where we're going next. Shuloma Station. We're looking for a priest, named Heyes. We went into phase while you were sleeping."

"You didn't think to discuss this with me?"

"You were asleep," she said, as if having to explain something straightforward and obvious. "There was no point in wasting time."

"So what's the reasoning behind Shuloma Station? What makes you think that's our best option?"

Behind him, someone began to laugh. Kinsella looked back over his shoulder. One of the crimopaths was standing in the doorway, watching. And laughing.

"Stop that," Kinsella said, but the laughter continued.

"All right," said Conway softly. "That's enough."

The crimopath immediately went silent. But he stood there, still, watching Kinsella. "Jesus Christ," he muttered, his skin crawling.

"You can go," Conway said. "I'll call you if I need you."

The crimopath obeyed. Kinsella shuddered. "You've not answered my question," he said. "Why Shuloma Station?"

Conway sighed, as though the question were impertinent. "How do you *think* I know where we need to go next?"

If Kinsella thought he'd felt chilled before, it was nothing to how he felt now. He looked back over his shoulder to where the crimopath had been standing moments before. "They weren't on Shard's World for us, were they? When did they arrive?"

Conway didn't answer, but continued eating.

"Conway, how long had they been there?"

"I don't know," she said, through a mouthful of food. "Long enough."

Long enough to get to Fredricks, and kill him. But not before extracting the information that they wanted from him. Kinsella shook himself to dispel the thought. He didn't want to dwell on how Fredricks might have died. He had seen crimopaths in action before, as a young man, before their use was outlawed. It had been a profound relief when the ban had come into force, and they were all retired. Kinsella had slept more easily at nights, knowing that they were locked in deep dungeons with miles of ocean above them. They shouldn't be on the loose now. "I know you think you can control them," he said. "But I swear to you—you can't. We... We never could. They'll be looking for ways to get away, and I swear—they'll find them. They are smarter than you—smarter than both of us—and they *will* get away from you."

Conway had lost interest partway through this speech and had turned her attention to a carton of juice. "The inhibitor will control them," she said offhandedly, sipping at the juice. "That's all I need."

"For now, but it won't last—I can tell you that. Don't you think they're going to be doing something about that? They'll work out how the inhibitor works, and disable it. When they've done that they'll coming looking for you to repay you." *And I*, he thought, *will be collateral damage.*

"So how would you have obtained the necessary information from Fredricks?"

Kinsella didn't hesitate for a second. "I would have paid him, of course. That was the language that Fredricks knew best."

Conway gave him a scornful look. "And he would have taken your money, lied to you, and sent you on your way. But he would not dare to lie to my people. Not if he knew he was bargaining for his life. And so now we are *en route* to Shuloma Station, rather than hanging uselessly in orbit around Shard, waiting for your computer to sift through files for information that might not even be there." She stood up, and began to gather together her empty food cartons. "I believe I prefer my way, Mr Kinsella. It gets results. We'll arrive on Shuloma Station soon, and when we get there, we will find Delia Walker, and then—" She stopped herself, as if she had suddenly remembered she had an audience.

"And then what?" Kinsella asked softly.

She looked down at him with her pale eyes. "What else? We will learn the nature and extent of her treachery."

Her cartons were now stacked in a neat pile. *Cold, cold*, Kinsella thought. *So very, very cold*. "Is this the future?" he said. "The future of the Bureau?"

"It is the future of the Expansion, Mr Kinsella," Conway said. "We live in a terrible time, a time of great danger. We must make hard decisions, and we must not be afraid to act on those decisions. Because otherwise we will be destroyed, consumed by a merciless enemy that cares nothing for our scruples. I do not wish to be destroyed. And so I will act to protect and preserve the Expansion."

Kinsella did not reply.

Conway, having taken her cartons over to the recycler, stopped briefly on her way out. "Good night, Mr Kinsella," she said. "You can sleep easily— truly, you can. The Expansion is safe in our hands."

She left, and Kinsella sat for a while alone in the empty room. What would be left of the Expansion, he wondered, by the time people like Grant, and Conway—and their damned crimopaths—were done? Who exactly would be left standing? And what would the Expansion look like? Like Braun's World, he feared; burned to the ground. He wondered whether they might be better surrendering to the Weird right now, rather than going through the terrible self-destruction upon which the people around him seemed set. He found himself thinking about the grey empty swirl of the void, that empty, soulless space, where nothing lived. Except the Weird. Once again, he found himself cursing Adelaide Grant, sending him to this hostile place, with such hostile companions. This world that she was set on creating—this was not what he wanted. Not what he wanted for...

His child.

Kinsella shook himself. That had come from nowhere, and he suppressed the thought as quickly as it had arisen. There was nothing there. He wasn't even convinced that Delia had told him the truth about the pregnancy.

About their child...

No, none of this was what Kinsella had wanted— but then he hadn't wanted Andrei Gusev dead either, and Walker, it seemed, had a hand in that. Maybe, he thought, as he rose wearily from his chair and went back to his quarters, there was nothing to be done. Maybe all the good guys were dead and buried. He lay on his bunk in the darkness in fruitless pursuit of sleep. Perhaps it was better to surrender to the inevitable, rather than fight. Better to go peacefully,

The Baba Yaga

rather than rage against the dying of the light. That way you might last a little longer. Long enough to save something that mattered.

WALKER TOOK LARSEN with her, and nobody else. Failt didn't want to leave her side ("*Someone* got to look after you, missus…"), so she told him she needed him to keep an eye on Yershov. Maria remained with Jenny, naturally, although this suited Walker's purposes. She didn't particularly want either of them to see the conversation that was about to follow. Let Maria remain idealistic about her for a little while longer.

The church was locked and dark, but that proved no barrier to finding Heyes. At the Crossed Keys, old Viola, sitting behind the bar and puffing on a small wooden pipe, watched them enter. She gave a slight nod of her head, and a big young man came from the other end of the bar and made himself quietly, but noticeably, present.

"I thought you'd gone on your way," Viola said to Walker. "Even I would say that there are better sights to see on Shuloma Station than the Crossed Keys, you know."

"I have some unfinished business with Heyes," Walker said. "Is she here?"

"I'm fond of that old woman," Viola said. "I don't want her to come to any harm."

"Neither do I. But she might be in trouble," Walker said, truthfully. "I want to make sure she knows what's heading her way."

"What kind of trouble?"

Walker smiled. "It's better that you don't know."

Viola sucked thoughtfully on the pipe. With another slight nod, she sent the big young man on his way. "Heyes is back there."

Walker nodded her thanks, and she and Larsen on into the bar. They found Heyes sitting alone in a quiet booth, eyes half-closed. There was a nearly empty tumbler in front of her. Walker sat down. Heyes looked at her glassily from under her eyelids. "Thought you'd be long gone." Her voice was slightly slurred. "Why aren't you gone?"

Walker slid in beside her, making the woman move along. Larsen sat down opposite. "I'm not finished with you yet," said Walker.

"'M finished with you. Never really got started. Got nothing for you." She waved at Walker, vaguely. "Go away."

Larsen turned to Walker. "This is your lead? Jesus Christ—"

"Don't underestimate this one, Kay."

"She's a drunk. A priest. A drunk priest."

"Maybe so, but she also caused a lot of influential people a lot of trouble back on Shard's World."

Slowly, but surely, Heyes began to slump forwards onto the table. "Look at her," said Larsen. "She's not even troubling that glass of whisky. Delia, we've got to go. We don't have much time and we're wasting it here—"

Walker shook her head. "This will be worth it. I promise." She snapped her fingers. "Hey! Heyes!" But the priest had started to snore. Walker banged her hand against the table. Heyes jumped.

"Stop tha'!"

"Wake up!"

"Wasn't aslee'…"

"All right, you're wide awake. So listen. Listen hard, Heyes You're in trouble. There are some bad people coming this way, and if they find out that you've met me, they won't take pity on you. They'll kill you."

Heyes put her head in her hands. "Let them come. Sick of this life. Be a blessing. God have mercy. Resurrection and the..." She hesitated. "What was it? 'I am the resurrection and the...' Oh, fuck it."

"For God's sake, Delia," hissed Larsen. "Let's get out of here!"

Heyes looked up and stared at her blurrily. "God help you. Never helped me. Only caused me problems. Made me try to live right. What good's that done me? I ask you." Her eyes narrowed as she tried to focus on Larsen. "Who are you? You're not that Vetch boy. Are you really Vetch? You don't look Vetch."

"Thanks for that." Larsen turned to Walker. "Whoever this is—she's not sober enough to help and we're wasting time we could use to get away."

Heyes slammed both hands against the table, sending the tumbler flying. Larsen caught it before it flew off the table. "The life!" cried Heyes. "That was it! The resurrection and the life." She stared at Walker. "Now what the fuck was it you were talking about?"

Walker put her arm around the big woman's shoulders. "Come on," she said. "Time to go. Time for you to take a little trip off Shuloma."

Heyes tried to shake her off. "Fuck off! 'M not going anywhere!"

"Oh, yes you are. You're coming with us. Otherwise some people are going to come and kill you. And they'll take their time over it."

"You can't fool me! Big con, that's what this is. Trying to find out about Stella Maris. Well, I won't tell you anything!"

Stella Maris... It might be enough, Walker thought. It might show up on a star chart somewhere. She could leave this drunken liability where she was. God only knew she had enough unexpected dependents right now...

But those people were still coming. And even if Heyes knew nothing about Braun's World, they might not believe her, however long they tormented her. In many ways, thought Walker, she was about to do Heyes a favour...

"You're going to tell me everything I want to know," said Walker, quietly and not pleasantly. Larsen frowned at her. "Listen, Heyes. My friend and I know a secret—a big secret. The kind that people don't hesitate to kill over."

"Bullshi'."

"There was a massacre on Braun's World. Millions upon millions dead. They said it was the Weird, but it wasn't. They lied, and murdered millions upon millions to make their lie seem true. They're killing everyone who know the secret. And the thing is—that includes you now, Heyes. They can't leave you alive. So they'll come and find you. They're already on their way. They're coming after us, and they'll know about you. Not least because when they catch up with me—and no doubt they *will* catch up with me, eventually—I'll tell them. I'll say to them, 'Your secret isn't safe until you kill the priest.' So you can't stay here. You have to come with us."

All through Walker's speech, Heyes had been coming more and more into focus. By the time Walker finished, she was stone cold sober. "You evil bitch..." she said, in a wondering voice.

"Yes," Walker agreed.

"Why the hell have you told me this? What have I done to you?"

"You haven't been as helpful as I needed," Walker said. "You know where this world is—where the Weird are living alongside humans. I want to go there. I want to..." Walker hesitated. Put bluntly, her quest seemed hopeless. "I want to talk to them."

"So to satisfy some fantasy of yours you've put the fucking *Bureau* on me?"

"They're already onto you," said Larsen. "You must have guessed what Walker is?" She smiled, almost cheerfully. "Look at it this way, Heyes. At least you've fallen in with the good guys."

"I'm trapped, aren't I?" said Heyes, desperately.

Walker nodded. "Best come with us. I'm sure it'll be safer in the long run."

YERSHOV WAS LESS than pleased to see Heyes. "I don't trust Catholics," he said, arms folded, feet planted firmly on the ground, as if to block her entrance to his flight deck. "And I particularly don't trust Catholic priests."

Walker gently pushed him out of her way. "You don't trust anyone."

"With good cause!" he yelled at her. "People don't tell me important things! Like the fact that they're having babies and all the rest of it!"

"Ah," said Heyes. "Did I let the cat out of the

bag? I'm sorry if I've caused any embarrassment." She thought about that. "That's not true. I'm not sorry at all."

Walker didn't reply, but simply gestured to Heyes to follow her to the flight deck. Heyes turned to Larsen. "I take it that your friend's condition is not a surprise to you?"

Larsen shrugged. "I'm her doctor."

"Handy." The priest lumbered after Walker onto the flight deck.

At least one member of the crew of the *Baba Yaga* was pleased to see Heyes. Failt bounded up to her. "Yershov don't like you," he said. "You must be okay."

Maria, however, was more pleased to see Larsen. "You promised you'd look at my little girl," she said. "See what can be done. Please. I don't know what they've given her and I don't know what harm it might be doing."

"I'm coming now," said Larsen. "And then I'd like to see you too, Delia."

Walker nodded. "Let's get out of here first," she said. She looked back over her shoulder to the doorway where Yershov was standing, sulking. "Sit down, soldier," Walker said. "We've got a job for you." She turned to Heyes. "So. Where are we going?"

Heyes sighed, as if this whole affair was against her better judgement. "The world is called Stella Maris, but you won't find it on any of your charts."

She'd been right to force Heyes to come. Well, it was probably tidier this way. And it might keep Heyes alive a little longer.

"Give Yershov the co-ordinates," she said. "It's long past time we were on our way."

* * *

By the time Larsen came to see her in her cabin, Walker was very nearly asleep.

"Your crew is certainly... interesting," Larsen said. "Did you intend to find yourself such a remarkable collection of waifs and strays?"

Walker gave a wan smile. "It was not in the original plan."

"Two children, two drunks, and somebody's mum," said Larsen.

"And a doctor," Walker pointed out. "At least you have a useful skill set."

"Hmm."

"How's the little girl?" Walker said.

"A lot better. She's still quite sleepy, and likely to be that way for a couple more days. But the drug hasn't permanently affected her. It would have—if they'd stayed. Maria made the right decision."

"She seems to make a lot of those," Walker mused.

"I took a look inside your pilot's head too," said Larsen. "If you're interested."

"I'm interested. Did you find anything there?"

"A whole lot of decaying tech. But you knew that already, I think." Larsen looked at her thoughtfully. "You know, every time he phases, a little more of his brain gets fried."

"I thought that might be the case. Can you do anything about that?"

"Not really. Pain relief—I gather you're controlling access to that."

Walker nodded. "Insurance policy."

"And I can tell him not to drink, because it doesn't help. But he won't listen. As for operating..." Larsen looked around the tiny cabin, which was still grubby, despite the efforts Walker had made when she first came on board. "Well, under these conditions, it would *certainly* kill him, but even if we were back on Hennessy's World, I don't think he'd survive it."

"So we carry on as we are."

"Well, most of us do. Yershov gets a little closer to a brain haemorrhage every time we phase. I'll be keeping a close eye on that, not least because we don't want it to happen while we're in the void."

"Christ, no!"

"I thought that might get your attention."

"We'll keep an eye on it," Walker agreed. "And, when this is over... Well, we'll take care of him."

"When this is over? Have you thought about what that might mean, Delia? There'll be no going back to the Expansion, you know."

"If the cover-up is exposed—"

"Who do we tell?" said Larsen. "Who will listen? And who do you think you can *trust* to tell?"

"There must be someone in the Bureau who would be appalled to learn about this. Who would be willing to have the perpetrators called to account for their actions—"

"Who? Who do you trust? That's powerful enough these days? You wouldn't believe the changes, Delia."

"There's Mark."

They stared at each other.

"Do you trust him?" said Larsen.

"Does he still have any influence?" said Walker.

Again, the silence. Larsen shrugged. "Let's sleep on this," she said. "I want to examine you—properly. See what's going on."

About half an hour later, Larsen sat back. "Everything's fine," she said. "Heartbeat good and strong. I wish I could take a look, but I didn't exactly pack for this."

Walker leaned back and closed her eyes. *Hey in there*, she thought. *Everything's fine. You hear that? Everything's fine.*

"I'm not even going to ask if you've thought about the birth."

"I have, a little," Walker admitted. "It worries and frightens me."

"So it should," muttered Larsen. "Let's hope that they can help us on Stella Maris. Heyes has sent women and children there before. Pregnant women too, she said. Surely they'll be able to help."

"That's good." Walker kept her eyes closed. She wanted to sleep, very much.

"The people coming after us," said Larsen quietly, "will not be good people. Whoever is involved in this—they'll throw all they can at us. They won't show any mercy. Not to those people out there—and not to you and..."

"Yes, I know," said Walker. She felt a touch upon her arm, and opened her eyes to see that Larsen had taken hold of her hand.

"At least you have a doctor with you now."

Walker smiled. "I'm glad you're here, Kay. I really am."

THE *BABA YAGA* passed through the void. All its crew were sleeping—the mother and child curled up together in their little bed; the Vetch as close as he could get to his mistress' door; the pilot in a drunken haze; the doctor sleeping the sleep of the just; the operative the sleep of the unjust. The priest was awake. She'd tried whisky, then prayer, then gone back to whisky. Now she was staring at the viewscreen, and the grey swirl of the void. She leaned over to the comm, and sent the message.

Stella Maris. On our way.

PART THREE

FIREBIRDS

CHAPTER ELEVEN

ON SPRING MORNINGS like this, when the sun was not yet high in the sky and there was still some coolness in the air, Shel Feuerstein would leave her home and walk out beyond the walls of the settlement, past the farmed fields, and out into the low red hills. This morning she left unusually early, as she had done for the past week, a fact she knew had not gone unnoticed in her long-house, but which had not troubled her unduly. Born and bred on Stella Maris, Feuerstein was not in the habit of defending her actions to anyone. Yes, there would be comments from her peers and her elders that her wanderings seemed to be starting earlier as the days grew longer, but, for the past week, Feuerstein had resisted giving any explanation. Every morning she went out, and every afternoon she returned, and she devoted herself to her tasks, and deflected questions, and wondered what the next day would bring.

Today she walked up into the hills again, as she had done every day this week, and she sat on the hillside by the source of a clear little brook, and she watched the sky. And today brought what she had been waiting for.

She heard it first as a rush of engines from far behind her, up along the valley. Jumping to her feet, she scrambled around the hillside, until she was looking north and west. And there it was, about two miles away, she guessed, creating a huge red dust storm as it came down: a ship descending from the heavens. Feuerstein watched it land, and watched the dust settle. Then she saw the hatch open, and some of the crew come out. She nodded to herself—she had been expecting this—but part of her watched what was happening with a deep sense of regret, and fear. This ship was bringing the oldest kind of enemy: conflict, violence, anger, aggression. Everything that the people of Stella Maris had been able to avoid, all these years. But now, Feuerstein knew, they would no longer be able to avoid any of it, no matter what they might tell themselves. The people of Stella Maris had fallen out of step with the rest of the settled universe years ago. Now that universe was coming to see them, and their world would never be the same again.

Feuerstein followed the little brook home. The countryside softened as she drew closer to the settlement. Grass began to grow, and then came the tilled, managed land that lay beyond the wooden stockade. The gate stood open, as it always did, but, as she passed through, Feuerstein made sure that the habits of the first settlers still remained in place, and that the gate could quickly be closed and barred.

No real threat had come to Stella Maris for a very long time, but runaway slaves valued their peace of mind, and often looked back over their shoulder. The settlement would be defended.

She did not go back at once to her long-house. She had duties at the far end of the settlement, where one of the old wells was being shored up, so she spent a few hours with the work party and then took a dip in the cold pond. It was late afternoon by the time she reached home. Work on the evening meal was already underway, and she joined her co-habitants in the preparations. Each of the long-houses in the settlement was home to fifteen or twenty people, of all ages, and both species. The peoples of Stella Maris mingled freely, and while some houses might be predominantly human or predominantly Vetch, there was not a house with fewer than three or four of the other kind. There were very few places in the settled worlds where humans and Vetch lived together so peaceably, and the people of Stella Maris were rightly proud of this. Everywhere else, as far as they knew, humans and Vetch were hostile, except as need demanded. Here, however, there was little in the way of dispute—as ever, the mood was calm and quiet, but Feuerstein could sense the air of concern among her housemates, and she knew there were many questions.

After the meal, the people of the long-house settled to their evening tasks: mending, fixing, playing, thinking, and sleeping. When the smallest were at last asleep, Feuerstein consulted her friends and fellow residents.

"The ship is here," she said. "There is a decision coming."

As she expected, the group was disquieted. They looked around each other, each of them understanding that something significant—and possibly divisive—was about to happen.

"The others will want to turn their backs," Feuerstein remarked. "They will want to send them back where they came from."

One of the group, a Vetch, older than many present, said, "Perhaps that might be for the best. We have a good life here. Why should others be allowed to disturb it?" One of the adolescents, speaking for the first time, disagreed. "We can't remain sealed off forever! There's a whole universe out there!"

The floodgates were opened. Others joined in to agree, or to disagree. There was a confusion—but not a clamour or a conflict—of voices. After a little while, during which many people spoke all at once, and which might have seemed to an outsider to be an uncontrolled discussion, the furore began to subside. All the ideas had now been given an airing. A decision was going to be made.

Feuerstein, as the instigator of the discussion, and as one known to hold a particular opinion, spoke next. "Many in this long-house, and in other long-houses, were born here on Stella Maris," she said. "But that is not true of all of us." As she said this, she glanced towards some of the older habitants, sitting and listening quietly. "For them," she went on, "Stella Maris was a haven. A place they came to in search of peace—and they found peace, despite expectation, and because of the secret this world holds. It is a long time since anyone has come looking for us. But it is my belief that this place should remain a haven for anyone who comes looking for peace and harmony.

Who are we to decide who is turned away? Who are we to decide that nobody else should share the peace and harmony which we are lucky to have?"

Some of the older people were nodding, perhaps thinking of what they might have done if they had been turned away from Stella Maris, and how different their lives might have been. Others looked more troubled.

"Other long-houses are free to choose what they want," said Feuerstein. "But I say that Stella Maris should welcome all."

The very oldest lifted a hand to speak. People turned to listen, because this was a person of great experience. "I lived somewhere else. The universe beyond this world is very different from what we enjoy here. We cannot assume that ships—and there will be more ships, I think—come in peace, and looking for peace. We may have to defend ourselves."

There was a ripple of muttering around the room: some were anxious; others excited. Some asked: *How can we defend ourselves?* Others said: *Let them come.*

"If people come to cause conflict, we cannot prevent them landing," Feuerstein pointed out. "And, yes, I say that we in this house join with all the other houses to defend ourselves. But if they come in peace, or in search of the same peace which we enjoy—I say we do not have the right to refuse them."

"Others may disagree," said the oldest one.

"That is their right," said Feuerstein.

"I fear a schism," said the oldest.

"It may happen," said Feuerstein, "but I do not fear it. We may disagree, and not be divided."

The oldest smiled. "With that, I agree. You have my backing."

Feuerstein looked around the group. "Are we in agreement?"

A single voice rose up in assent: *Yes*. The oldest turned to Feuerstein. "Then represent the decision of our long-house to the whole."

So HERE THEY were at last, on Stella Maris. The crew of the *Baba Yaga* gathered around the viewscreen and looked out on the world they had been hunting for so long.

"What a shithole," said Larsen. Maria tutted, nodding down at Jenny. "Sorry," said Larsen. "But it is. Do we think this is right place?"

Failt snuffled unhappily. "Don't look much, Missus Dee," he said. "Looks *bad*."

Walker looked at the dry, inhospitable world on which they had landed, and turned to Heyes. "You wouldn't have lied to us, would you? To defend your runaways?"

"You wanted to come to the place where I used to send them," said Heyes. "Well, this is it. You have to understand that I never came here," she went on. "There was a priest on Shard's World who ran the railroad before I did, and I took over when he died. As far I know there was someone before him, and someone before him... I inherited their work." She frowned. "One reason I felt particularly bad when the railroad was exposed."

Larsen was tapping controls alongside the viewscreen. "Have we found anything yet that passes for signs of life?"

Comfortably embedded in his pilot's sling, Yershov called out, "There's a settlement about ten miles from here."

They all turned to look at him. Walker, calmly, said. "Did you know that before you landed?"

Yershov shrugged.

Larsen said, "It didn't cross your mind to land any closer?"

Yershov closed his eyes and burrowed back further into his sling. "I was paid to bring you here," he said. "What you ladies do now is your own business."

Walker, Larsen and Heyes all looked at each other. *Ladies*, mouthed Larsen, and mimed strangling someone. "Well," said Walker, "it sounds like we have a walk ahead. Larsen, could you start hunting out some gear for the journey? Heyes, perhaps you could help. Maria, you should stay here with Jenny." She turned to the Vetch child. "Failt..."

"I stay here," he said firmly. "Don't know yet if Vetch are welcome."

Walker hesitated. She had got used to having her little guard dog around, and she realised she would miss his chatter, not to mention his unflagging belief in her and their quest. But she had to agree that Failt's presence might complicate matters unnecessarily. "All right," she said. "I guess that makes three of us. We'll wait until it's cooler, and then we'll set out."

Larsen, returning from the hold with water bottles and an assortment of hiking gear, took her aside. "Are you sure that Heyes and I can't handle this by ourselves? This is long walk, and we don't know what state the settlement is in at the other end. There might not even be clean water."

"Heyes is twenty years older than me," Walker

said. "If she can manage it, so can I. I assume you're not offering to go alone?"

"Not a chance," Larsen said. "Well, I can only advise, as your doctor. I can't pin you down and insist you stay."

"No."

She glanced around and lowered her voice further. "But are you absolutely sure about Heyes? I mean, she isn't exactly here under her own volition, is she?"

"I have confidence in Heyes," said Walker.

Larsen sighed. "Keep telling yourself that," she said. "If it helps."

They set out in the early evening. The ground was rough, rocky, and the heat of the day lingered, slowing their pace. There was no cover.

They'd trekked for about an hour covering a couple of miles, when they heard the rumble of an engine ahead, coming their way. Walker called a halt, to the obvious relief of her companions, not to mention her own. Heyes slumped down on the ground and drank liberally from her water bottle. Larsen, standing on one leg and rubbing at the other, watched as Walker took out a small set of binoculars. "Anything?"

Walker shook her head. "Whoever they are, they're kicking up a lot of dust."

They waited for a while until, at last, a large, old-fashioned lorry trundled towards them. It stopped some way distant, presumably to keep from covering them in dust. A courtesy Walker hoped boded well for the meeting about to happen.

They watched, tensely and in silence, as a party of five got out of the lorry—two humans and three Vetch, very big and imposing. Walker looked closely to see if any of them were carrying weapons. There were none that she could see; of course, her own weapon was concealed too. She rested her hand lightly against it.

"Well," said Larsen, quietly, "we were promised human and Vetch."

"So we were," replied Walker. She lifted her hand in greeting, and stepped forwards. "My name is Delia Walker," she said. "I come in peace, I guess."

One of the humans broke away from the group and came towards her. A woman in her mid-thirties with short dark hair, wearing what looked to be homespun clothes, she came close and then spoke without any further introductions. "Why are you here? What have you come for?" Her Anglais was excellent, but the accent was odd, as if it had drifted slightly from the mainstream in the time the people of Stella Maris had been set apart.

"Why are we here?" Walker took a breath. "That's difficult to explain. Perhaps you could take me to someone in authority?"

One of the Vetch made a low growling noise at the back of its throat. Thanks to her time with Failt, Walker recognised the unnerving sound as laughter. The woman fell back and spoke to the rest of the group; Walker strained to listen but could make out nothing. Eventually she woman walked back to them.

"We can't take you to someone in authority," she said. "But we think it would be best if you came back with us to the settlement." She gestured towards the lorry. "You can address us all properly there."

Walker looked at the lorry, unsure whether to trust these people. They were outnumbered and, as far as she knew, out-equipped. She didn't fancy being driven off into the desert, shot, and dumped. "Let me speak to the others," she said, and the woman nodded.

"Heyes?" said Walker, when the three of them were together. "You know these people. Any advice?"

The priest shrugged. "Don't ask me," she said. "I've never been here before."

"We *are* heading their way," said Larsen. "I do not say this solely because I think I am getting a blister, but in the spirit of full disclosure I think I should mention it. But it does seem a terrible waste of our time to walk where these people are going, particularly when they have taken the trouble to come and find us. In fact, I think it would be rude."

Walker looked at Heyes, who shrugged again. "I wasn't particularly looking forward to walking through a desert, not even at night."

"All right," said Walker. "We'll go." She led them over to the group. "It seems my friends and I are in agreement. We'd like to take you up on your kind offer of a ride."

As if there had been any doubt. The woman waved them into the back of the lorry, and they climbed in, grateful to get under the shade of the canopy. A long bench, with room for three, ran along each side, but there wasn't much room once they were all in. Heyes found herself sandwiched between two human guards, while the big Vetch lumbered into the seat beside Larsen and Walker, forcing them to push up close to each other. "If this is an arrest," Larsen muttered to Walker, "it's one of the most polite I've ever encountered."

The two other Vetch climbed into the front of the lorry, and they set off. The wheels set red dust flying behind them. Walker put her hand across her

mouth. "One of the most effective too," she said. "*If
this is an arrest.*"

THE OLD LORRY hardly moved at a great pace, but it
was certainly better than walking. Although there
was no clearly discernible road, the land through
which they passed became less bumpy, and the
journey was steady enough that Heyes fell asleep,
head tipped back, snoring gently. The sun slid
further down towards the horizon. Walker, looking
out, watched the red desert begin to change, turning
green and fertile, but she could see no water. "Is
there a river here?" she said. "An oasis?" But none
of their guards—if guards they were—replied, and
her question remained unanswered.

The sky was darkening when they reached
the settlement. The lorry slowed to a crawl, and
Walker saw a huge wooden fence, and an open
gateway, through which they passed. The driver of
the lorry sounded the horn, and, as they came to
a halt, Walker heard voices cry: "They're back!"
The message seemed to be passed around the whole
settlement rapidly; soon people were gathering to
catch a glimpse of the visitors. The Vetch sitting
in the back opened the hatch, and jumped down,
holding out his long arm and great paw for Walker
help her down. Heyes woke with a start and a great
snort. "What?" she said. "We here?"

"Come on, Mother," Larsen said, pushing the old
woman out in front of her. "Look smart. There's a
whole new congregation for you to minister to."

Some of the people gathering were carrying lamps,
and Walker was able to get a look at the faces of

those gathering. She saw many children—human and Vetch—and indeed there were more adult humans and Vetch here too, gathered together and not segregated, talking to each other about the arrivals. She saw them coming out of houses together too— did they even *live* together, sharing quarters?

"I wish Failt was here," she said to Larsen. "This was what he wanted to see, wasn't it? 'Living-in-peace-and-harmony.'"

"All looks too good to be true to me," said Larsen.

"What do you mean?"

"You saw the files from World. Looked like Eden, didn't it? All those people living together so happily. But in fact they were drugged to stupidity by the Weird and lived only long enough to be fed to the Harvesters."

"You think that could be happening here?"

"I think the people we've met so far are almost preternaturally calm."

"Perhaps they're all terribly well-adjusted," Walker said flippantly, but she began to look around her through different eyes. She remembered reading and watching the files from World, the first place where humans had encountered the Weird, and the horror and revulsion she felt as she realised how happily the humans were submitting to their terrible fate: to be consumed by the Weird. Could the same be happening here? Larsen was right: they had been greeted calmly, and now people were looking at them with curiosity, but with no fear, or *any* strong emotion. Had these people been assimilated too? Was she deluding herself that peaceful co-existence was possible? And yet the people on World had been in thrall; as if they lacked independent will. Here, there was clear purpose.

"Come this way," said the leader of the group

that had brought them to the settlement. The three women followed her, and Walker took her chance to look around the settlement. In the gathering darkness, she could see that it was well-kept and there was an abundance of life: big wooden houses, long and low, were set within trees and greenery and even flowers. Life on Stella Maris must be hard work, but the setting, at least, was pleasant. The door posts outside the long houses were carved with intricate designs, and this as much as anything made her doubt that the people here were in thrall to the Weird. No art could exist on a place like World, where all that was idiosyncratic had been eradicated from the souls living there, and no spark of creativity came from living and working alongside the Weird.

They came to a house that was larger, and higher, than the others they had passed, and the woman who had been acting as their guide said, "This is our main gathering place. It holds as many of us as wish to attend, and we have asked representatives from all the long-houses to come and hear you. Are you willing to speak?"

Now they were talking the kind of language that Walker understood: she could not count the number of committees she had attended during her career, and how often she had presented—and won—her case before them. She nodded, keen to explain her mission, and their guide led them into the building, and through into a big hall lined with seats, but otherwise empty.

"I thought we were here to speak to some committee?" Larsen said.

The woman nodded. "Wait," she said. "They're coming."

They waited a while. At last, a group of people began to file in, maybe as many as forty or fifty, and started to take their seats in rows at the front of the room. Soon Walker found herself facing them.

"May I speak now?" she said, and some of the people gestured at her to begin. So slowly, carefully, and with all her years of experience, Walker explained her mission: her belief that there was a Weird portal on Stella Maris, and that this was what allowed them to live so peacefully together. She explained how she wanted to explore the portal and learn whether peaceful co-existence could spread further. She explained that she believed that this was better than the war which was otherwise inevitably going to happen. "I want peace," she said. "It looks to me like you have peace. I want to understand how you've achieved it."

Walker finished her speech and looked at the faces lined up in front of her. Nothing. No reaction. Suddenly, she felt extremely tired. "All I want to know," she said, "Is whether the Weird are here on Stella Maris. Is there a Weird portal here?"

The group seemed to discuss something without words and then come to a decision. One of them, sitting on the far right, said, "Yes."

Thank God, thought Walker. Beside her, Larsen sighed with relief. "And will you tell me where it is?"

Again, that odd silent discussion. Were there telepaths here? Or was something else going on? Someone else in the group said, "No."

Walker was about to reply, and with some asperity, but before she could open her mouth, Larsen stepped forwards, and began speaking, very quickly. "Look, I don't know how much news you get out here in the boondocks—I'm going to assume not much—but the universe is busy changing. For one thing, humans and Vetch are no longer at war." There was some muttering at this news, and a few nods and looks exchanged between members of both species. Walker, who had been ready to pull Larsen back, decided to let the other woman speak for a while. She might have more success. "But it's a qualified peace," said Larsen. "We're all friends now, yes, but only because each empire thinks there's a greater threat out there. They're both—they're gearing up for war with the Weird, but I think they don't really understand what that entails. Anyway, they're coming out fighting. They're building bigger weapons, superweapons, and they're moving troops, and the killing has already started. There's been a great deal of death, already. We're here," Larsen spread out her hands in a gesture of openness, of friendship, "because we want to prevent more death. We want to find out how to live in peace. And harmony."

This time the discussion wasn't silent. There was much muttering around the group, which rose and fell and rose again, until eventually everyone was speaking. Then, suddenly, they all fell quiet. One of the Vetch sitting among the group stood up and said, "We must discuss this further, and privately. Please—make yourselves comfortable."

The committee—or whatever it was—filed out, leaving the three women sitting alone in the great hall. "Interesting," said Heyes.

"Interesting?" said Walker.

"Their decision-making process."

"They have one?" said Larsen. "They seemed to be making it up as they went along."

"No, there seemed to be some pretty clear processes at work there. I'd guess each of those people had the authority to speak on behalf of one of the long-houses. So some discussion must have happened already, before this gathering. I wonder if they do that for every decision, or whether less significant decisions are left to happen at grass-roots level. As I say, interesting. Needs more observation."

"God," said Larsen, "I'm hungry."

They sat and waited. Larsen stood up and paced around the room. Eventually, one of the side doors opened, but it was not the committee returning, only someone wheeling in a wooden trolley laden with food. That, at least, was cheerful, and they made a good supper of bread and cheese, fruits and vegetables. There was a clear wine too, which Walker didn't taste, but which Heyes and Larsen eventually agreed was 'saucy.' After about an hour, the committee returned and took their seats again. Walker approached them, and one of the Vetch, a female, rose from her chair, looming over her at an impressive seven-and-a-half feet tall. "We have discussed all that you have said. We have come to our decision."

Walker nodded, confident in the knowledge that she would soon be on the way to the Weird portal.

"We are not interested in wars beyond our world. We are afraid that you might bring these wars to us. We believe it is best if you leave Stella Maris."

Walker could hardly believe what she was hearing. "No," she said, shaking her head. "No, you've not understood—"

"We have understood."

"Then you've not listened. The war's coming to you whether you like it or not." She stared at the row of impassive faces in front of her. She couldn't have come this far, gone through so much, to be stopped by these... *idiots*. "You might not be interested in anything that happens beyond this world, but the rest of the universe is going to be taking an interest in you." She could feel her frustration growing; her voice becoming angrier. "Don't you see what's happening? Everywhere but here, the Weird are set on destroying whatever they meet—humans and Vetch alike. And now the humans and Vetch are set on destroying the Weird first. Your portal," she said, "is not going to save you! Quite the opposite. It will make these people fear you all the more. And *that* will make them hate you. They will come to *destroy* you. Do I have to tell them where you are to make you understand—?"

"Delia," hissed Larsen, "for the love of God, shut up!"

And then an old woman—a very old woman, leaning on a stick—stepped forward from the group, and she banged her stick against the ground three times.

The whole room went quiet.

"Listen to me," said the old woman, into the silence. "We have listened to you, and heard what you have to say, and we have discussed, and we have come to our decision. You may remain here and rest for the night. But then you must leave Stella Maris. You are not wanted here."

This message delivered, the committee began to file out of the hall. Eventually, only Walker, Larsen and Heyes remained. The priest looked around the room a few times, sniffed, and then headed for the door. "Threats," she said, "can only ever get you so far."

*   *   *

THE WOMAN WHO had been their guide since they arrived came to find them. She led them from the big hall upstairs to a small chamber where mattresses had been put down on the floor. There was water for drinking and washing, and some more food. "I hope you will be comfortable," she said. "Please remain here in this room and do not wander about. We will come for you in the morning."

When she left, Walker tried the door. It opened but, when she looked out along the corridor, she saw the shadow of a large Vetch against the wall ahead.

"Watched?" said Larsen, when Walker came back into the chamber.

"I think so," said Walker. She went over to one of the mattresses and lay down. She felt exhausted and sick. Larsen came over and made her drink water. "Why wouldn't they listen?" Walker said. "It's like they want to commit suicide."

Larsen shook her head. "No more now, Delia. Go to sleep. It's been a long day."

Walker closed her eyes, and fell swiftly into a dead sleep. Before dawn, they were woken, given food and water for the journey, and then, as the first pale light of the day began to inch across the sky, they were taken to the edge of the settlement. Their guide was still with them. "The day's coming," she said, "and it will be hot. Don't delay. Get back to your ship as quickly as you can. Your journey isn't long, but the heat of the sun can be cruel." Her eyes fell on Larsen, then Heyes, and finally on Walker. "Not all of you are suited for a journey like this."

"Well," said Larsen, as they set out, "at least once

we're back at the ship I can put my feet up for a while."

"Don't get comfortable," said Walker. "We won't be stopping at the *Baba Yaga* for long. Only long enough to see if we can pinpoint the portal. We know it's here. I'm sure we can find it."

Larsen frowned and glanced back over her shoulder. "You know, I don't think the people of Stella Maris will like that very much. They sounded pretty serious when it came to their portal."

"They can try stopping me," said Walker.

"They might just do that."

"Tell me, Kay—did you see any weapons back there? No? I didn't, either. I'm willing to bet you the ship that there's more firepower on the *Baba Yaga* than in the whole of that Girl Guide camp back there."

"It's not your ship," began Larsen, but Heyes was already speaking over her.

"Walker, I won't let you harm these people."

"You?" Walker looked her up and down. "I'm not sure you can stop me."

Heyes shook her head. "Are you capable of anything other than threats?"

"I only issue threats when it becomes necessary," Walker said.

"Yes, yes," said Heyes, with contempt. "That's always the excuse—"

"Ssh!" said Larsen. "No, I mean it! I think there are people coming."

Walker reached for her gun. "Could they have changed their minds?" she said. "Could they be coming after us?"

"I wouldn't blame them," Heyes said. "But I don't think they'd go back on their word." She gave a toothy smile. "Perhaps your friends are catching up with you at last."

Larsen blanched. "Christ," she said, "I hope not."

But the group that approached them were not from the Expansion. Going by their clothes, they were from the settlement. There were three of them in total, two human and a Vetch. Their leader, a small nut-brown woman, introduced herself as Feuerstein and said, "We are here to help you."

"To help us?" Walker looked at her suspiciously. "How?"

Feuerstein looked back with serious jet-black eyes. "You want to go to the portal. We can take you there." Turning away from Walker, she offered her hand to Heyes. "Mother," she said. "Welcome at last to Stella Maris."

Heyes stepped forwards and took the young woman's hand in her own. "You took your time," huffed the priest. "Didn't you get my message?"

"I did," said Feuerstein, "and I came as soon as I could." She looked at the priest with concern. "You are not well, Hecate. You should settle here for good."

Larsen and Walker glanced at each other. *Hecate?* Larsen mouthed. *Hecate Heyes?*

Heyes didn't miss the exchange. "Why do you think I turned to drink?"

Walker, turning to Feuerstein, said, "Your friends back there were pretty clear that we weren't welcome. Why are you helping us?"

Feuerstein glanced at her group of friends. "I was there at the meeting," she said. "My voice was heard, but I could not persuade them. They are frightened by your arrival, and want everything on

Stella Maris to remain the same. But not everyone here takes such a narrow view. We"—she gestured around the little group—"understood the content of your speech; although we did not like the anger that consumed it. You did badly there. You did not understand us. Nevertheless, we agreed with what you said, and so we are willing to take you to the portal."

Larsen said, "But what about the others?"

"What about them?" Feuerstein said.

"They were pretty clear that they wanted us gone. Won't they try to stop us?"

"No," said Feuerstein. "But it is a long journey, and we will not be helped."

Walker did not move. "I don't understand this," she said. "They told us to go. They *ordered* us to go—"

"They asked you to go," Feuerstein said. "They cannot order you. How could they order you?" She glanced down at Walker's energy weapon, still tucked away under her jacket. "What threat could they issue that would have an effect on you?"

"They were clear they wanted us to go. But now you want to help us?" Walker said. "I don't understand. What authority do you have to do this?"

"Authority?" Feuerstein looked genuinely baffled. "There is no authority. There is only my own will."

CHAPTER TWELVE

IT WAS WELL into the night when they reached the *Baba Yaga*. Feuerstein and her people had brought small tents that provided cover during the afternoon, when they rested and waited for the cool evening. The night sky was a blaze of stars, unfamiliar to Walker and her companions. When they reached the ship, they were greeted with palpable relief by Maria and Failt, who grabbed onto Walker's arm and wouldn't let go for some time.

After they had eaten and rested, they met on the flight deck to consider their next move. Feuerstein's people had made camp outside, but Feuerstein came on board, and she showed them on the viewscreen where the portal was in relation to their current position. "It's some distance," she said. "A few days' walk, even for the fittest amongst us. More of the red plains, then a great river, which we have to cross. Along a wide pass between the mountains. Then up to the portal itself." She eyed the crew of the *Baba Yaga*. "I would not advise bringing the children."

"We don't need to walk," Walker said. "Yershov can move the ship."

Yershov, who was lying in his pilot's sling, cracked open an eye. "I'm not moving this ship anywhere."

Walker ignored him. "How close can we land, Feuerstein? Mountainous, you said. There'd still be a walk, I guess—"

"I *said* I'm not moving the ship anywhere."

Walker turned him. "Now is not the time to get mutinous. We're nearly done. Then you can get paid and you'll be free to go. One last trip—"

"And I've said—I'm not going. I'm done." He swung round into a sitting position. "You're crazy, do you know that, Walker? A Weird portal? What do you think you're going to do when you come face-to-face with it? I bet you don't know. You haven't a clue. Well, I'm not interested in coming face-to-face with the Weird. I've heard about what they can do. Seen the same pictures and files you have—no, you didn't think I was paying attention, did you? Stupid old Yershov, the drunk, the junkie—he won't be listening. He won't be watching. Well, I *have* been listening, and I *have* been watching, and I'm telling you, lady—I'm done. You paid me to bring you to Stella Maris, and here we are and that's that. I'm not moving this ship so I can get my brains eaten."

"Eaten further," said Walker.

"Delia, that's enough!" said Larsen. Walker looked at her in surprise. Larsen wasn't one to lose her temper; more one to defuse with humour. "This man is in pain—real pain. He's brought us this far. Leave him alone."

"Yes, he's brought us this far, and he's going to be well paid for his trouble," Walker said impatiently. "He's brought us across star systems. I only want the damn ship parked up the road."

But Yershov wasn't budging. "You can whistle for it, lady! I've had enough. I'm leaving."

"By all means leave," said Walker, "but you'll be in agony within hours."

"No, he won't," said Larsen. "I can give him something for that. I won't withhold pain relief. Not even for you, Delia."

"Then he won't get paid," Walker said wearily. "Not until I get back. If you're planning to rid yourself of those troublesome implants, Yershov, you'll have to find yourself another client. And while these people seem to live the good life"—she jerked her head towards Feuerstein—"they don't seem to be rolling in ready cash."

Yershov rolled off his pilot's sling, He came up to Walker, stared at her, and then he spat at her feet. She stepped fastidiously backwards. "I'll see you in Hell before I move this ship," he said. The anger and humiliation were unmistakeable. "Fuck you, Walker!" Then he turned and stumped off the flight deck.

Feuerstein turned to Heyes. "Who are these people? Why have you brought them here?"

"You can trust the doctor," said Heyes. "She's sacrificed a great deal to come here." She sighed. "You need the full picture, Shel." She turned to Larsen. "Tell her what's going on. Tell her what we know about Braun's World."

In a neutral voice, trying not to over-dramatize, but unable to disguise her revulsion at what had been done, Larsen explained the secret of Braun's World: the portal that had never existed; the excuse it had given the hardliners to take over the Bureau; the cover-up that had followed; and Kit and Maria's escape, carrying the evidence to expose that cover-up.

Feuerstein listened carefully and without speaking. When Larsen done, Feuerstein sat for a while, studying the viewscreen, where Larsen had shown her a few of the files

"This here," said Feuerstein, pointing at the Sleer and the Flyers on Cassandra. "This interests me. We have seen things like this on Stella Maris—these flying creatures in particular. I had doubted that what we had here on Stella Maris was what you were looking for, but... Yes, the Weird are here. But different here." She sighed. "These people following you, Larsen. Will they come to Stella Maris?"

"I don't know," said Larsen. "I've done my best to cover my tracks, and I know Walker has done the same. But they're clever people, professionals, with the weight of a big organisation behind them, and very good motivation to find us."

"We don't have any defences," said Feuerstein. "We don't even have firearms. The lorry that brought you here is the only vehicle in the whole settlement."

"Your best defence is if we find a way of working with the Weird," said Walker.

Feuerstein looked at her steadily. "We already have that," she said. "But not in the way you mean." She turned back to Larsen. "Should I alert the settlement that people may be coming? If they've killed as many as you say—killed that many of their own people— they'll surely not hesitate to murder many of us."

"I can't answer that for you," said Larsen. "Would

it help them to know? Could they prepare some kind of defence? Would it only cause panic?"

Feuerstein thought a while. "There's little we can do now. If there are people coming, we will need all hands to defend our own group, I think. The quicker we can reach the portal, the better it will be."

They discussed their plans and, taking Feuerstein's advice, agreed that Maria would remain with Jenny and Failt on the *Baba Yaga*. Again, Walker was surprised that Failt was willing to be parted from her, but she didn't press. "Someone got to stay here and keep an eye on things, missus," he said, cryptically.

Maria said, anxiously, "How long should I expect you to be away?"

"If we're gone more than a month," said Larsen, "assume we're not coming back."

Maria took a deep breath. "And what should I do then? Yershov isn't going to wait forever. And there's Jenny..."

Feuerstein said, "Go to the settlement. Go to my long-house. Tell them that Shel sent you. They'll look after you."

"Will they let her in?" said Walker. "Even though you've come with us?"

"You still don't understand us." Patiently, Feuerstein said, "Of course they would help a woman and two children."

"Two women and three children," said Heyes. "You shouldn't come on this journey, Walker." She looked at Larsen. "You're her doctor. This isn't right."

"Do you think I can stop her?" said Larsen.

"She can't," said Walker. "Give it up, Heyes. I've come here to do this thing. I'm not giving up now." She turned to Feuerstein. "That lorry that took us to the settlement? No chance of borrowing one of those?"

Feuerstein smiled. "You've not been listening. There is only one. Listen, Walker, and understand. We have very little in the way of material goods, and nothing in the way of defences. All we have is hope that you've brought nobody in your wake. Because there is nothing to protect our people, if your enemies land at the door."

THEY RESTED THROUGHOUT the following day, and waited until the sun had set before beginning their journey. Maria, Jenny, and Fault watched them leave. Maria had given up trying to settle Jenny to sleep, and the little girl dashed between Larsen and Heyes, to whom she had taken a shine, holding hands and bestowing occasional kisses. Yershov was nowhere to be seen.

Fault clung to Walker's arm. "You take care, missus. You take care of you both," he said, and Walker, unexpectedly, found tears springing into her eyes. She folded her arm around the child, and hugged him. "I'll be fine," she said. "Believe me, Fault. I've come through worse than this."

At last their packs were shouldered and they were ready to leave.

"Goodbye," said Maria, holding the two children to her, an arm around each one. "Good luck. I'll be here, waiting. I know you'll come back."

They waved their farewells, and then Feuerstein and her people led them into the night. After five minutes or so, Walker looked back at the dark bulk of the *Baba Yaga* against the hillside. The road ahead sloped upwards, and then down, and when she looked back again, the *Baba Yaga* was gone, and only the bright stars ahead remained unchanged. Walker looked at the road ahead and moved on. After a while, she became aware of Heyes and Larsen, behind her, in quiet conversation. They were talking about her.

"Our leader," said Heyes, "presents some puzzles to me."

"Oh yes?"

"The loyalty of Maria; the love of Failt... There must be something about her to attract these people."

"It's not so difficult to understand, Mother. Walker is effective, but she isn't cruel. And she doesn't like waste. Life is messy, but killing is messier."

"Does that explain the baby?"

Walker listened with interest to hear what Larsen would say. But Larsen only sighed. "Now that," she said, "is a puzzle even to me."

After an hour or so, they stopped to rest. As they sat in a circle around their lamps, eating from ration bars taken from the *Baba Yaga* and drinking from the water bottles, Walker took the chance to ask Feuerstein more about the Weird portal on Stella Maris.

"The Weird have been here my whole life," said Feuerstein, "but they have not been here on Stella Maris as long as the settlement. That came first: a handful of escapees from a slave ship en route to a colony world. The ship docked at Shuloma Station, and some of them got free. One of them appealed to the priest there, and he helped them get away. Stella Maris was empty then. A hard bare time they had of it."

"So the green land around the settlement—the water, the crops?"

Feuerstein nodded. "That is all because of the Weird. When the portal opened, and the settlers made contact, the Weird promised that they would succour the community. As the settlement grew, we found that the land that was available to us to cultivate expanded too. We found wells and springs whenever and wherever we needed them."

Walker was amazed. "What are the limits, do you think?"

"We do not know." Feuerstein smiled. "Perhaps we could spread across the whole of Stella Maris, and the Weird might still be able to nourish us. Perhaps we could spread throughout the whole known universe, and still they would succour us. But I do not know."

Walker pondered this. "You've seen the images of other Weird portals opening on other worlds, now," she said. "Horror stories. Assimilation, consumption, absorption into a hive mind. But that doesn't seem to have happened here. At least," she said, "I'm assuming you've not been assimilated. You at least certainly seem to have your own will."

"Thank you," said Feuerstein, dryly. "And in answer to your question—I don't know. Remember, this is all I know about the Weird. Those pictures that I saw..." She shuddered. "They were a shock to me. But then your news of what had happened on Braun's World was horrific too. Murderousness," she said, "does not seem to be a species-specific trait."

I sincerely hope not, thought Walker. "So you've no idea what makes the Weird different here?"

"I've not communicated directly with the Weird, although others from the settlement have, insofar as one *can* communicate with something so very different. But from what I can understand of what they have said, there has been a schism of sorts within the Weird."

A schism? Walker's ears pricked up. This was language that she understood, and, if it was true, it would put a very different complexion on the Weird, whom they had hitherto believed operated under the control of a great mother-mind. But a schism meant that there was disagreement. That not everything was controlled as centrally as they had thought. "What was the schism about?"

"You must understand that I am only reporting what has been told to me. But I believe that there was a split between an assimilationist tendency in the Weird, and a tendency towards symbiosis. This is what has been told to me. I've understood very little of this, and perhaps thought the people were mistaken, but now, having seen the images you brought with you, I start to believe it. Some of the Weird wish to live by devouring. Others of the Weird wish to live by nourishing. Seeing the pictures you have brought, I now think this story may well be true. Here on Stella Maris, the Weird have succoured us. Elsewhere, they have murdered."

Larsen, who had been listening with great interest, said, "I have a question. On the other worlds we've seen, the Weird got a clear benefit from being living alongside humans. They got to consume them. So what are your Weird getting from you?"

"*Our* Weird!" Feuerstein laughed. "They are their own, I think!"

"Okay, but my question still stands. They don't eat you. So what are they getting in return for all the abundance they're lavishing on you?"

"I'll take an educated guess," said Heyes. "The settlement was here first, you said. People escaping slavery who found themselves on a barren world, and who had to work together or else they were going to die. Humans and Vetch, having to put the war behind them. I think the Weird—or those who tend towards symbiosis—saw this and were interested. The portal opened here because these Weird wanted to understand it. They saw humans and Vetch living side-by-side, and they wanted to know more."

Feuerstein smiled. "It's as good an explanation as any."

"You said that you haven't personally communicated with the Weird," said Larsen. "I know that back at the Bureau we've had no success—other than that telepaths were able to scan for mind-parasites. So how do you communicate with the Weird here on Stella Maris?"

"We have telepaths too," said Feuerstein. "Runaways from your government, who resented the use they were put to, having to spend their days immersed inside criminal minds. They are our channel of communication. But the Weird have been here so long now, and understand our needs so well, that we rarely have to resort to direct communication. Sometimes I think that a little of their mind-powers have rubbed off onto all of us here on Stella Maris." She shrugged. "I have no means of proving this."

Walker and Larsen were looking at each other in dismay. "Hold on," said Larsen. "You're saying we need a telepath to speak to the Weird?"

"I wish this had come up before," said Walker. "We don't have a telepath."

"Yes, we do," said Feuerstein.

"One of your people," said Larsen.

"No," said Feuerstein. "One of yours." She looked at Heyes.

Heyes looked blandly back at her companions from the *Baba Yaga*. "What? Oh, didn't I mention that?"

"No, you didn't," said Larsen.

"Anything else you haven't mentioned?" said Walker, scowling.

"That I don't like blackmailers?" said Heyes. "Oh, no, I think I have mentioned that."

"Once or twice," said Walker.

"Oh, shut up, Delia," said Larsen. "It's great we have a telepath. Hecate, I'm glad you're here. I can only wish you were better disposed towards us."

Heyes stood up. "I'm not ill disposed towards you."

"Could've fooled me," said Larsen.

"I'm not ill disposed towards *you*," said the priest, and she stumped off to look at the stars.

WALKER DID NOT go after her straight away. She sat some way back from the rest of the party, watching the stars and listening to the quiet conversation. At length, Larsen tapped her arm. "Will you go and apologise?" she said. "We'll be moving on soon."

Walker stood up, dusted herself down, and went in search of the priest. She found her sitting some distance away, hunched over her knees. She was twisting some beads within her fingers and her lips were moving, silently and rapidly. When she saw Walker, she stopped, touched something silver hanging from the beads against her lips, and slipped them into her pocket.

Walker sat down next to her. "Did you think of mentioning you were a telepath?"

"You know, Walker, you've done little to earn confidences."

"Is that how you knew I was pregnant?"

Heyes looked at her approvingly. "Well guessed. Yes, it was clear the moment you walked through the door. I only have low-level abilities but, well—not hard to spot."

"I guess not," Walker said thoughtfully. "Telepathy must come in useful for a priest. I imagine it makes you a good confessor."

"It also made me a drunk," Heyes said bluntly. "As to why I didn't mention it—you know better than to wonder why. Your own government—the one you've worked for so assiduously over the years—regulates telepaths."

"It certainly does."

"Controls their activities. Licenses them. Makes them do their dirty work."

"Not my area," Walker said, flippantly. "I was External Affairs. You'd have to take that up with a different office. Did you avoid all that? Have you always been a renegade?"

"No, not always. The Church has special privileges. It regulates telepaths too. Under licence from the government—more or less." She smiled. "The Church has always been good at being a jurisdiction within other jurisdictions. Empires rise, and empires fall, but the Holy Mother Church continues, a law more or less unto herself, century upon century, world without end." She smiled. "We've both dedicated our lives to something greater than ourselves, you know. And we both saw when the organisation we served no longer honoured the values that had drawn us to them in the first place."

"You pay me too kind a compliment in comparing us, Hecate," Walker said, almost harshly. "What you did for the people of Shard's World took real courage."

For a moment, Heyes' eyes softened. "I have never thought that you lacked courage," she said. "What do you want from me, Delia?"

"You know what I want. Feuerstein has said we need a telepath to communicate with the Weird. None of her party are telepaths, neither am I, and if Larsen is, she's kept that one up her sleeve for many years of friendship. I have no idea what it will entail, I have no idea whether it will be painful, or difficult, or traumatic—but I want you to communicate with the Weird on my behalf. Will you do that?"

Heyes studied her for a few moments. "I don't know," she said.

"Please, if you can, put aside our differences."

Heyes gave her a very narrow look.

"Please, if you can, put aside the fact that I blackmailed you and threatened your life to get you to come with me. For which," she added, as an afterthought, "I am sorry."

"Better," said Heyes. "Although you're not sorry."

"No," said Walker, "I'm not. I'd do it again. I know," she said, "that I am not the best advocate for my cause. Perhaps I have had a crisis of confidence. I thought I had won my case back at the Bureau, but I was deeply mistaken. But my cause is a good cause. It is the right cause. These people here are not in thrall to the Weird—that makes them unique, from all that I have seen. They may be, well..."

"Weird?" said Heyes.

Walker laughed. "A little, perhaps! But as far as I can tell they have not been assimilated. Not in the way that others living near portals have been."

Heyes looked at her thoughtfully. "You don't like the set-up here?"

"It confuses me. I don't see how it works." She shivered. "And it's... bloodless."

"You prefer things bloody?"

"That's not what I meant—"

Heyes waved her hand to stop her. "Leave it. Cheap shot. But when I say that I don't know about communicating with the Weird on your behalf, I'm being nothing other than honest. I simply mean that I don't know. I have no idea whether it's even possible."

"Feuerstein seems to think her own people have communicated with the Weird."

"Maybe so. And maybe the telepaths here have become used to communicating with the Weird, or being born here alters them in some way. And maybe they haven't been dulling their talents with drink for the past umpty years. Anyway, let us leave that aside. I'll try—of course I'll try." She gave Walker a dry look. "What? Did you think I was going to refuse?"

"I genuinely had no idea."

"Yes, well, don't judge everyone by your standards. Your cause, at least, strikes me as rational and righteous." Heyes gave a deep sigh. "Ah, now, there's Feuerstein waving at us. I guess it's time to move on. Ah!" She sighed again. "My poor old legs! Thirty years they've been kneeling in prayer, and now, at this age, when I should be sitting in a comfortable chair and putting them up, I've brought them out here to trudge up and down mountains and rest on hillsides! I should be at home, wherever that may be." Heyes stood and—wonder of wonders— offered her hand to Walker to help her stand. She looked at the other woman thoughtfully and with a strange expression that Walker eventually realised was compassion. "What *are* you thinking," said Heyes, at last, "coming on a journey like this?"

"Where else should I be? There's nothing for me back on Hennessy's World."

"No? You were rich, weren't you? Larsen told me how senior you were before they fired you—"

"Kay Larsen," said Walker, testily, "should start minding her own business. She's going to find herself in terrible trouble one day."

"—there could have been lucrative contracts; they'd pay for nannies, daycare, all the help you needed. Whatever you wanted. Not like poor Maria. Not like thousands I've seen on Shuloma— struggling to put the food on the table and pay the rent at the end of the month. And instead you found a rundown ship and a washed-up pilot, and dragged yourself out to the back of beyond to haul yourself up a mountain in the middle of a desert, all to chase down some aliens who may or may not be there, and may or may not be hostile. Anyone might think you weren't sure about this child."

"They can think whatever they like."

"Or you weren't sure about what kind of mother you'd be."

Walker turned away. "We should go," she said. "There's long road ahead of us yet."

"I'm praying for you," Heyes called after her. "Sorrowful Mysteries. They seemed the most appropriate."

No doubt there was a backhander there, but Walker was blessedly uninformed. "I haven't a clue what you're going on about," she said. "But thank you. At this point, I'll take whatever's on offer."

TO FIND A priest, you first needed to find her church, but the Chapel of the Immaculate Conception on blue level, section seven, was closed. That did not deter Conway's team; two of the crimopaths forced the door open, and the whole team went inside. Kinsella looked around with some distaste. Religion did nothing for him, and, in fact, he mistrusted those with religious belief. It had always seemed to him a kind of psychological failing; an inability to admit and come to terms with the meaningless of existence. There was no purpose, no grand scheme, and certainly no afterlife. This was all we had, Kinsella thought. We had better make the most of it.

Still, he could not easily watch what happened next. Whether from frustration at finding that their prey had escaped, or because they were bored, or because it amused them, Kinsella was not sure. But the crimopaths wasted no time in taking the church apart. Two of them worked their way around the walls, pulling down the hangings and tearing them into strips. The sound of the tapestries rending seemed to be funny, causing low laughter amongst them. Another of them kicked his way through the wooden chairs towards the altar. He stopped for a while to look at it—Kinsella almost thought it was veneration—and then the crimopath yanked at the cloth, screwing it up and throwing it on the ground. One of the women reached the statue of the woman in white and blue. The wooden flowers at her feet were thrown to the ground. Then she leaned forwards, put her hands around the woman's face, and began to kiss it. Red lipstick, like smears of blood, smudged the statue's marble face. Pleased with her work, she began to rock the statue to and fro, until it toppled from its table and shattered against the ground. Kinsella, watching in horror, turned to Conway.

"Jesus Christ! Stop them!"

Conway looked at him in surprise. "Is this offending you, Mr Kinsella? I'm sorry. I didn't know you were religious."

"I'm not," said Kinsella. "Not at all. But this is completely unnecessary!"

Conway did not make a move, and simply watched as the crimopath at the altar unhooked the crucifix hanging overhead and began to smash it with great force against the bare table. The cross began to splinter.

"Conway!"

Conway stepped forward. "All right," she said. "That's enough."

The crimopaths stopped immediately. But the damage was already done.

"What the hell is *happening* here?"

Kinsella turned to see who had spoken. An old woman, purple-skinned and wrinkled, with protruding lower teeth that reminded him faintly of tusks, was standing in the doorway. Her bright blue eyes were all ablaze as she looked around the ruin of the church. She took a step forwards. "Who *are* you people?"

"Criminal damage, Conway," Kinsella muttered. "You're not within Expansion jurisdiction now. The authorities aren't going to like this."

The old woman walked further into the church. "I said, who are you? What's been going on here?"

Conway stepped forwards. "We're looking for the priest, Heyes. Do you happen to know where she is?"

"She's gone. Settled her bar bill before she went." The old alien looked sad. "I guess that means she's not planning to come back in a hurry. And a good job—what have you lot been doing here?"

Conway, looking round, took in the destruction. "This? It was like this when we arrived."

The old woman scowled. "Don't take me for a fool, girlie," she said. "I run the bar next door. You could hear the racket halfway to purple sector."

Conway didn't look perturbed. She tugged at her earlobe, thoughtfully, and said, "I wonder whether you can shed any light on where Heyes has gone?"

Then it happened. The crimopaths, as if some instruction had been issued, turned as one to look at the old woman. Suddenly Kinsella felt a terrible sense of dread. He opened his mouth to speak—to warn her, to tell her to run—but his tongue seemed to be glued to the top of his mouth. The old woman looked at the crimopaths. "Who did you say you were?"

"I didn't," Conway replied. "But since you ask, we represent the government of the Expansion."

The old woman laughed. "You're a long way from the Expansion, girlie!"

"Not that far," said Conway thoughtfully. "But in many ways that works in our favour. We are not, for example, bound by the kinds of laws we might customarily have to follow if we were at home. We have what might be called leeway." She turned to her team. "I believe we should ask some questions."

"Questions?" said the old woman. "What kind of questions? What are you talking about?"

Conway did not reply. Instead, she turned to Kinsella and said, "You may like to leave now. This is not for the faint-hearted."

Kinsella hesitated, and, then, numbly, he turned away and began to walk through the mess towards the door of the church. The old woman watched him go, uneasily. "What's happening?" she said. "You!" she tugged at Kinsella's sleeve as he went past. "Where are you going?"

Kinsella stopped, briefly, to push her hand away. "For the love of God," he said roughly, "tell them whatever you know as quickly as you can. You might get out of this alive."

"Alive?" She turned away from him, to look at the crimopaths, heading towards her. A glimmer of fear was starting to enter those startling eyes. She said to Kinsella, "Help me!"

"I can't!" he choked out. "There's nothing I can do!"

He left the church, pulling the door closed behind him. He heard a scream, high-pitched and terrible, suddenly cut off. He stood uncertainly outside, staring at the closed door. Could he contact somebody? Who? Would they be able to help? Or would the crimopaths murder their way through Shuloma Station if he tried? Kinsella could well believe that the death count would rise rapidly, should the authorities become involved.

There was a bar next door to the church, the Crossed Keys. Kinsella went in, and sat in a booth towards the back. After about an hour (Did they really need that long? What were they *doing* in there...?), his handheld chimed softly. He nearly hit the roof. With a trembling hand, he checked the message. It was from Conway. *You can come back now.*

He finished his drink, paid, and went back round to the church. Unwillingly, he opened the door and went inside, terrified at what he might find.

There was, at least, no blood. The crimopaths had picked up a few of the chairs, and two of them, one of the men and one of the women, were sitting down, talking quietly to each other. Conway was standing beside them, and seemed to be busy with her handheld. Receiving more of her precious orders? The other two crimopaths were not to be seen, nor was the old woman. Slowly, Kinsella walked towards the altar. There was not much more damage that he could see, although the head of the statue of the blue-and-white woman had been detached from the body, and now lay on its side upon the altar. She still had red smears on her cheeks, and someone had painted her lips red too, with what Kinsella hoped was lipstick.

Behind the table where the statue had once stood there was a small door, through which one of the crimopaths emerged, whistling tunelessly. The other followed, and closed the door afterwards. "All done?" said Conway, and the pair nodded. "Good, good." Then she turned to Kinsella. "We're finished here," she said. "And we have our next destination. Follow the star. The star of the sea."

Kinsella finally found his voice. "I don't know what you mean."

"That's what we've been told," said Conway. "From a reliable source. The star of the sea. Mean anything to you, Mr Kinsella?"

Kinsella shook his head.

"Well, it does to me. Star of the Sea. Stella Maris." Conway waved the handheld about cheerfully. "I have the co-ordinates right here."

CHAPTER THIRTEEN

On the third day of their journey, the land started to become rougher and low hills began to rise and fall in front of them. Towards the end of the day's walking, the quiet hour before dawn, they came to the banks of a wide, slow-moving river. Here, Feuerstein told them, was where they would leave the desert plains behind them, turning north-west to follow the course of the river into the mountains. They still had several days of walking ahead of them.

They could perhaps have walked on for another hour or so before the cool dawn, but the riverbank seemed a natural break, and so they stopped and made camp. When the tents were up, and the food was eaten and cleared away, Larsen came to sit beside Walker. They sat together in silence, looking up at the stars.

"I grew up on Lindisfarne," said Larsen, at last. "Quiet colony world. Not much industry. All tourist trade and hospitality. Beautiful mountains and rivers and lakes. Adventure sports."

"Sounds exciting."

Larsen shrugged. "It was boring, actually. All highly-regulated and super-safe. Nobody wanted to risk getting sued. I came to Hennessy's World to study medicine. Never went back." She lay down on the ground. "I've spent so long on the inner worlds that I'd forgotten what the stars look like. How incredible they are. I'd forgotten there was so much to see."

"There's the quiet too," said Walker. "I don't think I've ever been anywhere so remote in my life. Even on Andrei's boat, you could hear the flyers in the distance and the throb of the city. I've never heard quiet like this. When I lie down to sleep it's as if I can hear the blood pumping around my veins. As if I can hear her moving within me..." She fell silent. Larsen's hand rested for a moment upon her arm, and Walker relished the contact and the gentle, wordless comfort. They listened to the soft sounds around them: the others settling down to sleep; some quiet coughs and muted conversation; Feuerstein moving to take the watch; and, below it all, the low steady rush of the river. At last, Larsen stretched and stood up.

"Get some sleep, Delia," she said. "Even an hour or so will be good for you."

Obediently, Walker lay down on her mat, curling up on her left side like Larsen had suggested. The child moved inside her. *Hello*, she thought. *Time to rest. Time for us to rest.* What she had said to Larsen was true. She had found herself, the past few days, in the silent emptiness of this desert, talking more to the baby. Listening for her responses. Feeling her. This journey had pared her down to the essentials. Down to the two of them. *Are you comfortable? Get comfortable. It's time for us to rest.*

She hovered on the edge of sleep. The child settled inside her, and she pictured her, legs and arms curled around her small self, sucking her tiny thumb, maybe. Suspended. Dreaming. Covered. Protected. *Loved...*

Walker woke, suddenly. There were voices at the edge of the camp, raised, and movement all around her. She sat bolt upright, clutching herself. Had they been found?

Larsen was leaning over her. "Don't worry," she said. "Everything's okay. But you'd better come. Your shadow is here."

Walker looked up at her friend in confusion. She thought, obscurely, of Kinsella, whom she hadn't thought of in ages. He had pursued her with courtesy and obstinacy; ever-present and persistent. He had said that he loved her. "My shadow?"

"Your Vetch shadow."

"Failt? He's here?"

"He's here and he very much wants to talk to you."

Walker scrambled to her feet and made her way through their little camp. Sure enough, Failt was there, sitting between Feuerstein and one of her people. Heyes was crouched down next to him, but when he saw Walker, he jumped to his feet.

"Missus Delia!" he cried. He ran towards her, flinging his arms around her. She found herself patting the top of his head and, then, more to her surprise, stroking his mane of hair, very gently.

"Well, Failt," she said. "I have to say that I'm glad to see you, but why aren't you back at the *Baba Yaga*? Has something happened?"

He looked up at her with his strange, blood-red, sorrowful eyes. "Bad news!"

Walker's heart clenched in her chest. From behind her, Larsen said, "Jesus Christ, what's happened? Where's Maria? Where's Jenny?"

"All safe. Leastways, I think so. Did my best, my very best, to make him follow. But, missus, he's on his way!" He clutched at her with his paws. "Couldn't shake him off!"

"All right," Walker said in a calm, clear voice. "Slow down. Back up and tell me what's happened."

Failt was shaking his head, sending his tentacles quivering this way and that. "Never trusted him. From the beginning, the very beginning. He had his eye on me. Wanted to space me! That's why I stayed. Keep my eye on him. Knew after you fought he was going to try something, and he has done."

"Okay, Failt, we're talking about Yershov, yes? What's he done now?"

"Been and gone and done it, missus. Heard him on the comm. Wants new implants. Wants to work again."

Larsen said, "I told him the op would probably kill him."

"Reason doesn't come into it," said Walker. "I imagine that whoever he's been talking to has been very convincing. But Failt—do you have any idea who it is he contacted? Who he's been talking to?"

Failt nodded. "Checked the comm when he was asleep. Didn't get a name, but they're Fleet. Come all the way from the Expansion. He's sold you out, missus. Told your bosses where to find you. Knew I had to keep an eye on him. He wanted to space me!"

Walker and Larsen turned to each other. "Well," said Larsen. Her voice was shaking. "I guess we knew this was coming."

"I know," said Walker. "Still, I hoped we might have enough time..."

Feuerstein was watching them closely. She stepped towards Walker and said, "Does this mean what I think it means?"

Walker hesitated before replying, and Heyes said, "Tell her the truth. You owe these people that much."

Walker nodded. "I'm sorry. I'm afraid so. If Failt is right—and I have no reason to doubt him—then it sounds as if our pilot has sold us out to the Bureau."

"And what does it mean for us? For Stella Maris?"

"I don't know," Walker said honestly. "But these people are prepared to do whatever it takes to protect their secret. And they have the capability to wipe out millions."

Feuerstein and her people gathered together and began to confer in soft, worried voices. Walker became aware that Failt was tugging at her arm.

"Missus," he said, urgently. "You gotta listen. Think I didn't shake him off. Think he's still coming after me. Tried my best but think he's here—"

He was right, and he didn't get to say any more. From somewhere in the darkness, an energy weapon was fired at them. The line of light burst overhead and hit one of the trees on the river bank, setting it ablaze. They all scrambled for cover; Walker pulling Failt after her and leaning over to protect his small body. From the distance, she heard Yershov, yelling.

"You little Vetch shit, I should have finished you when I had the chance! But I'll get you! I'll get you now!"

The weapon fired again. This time it hit one of the tents, right in the middle of the camp, where they had been gathered moments before.

"And you, Walker—do you hear me? I've got you now! I've set the Bureau on you, you bitch! They're coming for you, and I'm gonna watch while they tear you apart, and I'm gonna be *laughing!*"

THEIR PARTY RECONVENED under the cover of the trees. "All right," whispered Larsen. "That's definitely Yershov, and he's definitely angry, and he's definitely armed."

Another burst of fire flared overhead. "Missus Dee," said Failt. "Brought a couple of guns from the ship. Might come in handy?"

Another tree nearby caught fire. "Yes," said Walker. "I think they'll come in handy."

Feuerstein and her people knew the terrain best, so they began to creep forwards. Walker, preparing to follow them, was stopped by Larsen. "Now you're taking the piss, Delia. Get under cover. Stay there. Let us take care of this."

"You're not armed, Kay."

Heyes, beside her, stuck out her hand. "Then give me your weapon."

Reluctantly, Walker took out her weapon and handed it over to Heyes. A few seconds later, the sky above lit up—but not from a weapon being fired. Feuerstein's people had sent up flares. The whole area was as clear as if under floodlights—and there was Yershov. Heyes wasted no time. She stood up, took aim, and fired. White light flashed out in a great arc, bright even against the dying yellow of the flares. The night reasserted itself. Silence fell.

Walker whispered to Larsen, "What can you see? What the hell is going on? Is he dead?"

"No idea."

They waited a while, and then two of Feuerstein's people, who had gone out on a recce, came back and confirmed what they had guessed: Yershov was dead. Heyes' shot had beheaded him. The priest blanched and made the Sign of the Cross. "Bless me, Father," she whispered, "for I have sinned."

"God's work, Hecate," said Larsen, resting her hand on the priest's arm. She turned to Failt. "Yershov only mentioned the missus. Did he tell his contacts about me?" She glanced at Walker. "If it's only you he informed on, things might not be as we think they are."

But Failt was shaking his head. "Sorry, doc," he said. "He told them you were here too. Think they asked about you. He said, 'Yes, yes, she's here. The doctor's here.' But I think he was sorry he did that. He liked you, doc. He trusted you. But he still said you were here."

"Oh, Christ," said Larsen, with real fear in her voice.

Feuerstein and her people exchanged looks, and she turned to Walker. "Who exactly is coming?" she demanded. "We must know what this threat means for us. For Stella Maris."

Walker hesitated. Then Heyes, stepping forwards, offered her back her weapons. "I've killed for you now," she said. "Murder's a mortal sin. So stop prevaricating and give us real answers. You came here with a mission, knowing that it might bring danger after you, but you weren't ever able to protect us. I doubt you even thought about that—whether the people here might need protection. They have a right to know what hell is about to be unleashed on them."

"All right," said Walker, grudgingly. "Well, if it was me running the show, I'd be sending in a team to finish off me and Larsen."

"'Finish off,'" said Heyes. "A little more precision, please."

"Track down. Assassinate. Kill."

"And the people of Stella Maris?" asked Heyes. "There are over three thousand people in that settlement."

"I guess..." Walker looked up at the cold stars. "Interrogations would quickly find out whether they knew anything substantive about Braun's World. That's what I would order. But it's worth bearing in mind that I am what you could call the friendly face of the Bureau. I wouldn't, for instance, involve myself in the cover-up of a mass murder on a planetary scale."

"And I applaud your fastidiousness in that respect," said Heyes. "But tell us what your less considerate colleagues are likely to do."

"They're in a different league," Walker said. She looked directly at Feuerstein. "A few thousand people would barely count as collateral damage. A few well targeted missiles. A clean-up team on the ground to pick up any escapees. It wouldn't take very long, if that's any consolation."

Heyes recoiled. "Oh, sweet Jesus, Mary, and all the saints! What have I brought here? Shel, I can only beg your forgiveness!"

Feuerstein raised her hand to quieten her. "I don't blame you, Hecate," she said. "And neither, really, do I blame Ms Walker. The Weird are here, after all—and if the Vetch and the humans have decided to destroy the Weird, they would have come here to Stella Maris eventually. At least this way we have been forewarned. I can only wish we had had a little more time..." She shook her head. "We couldn't defend ourselves, of course, not against any kind of firepower. But time to move away, to hide ourselves..."

Failt piped up. "I sent Maria and Jenny. Slipped out when Yershov wasn't looking. Set him chasing me so they could get away."

Larsen took the child's paw. "You've been a lifesaver, Failt—you really have. So Maria is heading towards the settlement. That means they'll have some warning, at least, before the Bureau gets here."

"It's not enough!" said Heyes. There were red blotches across her face, and she was breathing very heavily. For a moment Walker feared the older woman might be having a heart attack. "We have to send them some kind of help?"

"What help?" said Walker, roughly. "What can we send them that would help them? A single ship from the Fleet would be enough to mount an air strike that would flatten that settlement in a matter of minutes. Do you have surface to air missiles that you can send to them? I know I don't. I can't work miracles, Heyes!"

Heyes subsided. Larsen put her hand upon the priest's shoulder. "Take it easy, Hecate," she murmured. "This is your doctor speaking."

"Yes, we need to warn them," said Walker. "We

don't know when the Bureau will arrive, and we don't know in what force they're coming. But there may still be time." She looked at Feuerstein. "A town founded by runaways, yes? Always on the lookout, checking back over their shoulders. There are escape routes, aren't there? Means to get out and get away. Get into the hills. I bet there are places to hide there, all ready for when the moment arose. Well, the moment's here."

Feuerstein nodded, but she looked grim. "Time has passed. It's a long time since anyone came our way as an escapee. Who knows whether these routes are still there, and the bolt holes still secure?"

"It's the best I can suggest from this distance," said Walker. "But I think we need to send a warning that trouble is on its way. Failt says Maria and Jenny are heading to the settlement..."

Larsen said, "Maria might be on her way, but she's carrying danger to them. Maria knows what we know—and she has a copy of the evidence about the massacre. Delia"—Larsen put her hand on her friend's arm—"we've got to assume that we're not going to survive this. Maria needs to be told—spread the word. Tell people what happened."

"How?" said Walker. "If they can only rustle up a single roadworthy vehicle, I doubt they've got comms technology powerful enough to send messages as far as the Expansion. Feuerstein? Is that right?"

The woman shook her head. "What we have is very limited in its range. I received messages from Heyes, but you were well within the Reach by then."

"So the secret of Braun's World is going to die with us?" said Larsen. "All of it for nothing. Poor Maria. Poor Kit."

"There's the *Baba Yaga*," said Heyes.

Larsen frowned. "Is her comm powerful enough?"

"Yershov was in touch with people in the Bureau," said Walker.

"Who may already have been halfway here—"

Heyes shook her head impatiently. "There's a lot of guesswork going on here. And even if you do get the word out—who are you going to tell?"

Larsen looked at Walker. "Time to call in a few favours, Delia?"

"Or issue a few threats," Walker said.

Heyes stared at her. "Threats? From here? You're in the middle of nowhere."

Walker shrugged. "A few timed messages. A few cover identities ruined, or secrets revealed. All very straightforward." She sighed, and reached for her handheld. "Kay, come with me."

After about an hour, their files and instructions were ready. Walker called Failt over to her. She took one of his paws in her hand. "I want to thank you, Failt. You saved my life."

He squeezed her hand. "You saved mine, Missus Dee. I said to you when you did: I'm yours. Whatever you want."

"All right. I'm going to hold you to that. I want you to go back after Maria and Jenny."

She felt the paw tighten its hold on her. "Oh, missus, not that. Anything but that! Don't send me away! Not now! Not when it's all coming to a head!"

"But do you understand how important they are, Failt? I know you do—and not only because they're Maria and Jenny, though God knows that would be enough. It's because Maria knows a secret—an important secret that needs to be told."

"I know about the secret," said Fault. "Know all about everything. The fire that came and killed all the people but there weren't any Weird there. I know all about it. But I don't want to leave you. I'm yours, missus. Yours."

She put her arm around his shoulders. "You're not, you know. You're not mine. You belong to yourself. I can't make you go—but I can ask you. Please. Go and find Maria and Jenny. Tell Maria—she has to let everyone know. Find a way to let everyone know." She dug into her pocket and took out her handheld. "Look," she said. "I'm giving you this. It's got a list of names on it. A list of contacts. A set of instructions. Maria needs this." At the sight of the handheld, Fault started whimpering, as if that above anything else convinced him that this was going to be goodbye. "Please, Fault."

Larsen, coming to sit on his other side, said, "It's important. We can't ask anyone else."

Heyes, too, nearby said, "They're right, Fault."

Fault looked up at Walker with his big lugubrious eyes. "Don't want to leave you, Missus Dee."

She held her to him. "I know," she said. "And I... I don't want you to go."

A strange smile passed over Fault's face. He hugged Walker tightly, and then he jumped up. He took the handheld from Walker's hand, and he said, "All I wanted to hear. I'll go. Go now. Tell Mama Maria she's to do what you said. Yours, Missus Delia. Forever."

And that was it. He was gone, in the blink of an eye. Walker stood up and followed after him for a few steps, but it was as if he had never been.

Heyes, coming to stand behind her, put her hand

upon Walker's shoulder. "Who would have thought? All he wanted to hear was that you loved him. And you did. You, of all people." She patted Walker's shoulder. "You might make a mother yet."

Walker looked into the distance. "I doubt that."

A SURVEY OF the planet's surface revealed a settlement of about three thousand souls in the middle of the desert. An odd place to put a town, Kinsella thought, but as he understood it, this place had been founded by runaway slaves, and perhaps they had thought that settling in the back of beyond might afford them some kind of protection. Still, he was not sure it had been a good decision. What did they do for water? What did they do for food?

The *White Horseman* came down a couple of miles from the settlement. "What now?" Kinsella asked.

"I think we can go outside and take a look," said Conway. "After that—I think we should wait."

The wait paid off. After about an hour, they saw a small a group of people heading in their direction from the settlement. One of the crimopaths began to pace around. "Wait," said Conway and, when he began to walk towards the group, she said again, "Wait," and made a show of reaching towards the inhibitor on her belt. The crimopath fell back and then walked, with a slow pace, round the back of Conway and Kinsella, up and down, like a tiger on the prowl. Kinsella felt his skin crawl; the hairs tingle. He could not prevent a flinch each time the crimopath came close. But Conway didn't even blink. She simply watched the road ahead; watched the little group come towards them.

At last they were close enough to speak. Four of them: two Vetch; two humans—a man and a woman. The woman addressed them. "We have come to ask you to leave," she said. "We have nothing that you want. We only wish to be left in peace, as we told the others."

Conway didn't reply. Instead, she turned to the crimopaths and said, "See to the Vetch, please. Leave the humans, for now."

The two Vetch were dead on the floor within seconds. All of the crimopaths had opened fire at once. One of the humans, the man, turned to run, and was shot in the leg for his pains. He fell to the ground in agony, and Conway nodded her approval at the careful attention to her orders. The woman cried out his name, but she didn't dare move towards him. Conway turned to her team and said. "Find out as much as you can."

Kinsella went back into the ship. He went to the empty rec room and filled the space with the sound of Thomas Tallis. *Human beauty*, he thought. *If I listen to human beauty, perhaps it will blot out the ugliness and the evil...* Eventually, Conway came to find him. He stopped the music at the sight of her, as if she might somehow sully its perfection.

"Yes," said Conway, "Walker and Larsen have been this way. Heyes was with them. They were asked to leave, but it seems that they haven't. A small party of malcontents are taking them up into the mountains to the Weird portal."

Almost to himself, Kinsella said, "She's still here..." Conway cocked her head to one side and looked at him with interest. "I mean," said Kinsella, "they're still here?"

"That's right. They have no weapons here," she said. "Nothing."

If Kinsella hadn't known better, he might have thought that Conway licked her lips. "Do we know which way they went? Do we know where the portal was?"

"That... was not easy to discover," Conway said. "This is clearly a secret they were keen to protect from us."

"I imagine your people persuaded them otherwise," said Kinsella with distaste.

"One of them refused to answer any questions. The other was able to see what that meant."

"Jesus," whispered Kinsella.

"So now we know where the portal is and, therefore, where Walker, Larsen, and the priest are." Conway studied Kinsella. "You seem troubled, Mr Kinsella. I would have thought you would be pleased to hear that we would soon be bringing the murderers of your mentor to justice. Andrei Gusev's death will not go unpunished."

As if she gave a shit about Andrei Gusev. As if any of them gave a shit. Only him, the last of Andrei's loyal lieutenants.

Conway stretched lazily, like a leopard contemplating making a move for dinner. "We should get going."

Yes, thought Kinsella. *A mob from the settlement might be too much even for your murderous lot.* "I thought I might remain here," he said.

Conway looked at him with pale expressionless eyes. "I'd like you to come with me, Mr Kinsella."

But I don't want to be part of this any longer. I don't want to see what you're going to do to them...

"Your knowledge of Walker and Larsen might

be crucial in taking them, if they decide to make a stand. People do that, in desperate straits. You may save lives if you come with us."

Fat chance of that, Kinsella thought, but he was cornered. "I'll go and pack."

"My team are seeing to that." She nodded to him to follow, and they went down to the hold. The crimopaths were hard at work, sorting out supplies and weapons, and packing not one but two of the land vehicles that the *White Horseman* carried. Kinsella turned to Conway. "Two? One of those is big enough to carry all of us."

"But we are not all going on the same journey, Mr Kinsella. You and I and two of my people will follow Larsen up into the mountains."

"And Walker."

She looked at him.

"Larsen and Walker," he said.

"Yes, of course."

"And the other two?" Kinsella said.

Conway rocked back and forth on the soles of her boots. "If they've been to the settlement, there's a risk of infection. I'm sending two of my team to find out whether that's the case. We may save lives," she said, keeping her voice just this side of pious.

Kinsella looked carefully at what was being packed into the second vehicle. It looked more like they were packing for a ground assault than for a mission of mercy. He wondered, if the plan was destroy the settlement, why they weren't simply going to fly the *White Horseman* overhead and fire a few missiles. That would surely be the quickest way to get the job done. And then he understood. They didn't want the job done quickly. They wanted to take their time.

Kinsella left them to it. He went back to his own quarters and packed his gear: clothes, a weapon or two which, he hoped, Conway had somehow not discovered. When he was done, he sat on the edge of the bed and waited for his summons to leave. His mind was racing. But chief amongst his unanswered questions was this: If Walker and Larsen had been crooked, if they had murdered Andrei for his money, then why the hell had they come here, to this miserable place? It had been easy to persuade himself that Walker's story of a world where humans and Vetch lived alongside each other in peaceful co-existence with the Weird had been nothing more than a pack of lies, a story to cover her escape from Hennessy's World. And yet he had seen them, before they were murdered—two Vetch and two humans. And here she was, Delia Walker, on this godforsaken world, chasing a rumour, a fairy story. Chasing a portal between realities that she alone, it seemed, had always believed existed.

STELLA MARIS WAS a long way from Braun's World, and Maria felt herself hardening further with every step she took. Jenny struggled on beside her, no longer complaining that her mother was insisting on yet another walk. The girl seemed to have accepted these hardships as part of life now. *If I thought about that too much*, Maria thought, *it might break my heart.*

She was still shocked at Yershov's betrayal, and, at least as much, she was saddened. It had been plain from the outset that the simmering tension between him and Walker was going to boil over at some point, and she had only hoped that she and Jenny would not be caught between them when it happened. Her loyalty was to Walker, who had rid the world of Amber and Springer, but she had not forgotten Yershov's willingness to intervene on her behalf. He had not struck her as a man given to selfless acts, but he had not wanted to see Jenny harmed and that, at least, had warmed Maria to him. And then Failt had come to her while she and Jenny were resting, and told her what the pilot had done...

Who would have thought too, back on Braun's World, that she would believe the word of a Vetch? But you didn't doubt Failt. You didn't doubt him, because he was devoted to Delia Walker, and he had her best interests at heart. So when he came and told you that Yershov had sold out Walker to her enemies, and that they were coming after her—well, you wanted to help. Whispering with Failt in her cabin, they had made their plans to get away—she to warn the settlement, Failt to warn Walker— and she had slipped out of the ship while the pilot was sleeping and hurried off with Jenny. Failt had left after her and, given that she had not yet been troubled by the pilot, she could only assume he had taken off after the child. She'd known that Failt was drawing the pilot after him in part to protect her and Jenny, but she had let him get on with it. One more reason to be thankful to the creature. One more reason to like a Vetch.

"Mummy," said Jenny. "What's that?"

The little girl was pointing ahead. Maria, looking to where her daughter was pointing, saw a great sleek ship coming to land. She knew immediately that these were their enemies and that they were in terrible danger. "Come on, Jenny," she said, taking her daughter's hand. "Let's get out of here."

But the ship had landed between them and the settlement. It would be a long walk round, and Maria wasn't sure that the plains offered enough cover. They inched on carefully to a little watering hole that she had seen, with a couple of trees around it, which gave some cover and a place from which to watch the new arrivals. Six people came out of the ship altogether—Maria did not know if there others inside—three men and three women. One of the women seemed to be in command; Maria, with her experience through Kit's long service in Fleet, recognised an officer when she saw one. Most of the others seemed to be military—they had the uniforms, at least—but something about the way they interacted with each other, and with their commander, made Maria uneasy. They seemed reluctant to follow orders, verging on insubordinate. But this was surely an important mission, one to be given to only the most trusted of people. Why send a crew that was on the verge of mutiny? Maria could not answer this, so she filed it away. There was no point in worrying over questions she couldn't answer.

One of the men was not military, Maria knew that. Not just the lack of uniform, but the bearing, and the general air of being slightly less fit than he might have liked. He hung back from the others and seemed, Maria thought, unhappy to be there. He didn't assist with the work, either, but watched as the five grunts—if that was what they were— brought out two ground vehicles, and then began to load them with supplies and hardware. Eventually, one of the vehicles was ready for departure, and the group split. The commander, and the civilian, and two of the grunts piled into one vehicle and set off into the desert. The other two remained behind, loading their vehicle. When they began to bring out ground cannon, Maria knew it was time to get moving. But how, she wondered, could she get to the settlement to warn them before they got there?

There was no point setting off before dark. The two soldiers would surely see her, and that would be the end of her mission. But as darkness fell, she began to regret her delay when she heard the sound of a motor vehicle coming towards them.

"Jenny," she whispered, "lie down on the ground."

The little girl did what she was told, and Maria looked round hopelessly for a weapon. Branches from the tree, she thought, hysterically. How good a defence would that be against their firepower?

The vehicle slowed, and then the engine stopped. Maria heard feet padding towards her, and got ready to fight, with tooth and claw if needs be. And then a familiar, ugly face appeared out of the darkness. "Mama Maria! Here you are! Come on, we gotta hurry!"

"Failt!" she cried, softly, and pulled the child to her. Jenny too jumped up from where she had been lying and wrapped her arms around her playmate. "How did you get here?" Maria said. "And where did you find this?"

She pointed at the vehicle. Failt gave a throaty laugh. "Pinched it from that big ship down there. Thought it wasn't fair they should get there first. Thought it would be better if we had it. They weren't happy, though," he said, and laughed again. "They weren't happy at all."

Maria couldn't help laughing herself. "But how did you know where to find us?"

His tentacles shook. "Sniffed you on the breeze. Humans smell. I know your smell now, yours and Jenny's." He pulled her hand, dragging her towards the vehicle. "We gotta go, Mama Maria. Those people down there—they're mean. They won't be good to us if they catch us. And we have a job to do. Promised Missus Dee that we'd see it done."

Maria lifted Jenny up into the cab, and climbed in after her. "You found them? What happened? Did you lose Yershov?"

Failt shook his head. Quickly—and with an eye on Jenny, God bless him—he explained what had happened up by the river. "Yershov won't be troubling us no more," he said, as he started the vehicle up again. Maria shook her head. He hadn't deserved this, she thought. He'd brought them here, after all, and all the time he had been in a great deal of pain. But it wasn't a good idea to betray Walker. Maria was thankful to her, and loyal, but she knew that Walker was not a person to cross.

As they sped on towards the settlement, Failt passed over Walker's handheld, and told Maria all that Walker and Larsen had said. "They said there were names on there, names of people you needed to contact. Messages you were to send. Instructions for what to do. They want you to spread word about what happened. Tell people what you know."

"If we want to do that, we should go back to the *Baba Yaga*," Maria said.

"But there's a problem," Failt said. "Before I took this thing"—he patted the controls in the cab—"I listened in to what they were saying." He glanced at Jenny, nodding off between them, and lowered his voice. "Bad things planned," he said. "Going to get to the settlement and finish off as many as they can. We've slowed them down, yes, but they're still coming."

So, a choice, thought Maria. Go back to the *Baba Yaga* and make sure the news got out, or warn the people of the settlement that they were in danger, and hope they survived long enough to return to the *Baba Yaga* afterwards.

"What you want to do, Mama Maria?"

There was no choice, not really. Maria was made of simpler stuff than the spies and spooks she had fallen in with. Not for her were the complicated games of ends and means. "Keep going, Failt," she said. "We have to warn those poor people down there."

CHAPTER FOURTEEN

THEY SPED OFF towards the settlement, darkness falling around them. Failt had found binoculars amongst the kit, and Maria kept watch on the progress of the pair behind them: they were running, incredibly, and making good speed, despite the heavy packs they were both carrying. There was no danger of the pair catching up with their party, but there was something relentless about them that frightened Maria. The sooner they could reach the settlement and warn the people of Stella Maris, the better.

"Can you make this thing go any faster?" she said to Failt. To Jenny, she said, "Sit still, sweetheart, and make sure you're holding tight."

Failt bumped and bashed the vehicle across the rocky plain. Closer to the settlement the landscape underwent a sudden change, becoming more fertile and managed. A road appeared too, taking them the rest of the way. Maria, turning to look at their destination, saw a wooden fence. She frowned. It didn't look like very strong. They had stolen the weaponry that their pursuers had intended to bring to attack the town, but who knew what they were carrying with them?

Failt slowed down as they drew nearer to the fence and, at last, brought the vehicle to a halt. The gateway was blocked, not by a gate, but by people: three lines, four abreast, humans and Vetch alike, preventing them from going any further. Failt sniffed. "They don't look pleased to see us, Mama Maria," he said. "Not very grateful, are they?"

Maria looked anxiously at the welcoming party. They didn't look ready to talk. Nevertheless, she had to try. She climbed down from the cab, lifting Jenny after her, and walked slowly towards the gateway, holding her little girl's hand. Failt hopped out and followed behind. She tried to look as non-threatening as possible—but, really, Maria thought, how much less threatening could she look? She was a young mum, with a little girl, and a stray Vetch orphan that had somehow come into her care. But these people seemed to be hardening against her with every step she took towards them: their arms locked together, their faces set, their eyes stern and unfriendly. She saw human faces, men and women; Vetch faces; even some children here and there—and not one of them was welcoming. At last she stopped, and discovered that not only was she holding Jenny's hand, but that Failt's hairy paw had somehow wrapped itself around her free hand. She squeezed it tight.

"Scared, Mama Maria," he said. "They don't look friendly."

Maria looked along the front line, but she couldn't see a single person to whom she thought she could appeal. The light was fading, and she was terribly aware that their enemies were drawing closer. She almost imagined she could hear their footfall, running unceasingly, getting nearer and nearer... "Please," she said. "I need to talk to you."

There was a soft ripple of murmuring through the assembled crowd, and then someone, a few rows back, called out, "Leave. You are not welcome here."

"I'm here to help!" Maria was aware as she said it how foolish it sounded. What could she do to help?

Someone else from the crowd spoke. "We know who you are. You came with the first ship. They brought discord and strife with them—"

"We mean you no harm!" cried Maria.

"Some of us left and have gone with the others from your party. This is the first time in our history that we have been split in this way. Before we have always agreed, in time."

"You've not faced danger like this before!" Maria said. "There are people behind us—chasing us— very dangerous people. They are armed, and they will kill as many of you as they can. Please, let us in! Let me explain what is happening!"

She took a step or two forwards, and the human and Vetch barrier again seemed to strengthen against her. *Oh, God,* she thought, *I'm never going to persuade them. I don't know what to say!*

Failt squeezed her hand. "Mama Maria!" he cried. "They're coming! They're coming! They got weapons! They're gonna shoot us, Mama! Going to shoot Failt!"

From beyond the fence, Maria thought she could

hear voices raised in anger, as if some kind of argument was going on behind the scenes. It was now quite dark, but there were lamps around the fence, casting light over the crowd. This was, she thought later, the reason they presented such an easy target. She heard someone from beyond the fence say, quite distinctly, "I don't care what you think! Two of them are *children*!" And then there was a burst of noise and a flashing light, and she heard a terrible yelp of pain. She realised that Failt, standing against her, was now on the ground, writhing and whimpering and bleeding. He had been shot.

"Oh, God!" she cried, reaching out to him. "I said they were coming! And you wouldn't help! Now look what's happened! Look what you've done!"

And this, it seemed, was the key to unlock the barrier ahead. All of a sudden, the rows of people melted, and moved to enfold her and the children. They were carried forwards, almost on a wave, Maria thought, and before she knew it, they were beyond the fence and within the settlement. She heard a gate being slammed, and saw people rushing about, and there was a general hue and cry. She fell to her knees beside Failt, clutching his paw, holding it to her. Jenny was hanging onto her arm, and she was crying. "Mummy? Is he dead? Is he dead like Daddy?"

A big Vetch was leaning over them. Maria, unable to stop herself, pulled away and tried to put herself between it and the children. "Go away! Go away!" she cried, through tears. "Aren't you satisfied? Haven't you done enough already?"

Slowly, gently, the Vetch made her pull back. "I'm a medic," it said. "I can help him. Please, let me help him."

Maria withdrew. The Vetch medic began to attend to Failt's injuries and then called for help to take the child away.

"Where are you taking him?" said Maria.

"We have a small hospital. We can help him there. I can help him," the medic said, "but you must trust me."

It seemed she would have to. Maria nodded, numbly, and watched as the child was taken away. Some people came to her, and led her and Jenny further into the settlement. "I need to talk to someone," she kept on saying, over and over. "You have to take me to talk to someone. Someone in authority..." But she didn't seem to be understood. "Please," she said, "I won't go any further. Tell me where you're taking me. You have to listen to what I have to say—"

She got no further. A great unholy light flared overhead, and then there were explosions. Grenades had been thrown over the fence. She heard screaming, and saw people running about her. Someone pulled her and Jenny away. The crimopaths had begun their siege of the settlement, and they were going to take their time about it, and derive as much enjoyment from it as they possibly could.

CONWAY'S PEOPLE CAUGHT up with Walker and her party mid-morning. It was not long after they had crossed the river and started making their way along the wide pass between two great rocky ranges of hills. According to Feuerstein, they would find the pathway leading to the Weird portal at the end of the pass. They had trekked some distance, when they heard the sound of a motor approaching from behind them. Feuerstein's people knew their business. They slipped ahead, hunted out defensive positions, and led Walker, Larsen and Heyes up the more northerly slope to safety. Then they set off back down the hill, two of them carrying the weapons that Failt had brought from the *Baba Yaga*.

About half-an-hour after they had departed, Walker and her companions heard weapons' fire from back down the pass. It went on, intermittently, for some time. Another hour or so passed. Then Feuerstein arrived, with one of her people. They were safe, she said, for a little while. They had brought the bridge down before the vehicle had crossed, and, given the width and speed of the river at this point, it would be some time before they would be able to ford it. "There are four of them," she said. "Most were in uniform. One wasn't."

Larsen, who had been looking back down the pass through Walker's binoculars, suddenly swore. "Jesus Christ," she said. "Delia, come here. Tell me if you see what I see." She handed Walker the binoculars.

Walker took them and looked back down towards the river. After a couple of minutes, she too said, "Jesus Christ."

"Is this a private prayer meeting or can anyone join?" said Heyes. "What have you seen?"

"There's a friend of ours down there," said Walker.

"A friend," said Heyes. "Shooting at you. Well, that makes sense."

"You say 'friend'..." muttered Larsen.

Walker passed back the binoculars. "Colleague, then." No, damn it, she thought, that wasn't fair. "He *was* our friend, Kay."

"Then what's he doing down there," said Larsen, "shooting at us, as Hecate rightly points out?"

"How would I know?" said Walker.

"You were fucking him," said Larsen.

"So were you."

"Not as recently."

"Ladies!" Heyes cut through the quarrel. "I hate to spoil this precious moment of friendship, but could one of you explain who this person is?"

"His name is Mark Kinsella," said Walker, wearily. "We were all very close, once upon a time."

"Some of us closer than others. Recently," Larsen muttered, but subsided at a stern look from Heyes.

"He's the father?" said Heyes.

"Yes," said Walker, "but that wasn't what I meant. Mark was one of us. One of our faction at the Bureau." She smiled mirthlessly at Heyes. "Remember, we were the good guys? Well, Mark was one of the good guys too."

"But now the father of your child has decided to hunt you down and murder you? You certainly pick them, don't you, Walker?"

Larsen was shaking her head. "I don't believe it," she said. "Not of Mark. He wouldn't switch sides like this."

"Perhaps he never switched sides," said Walker grimly. "Perhaps he played us all for fools for a long time."

"I can't believe that," Larsen said. "I mean, Mark could certainly be a bloody fool, but he was Andrei's man, through and through. Always was, always will be. I can't believe he'd side with Grant. Not willingly."

"There's one way to find out," said Walker. "Can I borrow your handheld, Kay?"

"My handheld?" Larsen looked suspicious. "Why?"

"Because I need a handheld, and you might remember that I gave mine to Failt so that he and Maria could try to bring down the government."

Larsen, with a laugh, passed the handheld over. Walker thumbed through the contacts, until she found the one she wanted. "Hello, Mark," she said.

His voice came back tinnily. "*Kay, is that you?*"

She didn't reply. After a moment, he spoke again. He sounded stunned.

"*Delia?*"

"Yes, it's me. What the hell is going on? Who are these people you've brought with you, and why are they trying to kill us? Kay's here too, you know." She frowned. "I'm guessing you knew that already." Her heart almost skipped a beat. Did he know about Braun's World? Was he *part* of it?

"*Delia, I can't believe this. Are you mad? Are you trying to get me killed?*"

"Why are you doing this, Mark? You're supposed to be on our side—"

There was a hiss that might have been interference, and might not. "*You've got some nerve. With the deaths on your hands!*"

Deaths? Walker looked at Larsen. There'd been that whore and her pimp back on Shuloma Station, but not anyone else. Fredricks only had himself to blame. "What are you talking about?"

"*What am I talking about? Andrei! I'm talking about Andrei! He loved you, Delia—like a father. Nurtured you. Advanced you. Why did you do it?*"

It was a body blow. In fury, Walker turned to Larsen. "Did you know about this?"

"What? What the hell, Delia! Don't you think I would have mentioned it?"

Heyes, beside them, said, "Who is Andrei?"

Larsen said, "He was second at the Bureau. Ran the place, really, for decades. Delia, and Mark, and I—we were, well, his protégés, I guess."

"And now he's dead," said Heyes, "and you all think that one of you must be responsible. Dear God." She shook her head. "What a happy little band you are."

"*Delia? Shall I take your silence as admission of guilt?*"

"I didn't know anything about this," said Walker.

"*You're a liar.*"

Walker began to regroup. "Oh, for God's sake, Mark," she said, impatience creeping into her voice. "I'm sure you've been lied to, but not by me. Why the hell would I murder Andrei Gusev? He was my route to power." *Let's leave aside the fact that I loved him like a father.*

There was a pause, then Kinsella said, "*I don't know. For his money?*"

"His *money?*" Walker burst out laughing. "There was no money, Mark! Andrei never had a bean! It was all smoke and mirrors, credit and debt. Dear God, if you think I murdered Andrei Gusev for his money, you're deluded! Besides," she went on, "if I'd recently become the recipient of his fictional fortunes, why would I be halfway up a hill on this dump of a planet? Everything I've said I've meant, Mark. I'm here to find a Weird portal. The people of this world are living in peace with the Weird. I want to find out how. Because we cannot beat the Weird, not by force. We cannot destroy them—not as quickly as they can destroy us. And if we don't find a way to communicate with them, to live with them, then our species will be extinct within fifty years. *That's* why I'm here, Mark. And that's why Andrei helped me leave."

There was silence from the other end. "Mark? Are you still there?"

"*I'm still here.*"

"Good."

Larsen mouthed: *I think we might be getting to him.* And then Walker said, "Dear God, Mark, Andrei! How could you believe I would do something like that?"

Larsen rolled her eyes. "For fuck's sake, Delia," she muttered. "Do you not know when to stop?"

"*There's a lot you've done that I can't quite believe,*" Kinsella shot back, bitterly. "*You know, I doubt you were ever even pregnant—*"

"You really are a piece of shit," said Walker.

"I hate to interrupt," said Heyes, "but listen. We have incoming."

She was right. Walker could hear them coming up the hillside. She cut the comm and tossed the handheld back to Larsen. "Take cover," she said.

FAULT'S INJURIES TURNED out to be considerably less serious than the blood had suggested. Huddled up in a small but comfortable bed in the little hospital at the heart of the settlement, he sat with one paw on Jenny's small hand, and Maria fussing beside him. "Sorry if I gave you a fright, Mama Maria. But it hurt!"

Maria stroked his forehead. Strange how you got

used to their funny ugly faces, she thought. She didn't even mind the grown-up Vetch that were here so much, any longer. The medic had been competent, calm, and kind. "Don't worry about any of that, Failt," she said. "All you have to worry about is getting better. What will Jenny and I do without you?"

His tentacles curled slightly in what Maria had come to recognise was pleasure, and affection. "Those people," he said. "The people from the spaceship. They still here?"

"They've fallen back for the moment," said Maria. "Someone had the presence of mind to get into the truck you brought and drive it inside the settlement."

Failt whiffled with laughter. "Full of all their guns and arms and all," he said. "Bet they don't like having that turned back on them!"

They hadn't, as far as Maria had been able to learn, and, to be honest, she didn't believe that this would send them away from the settlement for good. She had watched them running towards the town, and seen the fervour in their eyes... They had been given orders—to stop the spread of the secret of Braun's World—and they would keep on coming until those orders were fulfilled. Who knew what they were planning now? They could be heading back to the ship, getting more weapons, or preparing to fly the ship over and attack the settlement from the air... Whatever they were planning, they would be back eventually. And before that happened, she had to get the message out. If she was going to die here, at the hands of these people, she swore that it would not happen until the whole Expansion knew about the cover-up on Braun's World. Leaving Failt tucked up in his bed, and Jenny sitting with him, Maria went in search of the kindly Vetch doctor.

"Please," she said, when she found him. "I have to speak to someone—and I think that you all want to speak to me."

About half an hour later, Maria was led towards the great hall that Walker, Larsen, and Heyes had visited only a few days ago. A much smaller group came to hear Maria, however; most of the people of the settlement were busy organising the defence of the town, or else involved in the clean-up. Maria found herself facing no more than fifteen or twenty people, Vetch and human. They were stern and unfriendly. One of the women, an older human, stood to speak at once.

"Why has this violence been brought down on us?" she said angrily. She seemed to be addressing the room at large, or else making sure that an opinion was heard. At any rate, Maria sensed that she was not being asked to respond, not yet, only to listen and to hear. So she kept her peace, for the moment, and listened, and heard. "We have lived peacefully for many years," the woman went on. "We have kept ourselves isolated from the wider universe so that we might avoid the grief and bloodshed that seems to be the way that others work. And now this has been forced upon us!"

"Remember that we kept hidden away to protect ourselves!" another person cried. "Beyond Stella Maris, some of us are still owned! Some of us are still considered property! Does this mean that our isolation is over? Does this mean that Stella Maris is no longer secret? Will our old masters and owners be coming for us?"

There was a general sense of dismay at this. Maria, thinking that her moment might have come, spoke up. "It's worse than that, I'm afraid," she said, lifting her voice above the confusion. Hearing her, people turned, some calling out, "How? How could it be worse?" Slowly the room settled into silence, and someone gestured to Maria to continue. Her voice trembling, she started to speak.

"I know that you met Walker and Larsen," she said. "I know that they warned you that people might be coming here to find them. You have to understand why."

"We told your friend that we were not interested in her wars," someone called out.

"Then I am going to have to *make* you interested," said Maria. "A crime has been committed—a terrible, monstrous crime. A whole world—millions of people!—has been murdered so that a few people could make sure they stayed in power." A few more voices began to rise, calling out *We don't want to hear any of this!* and *These are your affairs, not ours!* But Maria kept on speaking, her voice becoming stronger as she did.

"It's a world called Braun's World. The government of the Expansion claimed there was a Weird portal there, and they sealed off the planet and killed everyone there; to stop infection spreading, they said. But there never was a Weird portal on Braun's World. It was a lie told to make people afraid, and to put the perpetrators of that lie in power. And everyone who knows this secret—they're being killed in turn!"

The anger in the room was now palpable. *Why have you told us this? Why have we been made a party to this?* Maria forced herself to keep on speaking.

"It doesn't matter that you didn't know! It's enough that you ever spoke to Walker and Larsen! That's enough to condemn you in the eyes of these people! Even if I hadn't told you—you're guilty by association! They can't let you live, in case you know!"

They might ignore us! There are so few of us, hardly any of us!

"They've killed millions!" Maria cried back. "Do you think they'll hesitate to murder a few thousand more to keep their secret? Those people who came today"—she gestured back towards the gate— "they'll be back, very soon, and they'll be armed again. They won't stop until you're all dead!"

All around her, Maria could hear the rage at the news washing around the room like a great tsunami; rage that this had all been brought upon them unwillingly, and that they were now in such danger. But the people of Stella Maris, like all those who'd known oppression, were nothing if not practical, and they had the will to survive. In among all the anger, Maria heard concrete plans being made: the people pulling together to preserve themselves. She heard plans for an evacuation being mooted, and then outlined, and then actioned. She heard names of people put forward to lead on this. She saw people start to leave to begin work.

"Please," she called out, "I know you have no reason to help me, but there is something you can do. Something that will truly wound this enemy of yours."

"What can we do?" someone called to her.

"You can help me get this message out—back to

the Expansion. The people who want to kill us will be exposed, and destroyed."

She felt the hesitation in the room, and a kind of debate seemed to ripple around her. "We cannot contact the Expansion," someone said. "There are no communications systems here on Stella Maris with the range."

"There are on the *Baba Yaga*," said Maria. "On my ship." She felt odd claiming it in this way, but she supposed she was the last of them. "Help me get back to my ship."

"We cannot help you! The enemy is at the gate!"

"You have evacuation plans," Maria said. "I know you can leave the settlement. I know there are safe routes out. This is your way to fight back!"

But people were rushing past her, and she was not sure that she was being heard.

THROUGHOUT THE DAY Walker and her party journeyed up the pass towards the mountain where the portal lay. Their pace remained slow: they did not know what weapons their pursuers were carrying or what their range might be, and so they tried to keep to the cover of the trees. Every so often, one of Feuerstein's people would look back to check on their pursuers' progress at the river. As they went on, Walker began to feel an overwhelming sense of dread; her journey was surely hastening to its inevitable end—an ignominious end, on a forgotten planet, with nobody to remember her, and her mission unfulfilled. The rest of the party too seemed sombre. Larsen was silent. Heyes kept her head down and plodded onwards.

Late in the afternoon they stopped to rest and eat. Walker sat a little distant, as if trying to prevent the direction of her thoughts from dispiriting the others. At length, Larsen sought her out and sat down next to her.

"I think we should try to speak to Mark again," she said.

"I've tried that already," said Walker. "I got nowhere."

"I don't mean you," Larsen said. "And I don't mean over a handheld. I mean face-to-face."

Walker looked back down the pass. "I'd like to see you try."

"I mean it, Delia. I can't believe that Mark is party to any of this. I can't believe he would betray us like this."

"They're down there shooting at us. He's there with them. How much more evidence of treachery do you need?"

"I heard him," Larsen said. "He sounded as bewildered as you and I. When he spoke about Andrei, he sounded bereft."

The thought of Andrei, murdered by these people, was almost too much to bear. Angrily, Walker said, "He thought we were responsible, Kay. You and me—guilty of Andrei's murder! I don't know what's happened to Mark Kinsella, but he's not the man that I..."

"That you loved?" said Larsen. She was sitting in the half-light, and it seemed to Walker all of a sudden that they were mirror images. Larsen looked so tired, wearied from the uncertainties of her recent life, running towards nowhere with assassins at her back; shocked by her sudden exile from her old way of life; knowing she had made the right decisions, but terribly conscious that a high price was being paid by everyone around her.

"I did love him," Walker admitted. "But that's over now."

Larsen gave a bitter laugh. "Then you're lucky," she said. "I never quite got over the whole affair. He did. Quite quickly, I thought. But then he never knew... He never knew the half of it."

Walker had known, if she hadn't admitted it to herself, that Larsen had been pregnant once upon a time. And she'd known who the father was.

"I don't regret my decisions," said Larsen. "Not even here, and now..." She looked around them. "Especially not here and now. But I wish that Mark and I had managed to remain friends." She stared past Walker, on down the pass. "I don't want to think that he's fallen in with Grant," she said. "I don't want to think that he's sold out, and so badly, and for so little. I wonder why I don't want to think that. Is it because I loved him, and I don't want to think that I'm the kind of person who would fall for a complete bastard?"

"None of us want to feel we've been taken for fools," Walker said. "I think... No, I don't think that Mark has betrayed us. I think that's he's found himself in a harder position than he ever expected. Andrei murdered, Grant running the show—and you and I gone. I imagine Mark had to make some tough choices to prove his loyalty to the Bureau. A little like the choice you made, to tell Latimer about the baby. And I don't think he knows in full what the people he's serving are really like." She gave a wry smile. "Because I don't want to think that I'm the kind of person who would fall for a complete bastard either. And I'd rather remember how he was, when I loved him—or thought that I loved him."

They heard footsteps coming towards them, and both turned at once. It was Feuerstein. Quietly, she said, "I'm sorry to disturb you both, but they're crossing the river. It's time we made some decisions about what to do next."

Walker, turning away from Larsen, nodded. "I need to press on," she said. "With Heyes. On to the portal. We'll need a guide."

Feuerstein nodded. "That will be me."

"And the rest of us?" asked Larsen.

"Provide cover," said Walker. "Hold them back for as long as you can."

"Oh, good," said Larsen. "That was what I was hoping you would say."

"Wait till you hear what's coming next," said Walker. "We only have three weapons between us."

"I'm guessing you're not going to let go of yours," said Larsen.

Walker smiled.

"There are four of them," said Feuerstein. "When the three of us leave, that leaves you, Larsen, and two of my people."

"And two guns," said Larsen. "You'll forgive me if I don't look delighted at those odds."

Walker studied her carefully. "You're not thinking of doing anything stupid, are you?"

"More stupid than anything else I've done in the past few months?"

"I was thinking on the lines of trying to speak to a mutual friend of ours in person."

Larsen began to walk back to the camp. "If I do decide to do that, Delia, it will be my own decision."

Walker followed her back to join the others. Feuerstein went to brief her people and say her farewells, and Walker, Larsen and Heyes stood together in an awkward trio. At last, Larsen spoke. "Well, Hecate, I know you don't have much time for her, and I can hardly blame you, but please take care of her—take care of both of them."

Heyes rested her hand gently upon Larsen's arm. "You know I will. You don't need to worry."

"I do worry," said Larsen, "not least because I intended to be there when the time came..." She sighed. "Oh, God, Delia. I don't know what's going to happen. I don't think we're going to get out of this alive, either of us. And yet... I can't help imagining her, all grown up, with a mind of her own, her own voice..."

She stopped speaking, and Walker drew her into a rough but deeply heartfelt embrace. "I'll take care," she promised. "I'll do my best. Perhaps I'll get back and perhaps when I do there'll be doctors down there, and she'll come out and be fine, and she'll live here on Stella Maris and be happy..."

Feuerstein came back. "We have to go," she said. "They could be halfway across the river by now."

Reluctantly, Walker and Larsen let go. Heyes said goodbye to Larsen, quickly and quietly, and then, following Feuerstein, they left the doctor behind in the darkness.

ALL DAY THE crimopaths had worked on building a raft and, as the sun set and the whole of this remote part of this remote world was bathed in glorious golden light, they set off to cross the river on their mission of murder. By the time it was full dark, they were well on their way in pursuit of Walker and Larsen. Conway, satisfied again that they were making headway, went on ahead with one of her team.

And then the firing started. The battle that followed was scrappy and short, and, at the end of it, two people lay dead, and one of their assailants had been captured. One of the dead was one of Feuerstein's people. The other was Conway.

Kinsella watched as two of the crimopaths brought their prisoner forwards. It was Vetch. His gut clenched in fear and pity. Conway was the only thing that had been controlling them. Now they were free to act upon whatever impulses grabbed them. This Vetch they had captured would be dead, eventually, but it was going to be agony. Realising that the crimopaths had their attention entirely on their prey, he turned away and, as quietly as he could, slipped away beneath the trees. When the screaming started, he sat down, put his hands against his face and began to whisper to himself. Snippets of poetry. Witty responses he had never made in arguments long lost. Bits of songs. It blocked out hardly anything, and nowhere near enough, but it did mean he didn't hear the person coming up quietly behind him. The next thing he knew there was a knife against his throat and a voice whispering in his ear.

"Hello, lover-boy," said Larsen.

CHAPTER FIFTEEN

KINSELLA LAID HIS hands, palm down, flat upon his knees, so that Larsen could see that he wasn't going to try anything. If she was a traitor, and if she was responsible at all for Andrei's death, then she was more calculating and more dangerous than he had ever guessed. Or perhaps it wasn't her. Perhaps Delia had been the instigator, and Larsen was now caught in a bind... Softly, he said, "I can see you've been spending time in Walker's company."

From beyond the trees there was a blood-curdling scream.

"You're the one that's brought crimopaths after us," hissed Larsen. "That's what they are, isn't it? Crimopaths?"

"I'm not going to deny it," said Kinsella.

"I thought you'd seen enough of what they could do. I know I did. Cleaned up afterwards. That's what doctors have to do, you know. Clean up after the mess left by other people—"

"I didn't bring them!" Kinsella shot back, and had to wonder why it mattered to him that Larsen did not have a bad opinion of him.

"We never wanted to see anything like that ever again."

"It wasn't me! What do you think I am? It was Conway!"

"Who the hell is Conway?"

"She's Grant's person. Or she was. Your people killed her. She was the only thing keeping those damned animals on their leash, and now you've let them loose."

The cries from the crimopaths' victim came again. Cries for mercy, and for pity.

"You didn't have to come with them, Mark. You didn't have to bring them after us!"

"Do you think I had a *choice*?" He could feel her, tense and angry behind him, her knuckles white around the shaft of the knife. "Jesus, Kay, will you put that damn thing down? I'm not your enemy! You and Delia—you were the ones that ran! And then Andrei's fucking corpse turned up!"

"If you think we were responsible for that, you're more of an idiot than I ever gave you credit for."

"I'm flattered—"

"You need to listen to me, Mark. There's much more at stake here than you know about. Listen to me. The portal on Braun's World was faked. It was an excuse for Grant and her people to depose Andrei and Delia. They murdered millions to cover up their secret, and they're still murdering to cover it up. That's why they've come after me. And you've swallowed everything they've told you, haven't you?

You were ready to believe that Delia and I were capable of murdering Andrei rather than thinking that we might have reason to leave. Christ, Mark, she's having your baby!"

Kinsella sat for a while. Snippets of poetry and bits of songs. Witty responses in arguments long lost. "Do you have any proof?" he said, at last.

"Do I have *proof*? They've sent crimopaths after us! But, yes, I do have proof. I did have proof. One of the people who travelled with us has it all on datapin."

"And where is she now? She's not up ahead, is she?" Cold washed through him. "They're going to catch up with them, you know. Whoever you sent off up that pass. It's only a matter of time."

"No, she's not up there. She's heading back towards the settlement. She's going to try to get the message out."

"Back to the *settlement*?" Kinsella frowned "There's another pair of crimopaths heading that way."

"We know. We've sent her to warn them—"

"And does she know that they've been instructed to wipe out the settlement? They'll blast her and her proof to oblivion."

Larsen didn't reply at once. Then she said, "Are you on our side now, Mark?"

"What? I've always been on your side! Or you've been on mine—"

"Be careful what you say next."

"Look, I'm not on the side of mass-murdering crimopaths and the mass-murdering bastards that send them. Will that do?"

She sighed. "I guess it's going to have to. You're still a shit, though. The things you said to Delia—"

"I know," he said. "But she said some pretty foul things too, you know—"

"Stop now," Larsen advised.

"All right, I'll stop. So will you put the knife down now, Kay?"

He watched as her death-grip on the handle relaxed slightly, and then she pulled her hand back. "Don't move," she said. "I've still got this thing ready."

"I won't move until you tell me." And he didn't, but stayed sitting on the ground while she scooted round to sit down facing him. She looked older; tired and worried. He was conscious, suddenly, of the sacrifice she had made, throwing away her old life to run from danger into danger. He felt he owed her an apology, but he wasn't sure how to offer it, and he wasn't sure how well it would go down.

"All right," she said. "What do we do next?"

"We came here by ground vehicle," said Kinsella. "It's back on the other side of the river." They could hear low moaning coming from beyond the trees. "I think we should take it while those bastards are busy."

"I think I agree with you," said Larsen. "Then what?"

"Who's with Delia?"

"Someone else from the settlement. A priest called Heyes."

"I've heard of Heyes." He shivered to think of the ruin of the church and the tortured old woman that the crimopaths had left behind. That he had stood by and allowed... "Where are they going?"

"There's a Weird portal up in them there mountains, Mark. Helping everyone here live in peace and harmony."

He laughed to himself, softly. "So she was right along."

"Of course she was."

"And are they armed? Delia and her party?"

"They've got a couple of weapons between them."

He thought for a while. "No point going after her," he said, eventually.

"I'll make sure I mention that if we see her again."

"I hope she'll take it as the compliment it's meant to be. Delia has to take her own chances now. But we have to make sure that the information about Braun's World gets through. Which means getting back to our ship as quickly as we can. We've one point in our favour, there."

"Which is?"

He gave a grim smile. "They like to take their time about things."

Larsen nodded, and then, suddenly, she gave a dreadful gasp of pain and rolled onto the ground, clutching her leg.

"Kay? What is it?" He reached out for her, tenderly. "Are you okay?"

"Yes, I'm okay!" she snapped back. "But I'm bloody glad you changed your mind when you did. I've got horrible cramp."

LONG BEFORE DAWN, Maria left the settlement. Failt had insisted on coming with her, and it was this, more than any appeal that Maria could have made on her own account, that meant that she was loaned the old lorry. The great old bulk of the *Baba Yaga* loomed large in the desert, and Maria was glad to see it. She helped Failt down, and up through the hatch, and then they scooted through the deserted ship to the cockpit.

Failt hopped up into the pilot's sling, as if he was born to it. "Watched him close," he said. "You keep an eye on someone wants to space you. Soon get this message sent, Mama Maria."

Maria sighed. "I almost wonder if it matters, Failt."

"What?" His big eyes stared back at her. "Course it matters! What are you saying now?"

"I mean... I don't know what people will do when they hear our story. Perhaps they'll ignore it."

Failt was shocked. "They can't ignore it!"

"Some evils are too big," Maria said. "People can't admit to them. They stare them in the face and deny they exist."

Failt thought about this for a while. "Still," he said, "we have to try."

IT WAS NEAR dawn when Walker, Heyes, and Feuerstein reached the mouth of the cave that contained the portal. Feuerstein put out her hand. "I'll take the weapon now, please," she said.

"I don't think so," said Walker.

"I think it will be best," insisted Feuerstein, quietly. "People are still following us and they are gaining on us. I intend to remain here, to slow their progress."

With a sigh, Walker handed over her weapon. "You aren't a match for them."

"That's my business," said Feuerstein. "Your business is in there."

"I'm grateful," said Walker.

Feuerstein nodded. "Let's hope it's worth everything we've given."

Bending their heads, Walker and Heyes went through the narrow entrance to the cave. Inside, the roof opened up a little so that they were able stand up again. They were in a passageway into the mountainside.

"Guess we go that way," Walker whispered.

"Guess so," Heyes whispered back. "Funny that we're whispering."

"Funny?" whispered Walker.

"Like we're in a cathedral."

Walker grunted, and started to move on. Heyes followed. The passage was too narrow for them to walk side-by-side, and Walker was grateful she had never been troubled by claustrophobia. After about five minutes' slow progress, the passage opened out into a huge cavern. Walker took a few steps inside and halted. There, falling away in front of her feet, was the portal.

It lay inside a great chasm plunging deep into the earth. Through it could be seen what looked like a huge sea, a great grey ocean swirling and twisting around. Little bulges of purple, like blood clots, rose up and down, coagulating and dissipating and then reforming. Walker stuffed her hand into her mouth and steadied her stomach. Left to grow, she guessed, they would become Sleer, the human-shaped bodies that the Weird had used, on other worlds, to murder humans and Vetch alike.

Heyes, coming out of the passageway, saw the portal and staggered forwards. Walker, grabbing her arm, pulled her back. "Christ, Heyes, now's not the time to start genuflecting!"

"Oh, Jesus," whispered the priest. Her hands were

pressed against her forehead. "Oh, sweet Mother of Mercy, I can *hear* them!" She turned to look at Walker. Her eyes were wet with tears. "Yes," she whispered, "Yes, I can hear you! I can see you! The whole of creation!" And then she spoke no more.

DAWN WAS APPROACHING as Kinsella and Larsen reached the *White Horseman*. Kinsella drove the ground vehicle back into the hold and soon the ship was in flight, heading towards the settlement.

He and Larsen had not spoken much on the way back. So much still hung between them. But as the settlement came into view, Larsen said, "She really is pregnant, you know."

"What?"

"Delia. She didn't lie."

Kinsella felt sick to his stomach. "I regretted that almost as soon as I said it."

"I'm glad," said Larsen. "I didn't make the same choice as Delia, and I would make the same choice again, but she didn't deserve excoriation."

Kinsella turned to her. "I didn't know," he said. "Kay, I had no idea."

She gave him a wry smile. "Well, it was my business, really, wasn't it? Like I said, I wouldn't change anything. Not even this."

The crimopaths had seen the ship. They watched as they turned the ground weapons their way.

"Still," she said, "I would have liked to have been there for Delia, when the time came."

And then everyone opened fire.

* * *

HEYES REACHED OUT to grasp Walker's hand. *Listen*, she said. But her mouth wasn't moving.

"Heyes?" Walker took a step back. "What the hell's going on?"

What do you think? The priest's voice was as tetchy as ever. *For pity's sake, Walker, use that brain of yours!*

"You couldn't speak to me directly before, could you?"

Of course not! The Weird are amplifying my powers... Dear God. It's like having a whole candlelight procession march through your brain... Yes, all right, I'll let you speak to her!

"That wasn't to me, was it?" said Walker.

No. Listen, Walker. They're going to speak to you now...

Walker felt the priest's hand began to shiver within hers. Her eyes went glassy.

Walker.

"I'm here," she said. "I want to talk."

Don't talk. Listen. We have been we are we will be watching. We see you and we hear you. We are part of the whole we are separate.

Walker thought quickly. Was this what Feuerstein had meant when she talked about a split in the Weird? In the Bureau, they believed that the Weird had a mother-mind, a controlling central intelligence. But this Weird was different. Part of the whole, but separate.

We are part of the whole we are separate we see this in you too you two.

Well, what the hell did that mean? Did they know about the factions within the Bureau? Did they know that she and Larsen were on the run?

Walker's spook-mind began running through the ramifications of that: where their influence must be; who their people must be within the Bureau...

"Walker," said Heyes sharply. "Stop that. None of that matters now. Listen."

She is part of you she is different she is part of the whole she is separate.

"Oh," breathed Walker. "You mean the baby."

"Yes," said Heyes. "They mean the baby."

She grew she is growing she will grow she is part of you she will be separate she will be part of the whole but separate. Be part of the whole be separate be part of the whole be separate...

"Yes, all right, I'm pregnant—but that's not what I'm here to talk about—"

"Oh, for God's sake, Walker, stop being so bloody obtuse!"

Be part of the whole be separate be part of the whole be separate be part—

The voice in her head stopped, suddenly. Heyes had withdrawn her hand. "Sorry," she said. "Too much. Couldn't go on any longer."

"Heyes!" Walker grabbed her hand. "You can't stop now! We've barely started! They wanted something from me. I need to know what they want!"

"Oh, Delia," said the priest sorrowfully. "Do you really not know?"

"'Be part of the whole be separate.' But what does that *mean*?"

"They're a shared mind, Walker. They see you and the baby, symbiotic but growing apart. Separating. They want to find out more."

"So give me your hand and I'll tell them."

Heyes shook her head. "They want more than that." She looked into the swirl of the portal. "They want you to go to them."

"WHAT'S OUR STATUS?" said Kinsella. "Larsen, what's the state of the ship?"

"I believe the technical term is 'fucked,'" said Larsen. "Mark, we're not getting out of this."

Kinsella nodded grimly, and began to turn the *White Horseman* around to fly over the settlement.

"What are you doing?" cried Larsen. "We could go up at any second—all those people below—"

"If we're going," said Kinsella, "we're taking those bastards with us. They're not going to do any more harm."

He was a good enough pilot, just, to be good as his word. The *White Horseman*, now burning fiercely, passed over the settlement, and Kinsella pointed it towards his enemies. As the ship began its last descent, Kinsella reached for Larsen's hand. "I'm sorry, Kay. Sorry for everything. Please, forgive me."

She held his hand tight. "I forgive you," she said. "I hope they make it. Delia—and the little girl."

Kinsella smiled. Their little girl, he thought. *His* little girl.

And the *White Horseman* reached its destination.

FAILT AND MARIA watched as the information streamed from Walker's handheld and out, out, into the universe beyond. Onto multiple channels, to all the people named by Larsen and Walker—out went the evidence that proved that the Weird had never been on Braun's World, and that the bombardment was mass murder.

"What happens now, Mama Maria?"

"I don't know. But I think this means the end of life as they know it for the people of Stella Maris." *And perhaps for the universe beyond.*

Failt sniffed. "No living in peace and harmony?"

"Who knows? Perhaps it will mean peace and harmony for more than us. Perhaps it'll mean more war. We'll have to wait and see."

"GO TO THEM? Into the void?"

"Past the void," said Heyes. "Beyond the void."

"How do you know this, Heyes?"

Heyes smiled. "I saw what they had to show me, Walker. I've seen... creation." Tears were running down her weathered cheeks. "God is good."

From back along the passage, they heard weapons fire, and a high scream. "Feuerstein," said Walker.

"It's time to go, Delia. Time to take the plunge."

"Into Hell?"

"God knows you deserve it." Heyes lifted her hand and, in the air between them, made the sign of the cross. "There," she said, "absolution."

"I'm not a Catholic. And you're not a priest. They booted you out, remember?"

"Well, you never know." Heyes leaned forwards, and, cupping her hands around Walker's face, leaned in to kiss her on the brow. "For the sake of the little one, I hope you both make it."

Walker glanced back over her shoulder. Were those shadows on the wall beyond? "What about you?"

"I can take care of myself."

"Come with me."

"I don't think they'll take me."

"They'll kill you. The people coming. They'll kill you."

"Who knows," said Heyes. "Maybe I'm smarter than I look." Her eyes glazed for a brief moment. "They want you, Walker. Now or never."

"But how will I talk to them? I'm not telepathic—"

"You'll find a way." Heyes pulled away and started to walk back towards the passage. "Go on! If you're going! Goodbye! Godspeed! God is good!"

Walker turned and looked into the void. *Here I am*, she said. *I'm coming*. She pressed her hands around her stomach. *Here we go, little minnow. Here we go.*

And they fell.

Some weeks later

MUCH HARM HAD been done to the people of Stella Maris and their settlement, but the work of repair went on steadily. Maria was glad to help, grateful that these people had put aside their animosity towards her and had begun to accept her. She knew their welcome was for the sake of Jenny and Failt more than anything, but she hoped that in time, they could come to accept her too. She could not see herself leaving Stella Maris, not in a hurry. Perhaps she could learn to fly the *Baba Yaga*, but where would she go? If people were still coming after her, they would catch her eventually. And if she was to be left alone, there was nothing back for her in the Expansion. Not without Kit. Jenny was happy here, and there was Failt. For his sake alone, Maria would remain on Stella Maris. He had quickly settled in and he loved the place. He loved to live-in-peace-and-harmony. He had dreamed of it, and it had come true. And it was not that she could take him back with her to the Expansion. A human mother and a Vetch child would not be accepted there.

Feuerstein's long-house had given them a home, in memory of their house-sister. After the dust had settled, a party from the settlement had journeyed up to the portal to communicate with the Weird, and to find out what they could about what had happened to Walker and her party. Crossing the river, they had found Conway's body, and then, at the entrance to the cave that housed the portal, had found Feuerstein. Heyes, too, lay in the passageway leading to the portal. Both women had been shot dead. Beyond Heyes they found the bodies of two crimopaths, but they could not determine who or what had killed them. Received wisdom back at the settlement was that the Weird had dealt with them. Maria had no idea if this was possible—or how—but at least they would not be haunting her dreams. The bodies of Conway and the crimopaths were buried, quickly, up in the mountains, but Feuerstein and Heyes had been carried back, and laid to rest in the little graveyard at the west end of the settlement. Using the databanks on the *Baba Yaga*, Maria had found some words to say over Heyes' body.

> *All praise to you, Lord of all creation.*
> *Praise to you, holy and living God.*
> *We praise and bless you for your mercy,*
> *we praise and bless you for your kindness.*

You sanctify the homes of the living
and make holy the places of the dead.
You alone open the gates of righteousness
and lead us to the dwellings of the saints.

Almighty and ever-living God,
in you we place our trust and hope,
in you the dead whose bodies were temples
   of the Spirit
find everlasting peace.
As we take leave of our sister,
give our hearts peace in the firm hope
that one day Hecate will live
in the mansion you have prepared for her
   in Heaven.

But she did not know if the words were right, and she could not be consoled when the old woman's body was lowered into the ground.

There was no sign of Walker's body, and none of the people of Stella Maris had any idea what might have happened to her. She had disappeared, as if a hole in the ground had opened up and she had fallen into it. Maria found that she could not get Walker out of her mind. She kept expecting her to turn up, suddenly, out of the wilderness, calm and calculating and hard-eyed and with a baby tucked under her arm. She dreamed of her, often, like she dreamed of Kit, too, arriving out of nowhere. But neither of them came. Eventually the dreams left her. Maria supposed this meant she was healing.

There was much discussion about what these events might mean for the future of Stella Maris. The telepaths with the party had tried to communicate with the Weird, but it had been oddly silent. There was some fear that the Weird had gone, and that all the nourishment it supplied, that kept the water flowing and the foodstuffs growing, might suddenly disappear, but that had not happened. Spring bloomed rampantly in and around the settlement, and then became a glorious, bright summer. But there were other worries too: whether it had been wise to send out the messages that Maria had sent; whether anyone else might come from the Expansion as a result; and who—friends of Walker and Larsen, or friends of those who had sent the crimopaths. Whatever happened, there was a will to defend the portal come what may. The ruins of the *White Horseman* had been ransacked for material to assist in their defence, and the *Baba Yaga* too would play her part, if necessary.

But nobody came. The summer advanced, reached its full height, and then began to ripen into a rich and varied autumn. And then, one cool morning that carried with it the first suggestion of winter, they came: seven bright stars in the sky that quickly turned into ships, landing in the distance. Maria recognised ships from the Expansion.

But they were not the only people to come to the settlement that day. Someone was spotted walking along the road towards the gate. At the gate, she was stopped, her way barred. Maria, slipping through the crowd, came to the front and saw a girl of about fourteen or fifteen, bare-foot, wild-eyed, and strange. When she saw Maria, the girl lifted her hand, as if in greeting, and then she spoke, in a clear voice.

"My name is Cassandra," she said. "My mother was called the Walker."

ACKNOWLEDGEMENTS

GRATEFUL THANKS TO Eric Brown for inviting me to explore *Weird Space*, and for greeting every shift I made away from his original conception with enthusiasm and generosity.

Thank you also to my head of department at ARU, Farah Mendlesohn, for granting me teaching relief so that I had the time to complete the book. The coffee shops of Cambridge – particularly Hot Numbers, Espresso Library, and Afternoon Tease – provided the space in which I could work and enabled me to spend my advance in style.

My thanks and love, as ever, to Matthew, who gives me the support to enable me to be teacher, writer, and mother. And all of my love, of course, to beautiful Verity, who already likes rockets.

Una McCormack

ERIC BROWN

Eric Brown began writing when he was fifteen, while living in Australia, and sold his first short story to *Interzone* in 1986. He has won the British Science Fiction Award twice for his short stories, has published over forty books, and his work has been translated into sixteen languages.

His latest books include the SF novels *The Serene Invasion*, *Satan's Reach*, and the crime novel *Murder by the Book*. He writes a regular science fiction review column for the *Guardian* newspaper and lives near Dunbar, East Lothian.

His website can be found at
www.ericbrown.co.uk

UNA McCORMACK

Una McCormack is a *New York Times* bestselling author of novels based on *Star Trek* and *Doctor Who*. Her audio plays based on *Doctor Who* and *Blake's 7* have been produced by Big Finish, and her short fiction has been anthologised by Farah Mendlesohn, Ian Whates, and Gardner Dozois. She has a doctorate in sociology and teaches creative writing at Anglia Ruskin University, Cambridge. She lives in Cambridge with her partner, Matthew, and their daughter, Verity.

'Eric Brown spins
a terrific yarn.'
*SFX on Guardians
of the Phoenix*

Eric
Brown

WEIRD SPACE
THE DEVIL'S NEBULA

Ed Carew and his small ragtag crew are smugglers and ne'er-do-wells, thumbing their noses at the Expansion, the vast human hegemony extending across thousands of worlds... until the day they are caught, and offered a choice between working for the Expansion and an ignominious death. They must trespass across the domain of humanity's neighbours, the Vetch – the inscrutable alien race with whom humanity has warred, at terrible cost of life, and only recently arrived at an uneasy peace – and into uncharted space beyond, among the strange worlds of the Devil's Nebula, looking for long-lost settlers.

 WWW.SOLARISBOOKS.COM

Follow us on Twitter! www.twitter.com/solarisbooks

Eric Brown
WEIRD SPACE
SATAN'S REACH

'It's a runaway success.'
SciFiNow on Weird Space: The Devil's Nebula

Telepath Den Harper did the dirty work for the authoritarian Expansion, reading the minds of criminals, spies and undesirables, for years. Unable to take the strain, he stole a starship and headed into the void, a sector of lawless space known as Satan's Reach. For five years he worked as a trader among the stars – then discovered that the Expansion had set a bounty hunter on his trail. But what does the Expansion want with a lowly telepath like Harper? Is there something in the rumours that human space is being invaded by aliens from another realm? Harper finds out the answer to both these questions when he rescues a young woman from certain death – and comes face to face with the terrible aliens known as the Weird.